Praying for Sunlight, Waiting for Rain

a New Guinea story

Kieran Donaghue

Published in Australia by Sid Harta Books & Print Pty Ltd,
ABN: 34632585293
23 Stirling Crescent, Glen Waverley, Victoria 3150 Australia
Telephone: +61 3 9560 9920, Facsimile: +61 3 9545 1742
E-mail: author@sidharta.com.au

First published in Australia 2024
This edition published 2024
Copyright © Kieran Donaghue 2024
Cover design, typesetting: WorkingType (www.workingtype.com.au)

ISBN: 978-1-922958-65-5

Contents

About the Author

Kieran studied philosophy in Australia, the United States and Germany in the 1970s and 1980s. He taught for a short period at the Australian National University, then spent nearly twenty years working for the Australian Government's overseas aid program. During this time he made numerous visits to countries in Africa, Asia and the Pacific, learning much from local people and from many fine aid workers dedicated to improving the lives of others. *Praying for Sunlight, Waiting for Rain* has its genesis in the visits Kieran made as an aid official to the highlands of Papua New Guinea.

Further biographical details, along with information about Kieran's first novel, *German Lessons*, and his contribution to an anthology on the 2019–20 Australian bushfires, *Continent Aflame: Responses to an Australian Catastrophe*, can be found at: **www.kierandonaghue.com**

Other titles by the author:

German Lessons

Contributed to:
Continent Aflame:
Responses to an Australian Catastrophe

For Mariko – and in memory of Toshio.
Once again.

Acknowledgements

I would like to give special thanks to my niece Ngaire Donaghue, who convinced me that a story worth telling lay buried within the original manuscript and suggested ways of unearthing it. Thanks also to Mariko Nakamura, Brian Donaghue, Barry Donaghue and Michael Main, who provided subsequent support and textual advice, and to Chris Ballard, who introduced me to the wide range of fiction set in New Guinea. I also thank Jenn Zabinskas and Bronwin Dargaville for their expert editorial assistance.

Author's Note

While *Praying for Sunlight, Waiting for Rain* is a work of fiction, in writing the story I tried to stay true to the broad contours of the history of the early years of European contact with the New Guinea highlanders. I have listed in the Bibliography the main texts relied on to this end. The story should not be read as a substitute for the historical accounts contained in these and other works.

Certain words with racial or ethnic meanings that some readers may find offensive are used in the story. I did not take the decision to use these words lightly, doing so only when I judged their use to be integral to the task of conveying the mores of the times or depicting the personalities of specific characters. I trust that the use of these words will be seen in this light.

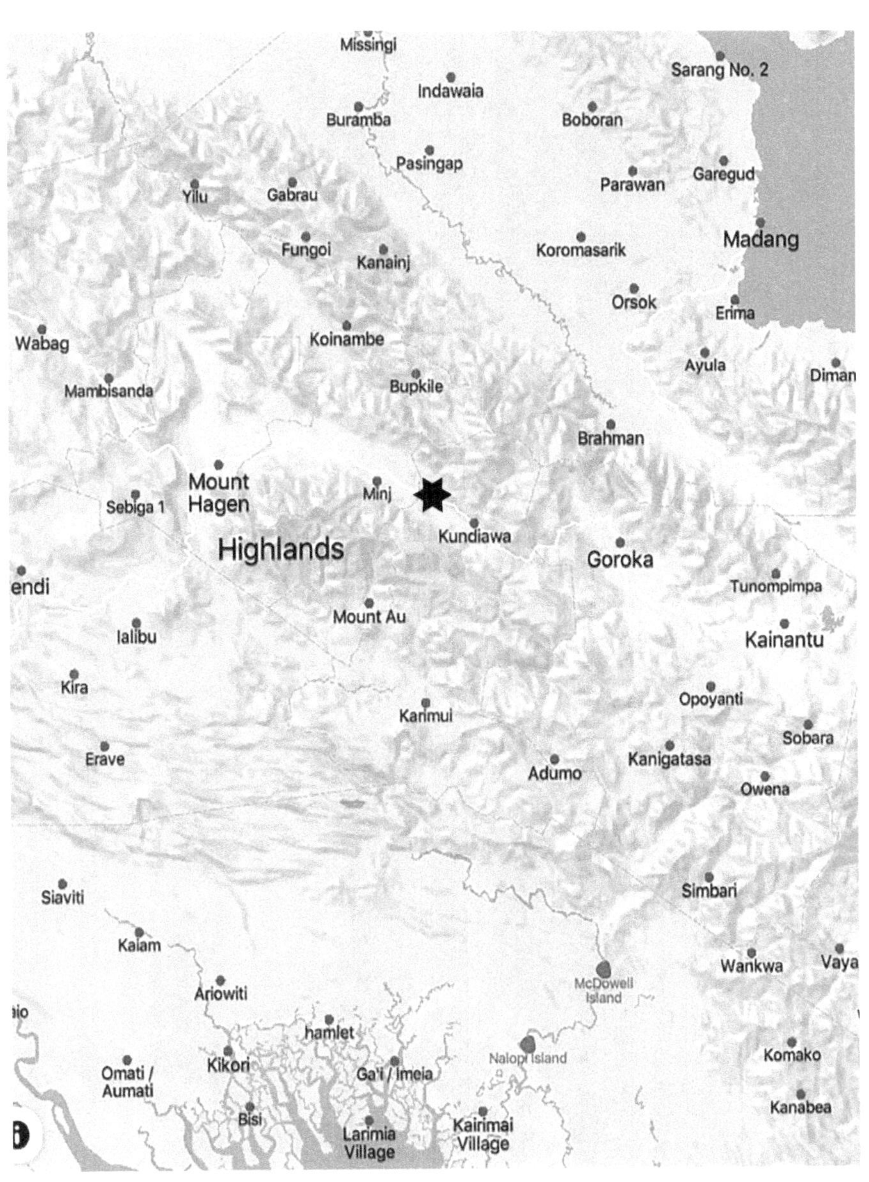

*Carl Starck's mission house is located between
Kundiawa and Minj (marked by star)*

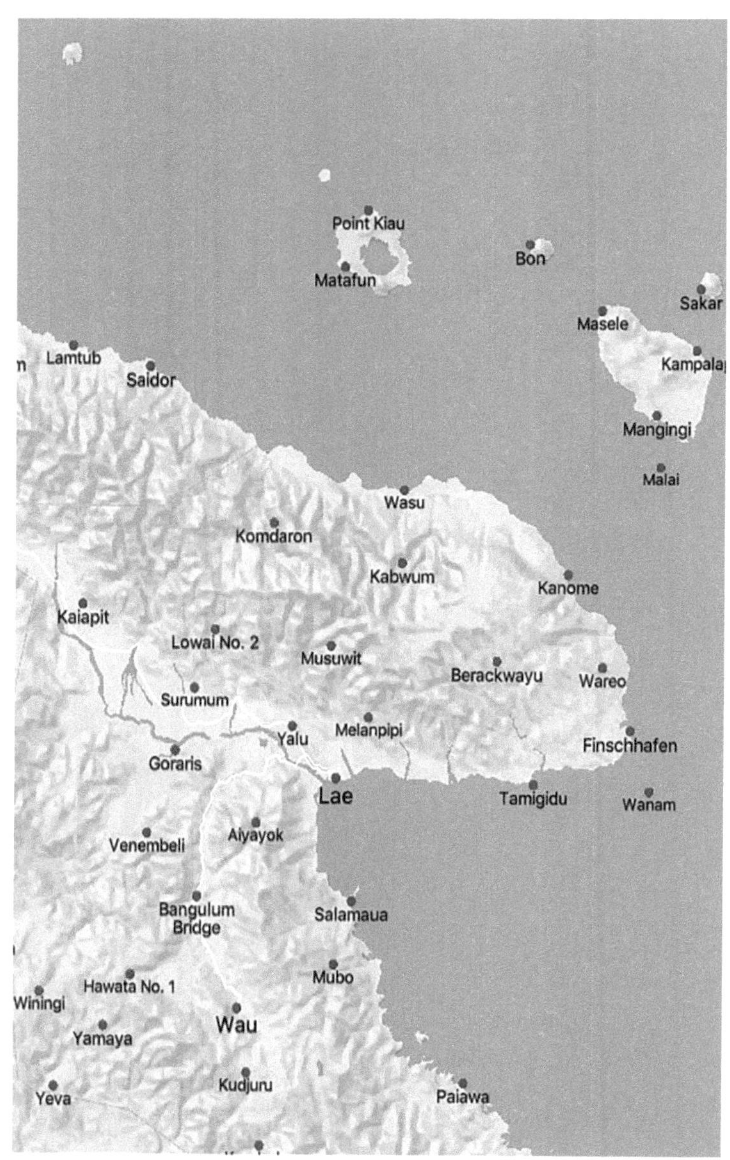

© OpenStreetMap, Mapbox and Mapcarta

Reunion

(1937)

One

Ellen removed her goggles and leather helmet and looked around in the bright sunlight for Carl, but before she could fully register his absence a chanting mass of glistening bodies surrounded her.

'Misis! Misis!'

She looked around again for Carl, then allowed herself to be manoeuvred onto an improvised chair secured between two long poles festooned with flowers. She struggled for balance as the whole apparatus was jerked into the air and carried off on bare shoulders at a pace between walking and running. As she looked back, the only white face she could see belonged to the pilot, Len, who was supervising the unloading of the tiny plane—suitcases of clothes, boxes of medical supplies, newspapers and books secured by leather straps. Len gave her a wave and a thumbs up. She returned the wave half-heartedly and wondered what she must look like, stuck up there like a stranded bird.

They crossed a fast-running creek and a deep gully and jogged their way into higher land, the backs and shoulders of the carriers rippling with sweat. Ever more bodies and voices added themselves to the procession, the din waxing and waning in the thin air. Then several arms pointed up and away and she saw a white man standing on a ridge, in baggy short pants and long socks, a short-sleeved shirt and wide-brimmed hat, a hand raised in greeting. Behind him further up the hill was a sloping roof covering a structure raised from the ground on squat supports. She smiled at the thought of her husband and at this first sight of her new home.

As the cavalcade ascended the hill she watched as Carl came forward to meet it. He lifted her lightly to the ground and stood beside her as the crowd ebbed and flowed, singing and clapping, bright teeth scattering the clear light. Several hands pushed through the melee to poke and prod then quickly withdrew, seemingly assured that the slender white woman was indeed made of flesh.

After several minutes, Carl raised his hand and uttered a series of guttural sounds. The singing and dancing gradually stopped, replaced by an expectant silence. Again Carl spoke, and Ellen sensed through the indecipherable words that gratitude was being expressed on her behalf. She offered a smile in confirmation. Then the crowd began to dissolve, several of the men touching Carl's hands or bits of his clothing as they left.

'I need the toilet,' Ellen whispered as Carl leant to embrace her.

There was something that looked like an outhouse a short distance from the main building. Inside there wasn't a toilet bowl, just a hole surrounded by a rectangle of pieces of timber. Carl left Ellen there to squat, holding onto the wooden struts that formed part of the side walls. The hole was deep and the smell bearable, but there were flies everywhere and Ellen hurried to finish the task as quickly as possible. When she was outside, Carl had disappeared and she could not see a tap, so she used a handkerchief to clean her hands. She wondered if she would ever get used to this.

*

Ellen smiled at the young man standing in the doorway, dressed in shorts and a shirt similar to Carl's but with nothing on his feet. She looked to Carl for an explanation.

'This is Aijang, our cook-boy.'

She held out her hand. The man gave a loose-limbed curtsey then brushed his hand against hers.

'Aijang understands some English, if you speak slowly.'

Ellen nodded but could think of nothing to say. She left Carl to save her embarrassment by instructing Aijang to prepare something to eat and drink.

When Aijang had gone Carl took Ellen on a tour of the house. There were just four rooms in the main part, all leading off a wide central hallway. The living room at the front contained two sitting chairs, a sofa, a large desk covered in papers and supporting a sturdy typewriter, a desk chair and several well-stocked bookshelves. A wind-up phonograph stood on a small table next to the desk, a collection of records stacked neatly beside it. The room was full of light, thanks to the open window that gave a wide view down the hill to the bottom of the valley. A second room on the same side of the house was a dining room, furnished sparsely with a table and chairs and a pair of small matching cupboards for crockery and cutlery.

On the far side of the hall were two bedrooms, the one at the front with a double bed, a chest of drawers, a wardrobe and a view that paralleled that from the living room; the other bedroom had a single bed, a radio transceiver on a small table, a bicycle-like machine that Carl said was to charge the radio's battery, and a tangle of camping equipment.

The final room was a kitchen, separated from the main building by a short, covered walkway. Sounds of activity could be clearly heard and Carl said that Aijang did not like to be interrupted in his work, so they would leave the inspection of the kitchen until later.

Ellen asked about a place to wash and Carl led her in the direction of the latrine to a canvas-covered arrangement. Inside was a bucket attached to a small chain propped at head height on a wooden frame. Carl demonstrated how the improvised shower worked, deftly avoiding the cascade of falling water.

'It freshens you up in the mornings like nothing else.'

Ellen shivered in anticipation as they walked back around the side of the house, past a copper, a rinsing tub bordering a neat pile of cut wood and a corrugated iron water tank that Carl touched with affection. 'The rains are good here,' he said. 'We're never short of fresh water.'

A small table on the verandah was set for lunch and Ellen immediately recognised the cups and plates that had been sent from home more than three years previously. She thought of the day her mother had packed them, taking exquisite care but with the set of her mouth showing unmistakably her unhappiness at the step Ellen was about to take.

'You'll help Misis, won't you Aijang?' Carl spoke slowly as the young man laid food on the table. 'You'll explain how things are done here.'

'Explain to Misis, Pastor Carl.'

'And when Misis asks you to do something, you'll do it straight away.'

'Straight away, Pastor Carl.'

Aijang disappeared and Ellen asked, trying to keep the concern out of her voice, whether the cook-boy would be with them in the house all the time.

'He sleeps in a hut out the back,' Carl reassured her. 'And when I'm away he comes with me.'

'But you're not going away, Carl? Not without me?'

Two

The heat on the coast had been like nothing Ellen had ever experienced, the sun a brutal ball of fire suspended over her shoulder, the only protection a few ramshackle buildings with interiors like furnaces. She had waited impatiently for the night, but it had offered little relief, just airless clouds of insects, implacable rain and the guttural sounds of men in pursuit of pleasure or oblivion. By contrast, the highland morning into which she had woken was crisp and cool, and the sweetness of the night still saturated her body.

As she sat with Carl on the verandah at a leisurely breakfast a line of women climbed the hill to the house, moving and conversing easily. They were carrying net bags full of sweet potatoes, leafy vegetables, beans and corn, and some had eggs, bananas and sugar cane. When they reached the front of the house they pushed their way forward, extolling with their arms and voices the virtues of their offerings, exhorting Ellen to come closer, to look and to touch. Aijang intervened and began to negotiate, obviously intent on driving a hard bargain, and Ellen sympathised with those women who were forced to retreat down the hill with their wares unexchanged. Those who had been successful showed themselves delighted with the salt, matches and bright baubles that Aijang had carefully doled out, and Ellen told herself that she had no right to belittle their simple pleasure.

After breakfast Carl suggested they visit his black mare Onyx, which was corralled in a small patch of ground to the side of the house. Ellen held back, not wanting Carl to see her nervousness in the presence of the animal. When prevailed upon to touch the horse's flank she hesitated then withdrew her hand quickly from the heavy, pulsating flesh. Carl held a bag from which Onyx was feeding as he spoke to her playfully. 'The people up here had never seen anything like you, had they girl? They thought you were some sort of giant pig.'

Ellen asked whether the surrounding country, with its mountains ranging up sharply from the valley floor, was not too demanding for a horse. Carl explained that the valley broadened out as it extended to the west, that several bridle paths were planned, and even where the terrain was difficult Onyx was a wonderful pack animal, worth her weight in gold.

'And the rivers, Carl? Aren't there tributaries of the main river? How do you cross them?'

'We find a way.'

Carl led Ellen further up the hill to a rectangular piece of terraced land. Inside a fence were several tidy rows of small shrubs, well-spaced to accommodate future growth. At one side a trellis was already partly covered by climbing plants, while furrows of rich dark soil were populated with seedlings of various forms and shades of green. Carl guided Ellen through a gate and stood gazing at the display. At the far end of the garden a man and a woman were working quietly on hands and knees, and Carl called out to them.

Ellen's first impression of the young man who stood up and turned towards them was of disproportion, of legs too short for the trunk, an impression that remained as the man moved stolidly forward. He exchanged some words with Carl then offered a soft hand to Ellen.

'Good day, Misis,' he said.

The angle of the man's head cast his face in a deep shadow, leaving Ellen unsure whether the set of his mouth constituted a smile or not.

Carl called out to the woman and she too got to her feet and came forward. She was older than the man, approaching middle age, with a deeply-lined, narrow face. She held out both hands to Carl and then to Ellen, who responded in kind, averting her eyes from the woman's near nakedness.

'Kubun and Yere look after the garden,' Carl explained. 'We're experimenting with new plants that might have a future as cash crops.'

The man and the woman returned to their work and Carl and Ellen walked slowly around the garden, every now and again stopping at a plant that Carl bent to touch. Ellen had not seen a coffee plant before and she listened as Carl praised its potential, while cautioning that the first fruit would not appear for several years. But they should get passionfruit the following year, all going well, and peanuts very soon. There were tea plants too, which were more speculative, and cinchona, the source of the quinine used to treat the malaria that was endemic in the lowlands but largely absent from the highlands.

'Malaria is a curse and a blessing,' Carl explained. 'It causes a lot of ill-health and early death among the lowland people, but it has also offered protection from European invasion.'

Ellen took Carl's arm and they moved on, Carl remarking casually that Kubun would come to cook when he was away, and to wash and clean. Kubun was as close to being a Christian as any of the local villagers; he knew some English and was of placid temperament. He would serve her unobtrusively. Apart from Yere, who was his aunt, Kubun had no close relatives, which meant freedom from the incessant importuning that relatives of servants often occasioned. Ellen was determined to go with Carl when he travelled, so she gave little thought to Kubun and his circumstances. Instead, she asked about Aijang.

'His first language is Kâte, one of the languages favoured by the mission, and he was delegated to teach me when I first arrived. He has a great talent for languages; he has picked up the language here in the Wahgi much more quickly than me. And he senses thoughts and emotions in the people that are hidden from me, although he considers himself superior to them.'

'He cooks all your meals?'

'In the early days I tried numerous cook-boys, but none proved suitable. Aijang offered to take on this task as well. He observed the cook-boys of other whites, learnt from them and extended their repertoire. He's proved very capable.'

They left the garden and walked higher up the hill to where the vegetation began to thin out. There they stopped and looked down along the valley to the distant mountains. Thin columns of smoke were clearly visible in the middle distance, holding their shape until they were high above the ground before gently dissolving. Here and there human figures could be seen moving about softly or bending tenderly over the ground. The Wahgi river sat shining in the grass matting of the valley floor. There was hardly a sound, but the air shimmered with a gentle pulse. The couple stood pressed together above this scene, speaking in short sentences about how much they had missed each other. Ellen leant her head on Carl's shoulder.

'Nature here seems so young and fresh,' she said. 'Not old and tired like at home.'

Carl mentioned the Barossa Valley as a counter-example. He said his childhood there before the Great War had been idyllic in a way that was now hard to imagine. But while the war had left no mark on the New Guinea highlands, the highland people had violent confrontations of their own that meant their life was hard. He added that despite the beauty and fertility of the landscape, the Wahgi Valley should not be confused with Shangri-La.

When they got back to the house Aijang was waiting. He said that Pastor Fiebiger's wife had been on the radio, asking if Misis had come yet.

'Lotte Fiebiger from the mission to the east,' Carl explained to Ellen. 'She's keen to meet you.'

'Oh, not yet, Carl. We need more time to ourselves.'

Three

Ellen was dressed almost entirely in white, her face shaded by a wide-brimmed hat, her slim body submerged beneath layers of gauzy material drawn in at the waist by a blue ribbon. Carl was wearing a light suit, a white shirt with a dark tie, and brown shoes. Ellen brushed down his jacket, smoothing out the creases and adjusting it so that it sat properly.

'You're not wearing your cassock?' she asked.

Carl took her hand and placed it on his arm as they began to walk down the hill. 'I don't lead the service; my command of the language doesn't allow it. And it isn't a proper service, just a foretaste.'

The village they arrived at after a five-minute descent to the bottom of the hill and a longer ascent of an adjacent rise consisted of twenty or thirty rough dwellings strung out unevenly along a verge, some obviously lived in, others run-down and apparently abandoned. The makeshift church, a men's long house, Carl had told Ellen, was distinguished by a rough wooden cross above the entrance. As they approached, they could see several women scouring the surrounds with improvised brooms, while others watched and offered advice. Then the group dispersed in such a way that the numerous piles of rubbish were hidden from view. But no attempt was made to hide the bows and arrows, spears and shields that were strewn on the ground beside the building.

It was still early morning and the outside air was cool, but the press of bodies in the church, most sitting on the earthen floor, generated a heavy warmth. There were flowers woven into the roof and the walls in a gaudy display, but any scent they might have exuded was overwhelmed by the stench of the pig grease that the people used liberally to bring their skin to a high gloss. Ellen followed Carl towards a simple altar and sat down on a wooden trestle then found a handkerchief and pressed its faint perfume discreetly to her nose. She was aware of the man and woman from Carl's garden, the man on one side with the other men, the woman with the other women, but she felt unable to turn to acknowledge them.

Carl went to an old harmonium and started to pedal, and the instrument began to groan. Voices called out; there were bursts of laughter and a slow clapping. A young man dressed in a fresh *lap-lap* and a clean shirt that set him apart from the others went up to the front and began to sing. Soon the entire congregation, Carl included, had joined in the singing, making the air shake.

Several hymns were sung, but even the ones Ellen recognised struck her as pagan in their exuberance. At times the pace seemed too much for the harmonium, and she watched with a mixture of embarrassment and amusement as Carl's legs pumped harder and harder at the pedals and the droning chords fell further and further behind.

Suddenly there was quiet, then the young man in the shirt

started to speak. At first his voice was almost an undertone, lulling the aroused feelings. Then his pace quickened, the volume increased and the gesticulations became more pointed until Ellen thought he was about to lose his self-control and fling himself onto the ground and writhe about. She felt herself gripped by a strange fascination and was almost disappointed when the man regained his composure and moderated the flow of his words, which then faded away to almost nothing.

*

'The young preacher got very excited, Carl. What was he saying?'

They had returned from the church and were sitting at the table on the verandah of the house. Aijang was a shadowy presence in the background.

'Kanbangi is one of our newer helpers. Like all the local people he is yet to be baptised, but he has a grasp of the rudiments of the Gospel, so I allow him to preach occasionally.'

'What did he say?' Ellen asked again.

'He spoke very quickly. I didn't catch everything.'

Ellen waited and eventually Carl continued. 'One of our villagers recently fell sick and died. His family blamed an old woman from another tribe; they said it was sorcery. A young man was designated to lie in wait; he ambushed the woman and clubbed her to death. Kanbangi was explaining that Christians must not retaliate in this way. We should forgive those who have wronged us.'

Ellen wiped the distaste from the corners of her mouth. Aijang was standing with a teapot and she held out her empty cup. Her hand shook.

'Bush *kanakas*, Misis,' Aijang said as he poured the tea, 'know nothing much.'

Carl said something sharp and Aijang turned on his heels and went away.

After a short pause Carl said, 'Since he was a boy Aijang has lived in close proximity to the white world. It's inevitable that he shares our prejudices.'

'He seems quite forward for a servant,' Ellen commented. Then she asked about the villager who had committed the murder. What would happen to him? Would he be brought to justice?

Carl left these questions unanswered, instead returning the conversation to the preacher in the church. 'Kanbangi was haranguing the people, but that just makes them sullen and unwilling to listen. I've tried to tell him this.'

'You should preach yourself. I'm sure you could make them understand.'

'I've enough of the language only for simple thoughts and feelings. Nothing more.'

Ellen took Carl's hand. She stroked and kissed it. She said that she was proud of him.

Carl eased his hand free. 'At the end, Kanbangi warned the men not to look at you, and especially not to catch your eyes. He said it is a terrible temptation to look into the eyes of a white woman, especially one so young.'

Ellen sat back in affected surprise. 'Am I such a dangerous thing?' she asked.

Carl leant across the table and kissed her lightly on the lips. 'A very dangerous thing,' he replied.

Four

For the next week Carl stayed close to home, working mainly at his desk. From time to time he stopped to tell Ellen something of his experiences in this new country or to ask for details of what had changed at home in the time they had been apart. The easy rhythm of these conversations helped to reassure Ellen that Carl was still the same person she had come to know in Adelaide.

Inevitably, the initial euphoria of the reunion ebbed away and soon Ellen found the days beginning to drag. She had done some nursing training at home while waiting for the New Guinea administration to allow her to enter the country, and she told Carl that she wanted to put this training to use. He said there was certainly plenty of sickness in the villages round about, but she would need to be careful not to promise more than she could provide. If a treatment went wrong or was ineffectual and a villager died she would be blamed, with untold consequences for his missionary work.

'But there must be everyday illnesses where I could help with little risk,' Ellen countered.

Carl said that the first step would be for her to learn the rudiments of the local Wahgi language. He would arrange for someone from the village to come and spend time with her. He showed her a dictionary he was working on and explained the accent marks he had designed to capture the distinctive sounds of the language.

Ellen nodded her appreciation of Carl's work. Then she said, 'On the coast I heard Europeans speaking pidgin English to the natives. Wouldn't that be easier to learn than the local language, and more practical?'

Carl said that the people in the Wahgi Valley did not speak pidgin, which was an artificial language incapable of capturing anything but the most banal thoughts. His tone was dismissive. 'Pidgin speakers inevitably become caricatures of themselves.'

*

That night a figure came into the front room of the mission house unannounced and took up a seated position on the floor. Ellen gave a short cry of shock, but Carl's only reaction was to move his hands in a reassuring gesture. The figure, a mature man of Carl's age or perhaps a little older, brought with it a smell of wood smoke and a silence that accentuated the sounds of the night and of the house. Distant singing gradually revealed itself to Ellen, concerted women's voices from lower down in the valley; there was the shrieking of a lonely bird and the audible adjustment of the floor to the intruding man's weight.

'This is Mbagl,' Carl said softly.

On hearing his name the man moved forward on hands and knees and took up a kneeling position in front of Ellen. With his head bowed he felt first for her ankles, then for her knees and forearms, at each point making small stroking movements with his hands. Ellen tensed at the papery touch that penetrated her clothing. She wondered if she should reciprocate the man's greeting and looked at Carl for guidance, but his face remained impassive.

Mbagl returned to his place. He began an exchange with Carl, the sounds seeming to Ellen devoid of any structure or shape, like a shallow river with no banks. Then the talk ceased and the silence returned.

'Should I make something?' Ellen whispered.

Carl shook his head. He took a tobacco pouch and a thin piece of white paper from his pocket and conjured up a cigarette that he handed to his guest. A second cigarette was made; a single match served to light both cigarettes and the two men sat smoking for several minutes, with only an occasional exchange of words or other signs of communication. Ellen felt superfluous, but she did not trust herself to move.

When at last the man had gone Ellen asked Carl when he had taken up smoking. He answered that he did not smoke much, only occasionally in the evening.

'When that man comes?' Ellen asked.

'Yes, I suppose so.'

Ellen took her time preparing for bed. When she finally lay down Carl reached for her, but she whispered that she was too tired. It was the first time since her arrival in the highlands that she had been too tired.

Five

The young preacher came in a rush and there was an intense conversation with Carl. When the man had gone Carl explained that some of his native evangelists who were stationed further to the west had apparently fought with local helpers of the Roman Catholics. Huts had been burnt down and gardens vandalised. If the administration got wind of this the evangelists would be banned from working in the villages and the mission would shrivel and die. He would have to go and sort things out.

For several minutes Ellen watched as Carl spoke on the radio, huddled over the microphone with his ears encased in headphones. At the end of a series of conversations he said that Lotte Fiebiger had agreed to come and stay; the mission's aeroplane would be available to bring her the following day.

'But can't I come with you, Carl?'

Carl explained his need to travel quickly and the possibility of danger. He added that Ellen would inevitably have bouts of sickness as her body adjusted to the new environment; she should be close to the mission house and its comforts when sickness came. He assured her that Mbagl would watch over her and the house, so she had no need to fear any intrusion while he was away.

When Carl and Aijang had gone, the man from Carl's garden appeared, indicating by words and gestures that he had come to help. She asked his name again and wrote down 'Kubun'. She set him to work giving the house an additional clean while she aired the linen for the single bed. She put on display the full complement of decorative things that had been sent long before from Australia but had not yet been unpacked. She made a careful assessment of the store of tinned food in the pantry and found a bottle of sweet sherry that she dusted off and put within easy reach. She asked Kubun to ensure that there was a constant supply of fresh vegetables from the village gardens, then explained as best she could how he should behave when the guest came and how he should set the table. Then she observed as he prepared a meal, making suggestions for improvements. She gave particular attention to the way the prepared food was arranged on the plate, telling Kubun that presentation was almost as important as the food itself. She emphasised that his hands must be well washed at all stages of the preparation and serving of food.

After dinner she covered her shoulders with a shawl and sat down in the living room to review the day's work. In the light of a kerosene lamp she allowed her eyes to follow the contours of the room and her mind to picture the rest of the house, and she realised how skilfully it had been constructed. The lengths of sawn timber used for the walls fitted perfectly with no gaps. The doors had been ingeniously hung to shut silently and surely, the wooden slats of the window shutters closed smoothly to keep out prying eyes while still allowing a light flow of night air, and the contrasting colours and textures of the floor, walls and ceiling complemented each other and pleased the eye. A woman's touch was needed to create a more lived-in atmosphere, but this would be her task. With this thought in her mind she went confidently to bed and was quickly asleep.

There was a heavy mist the next morning and Ellen held her breath as she listened to the sound of a small aeroplane searching for a way through. The sound of the engine disappeared and she thought that the plane might have turned back, but before long voices at the front of the house indicated that her guest had arrived.

Ellen knew from Carl that Alfred Fiebiger's wife had been one of the first white women in the highlands and was no longer young. She was expecting a heavy frame with clear signs of wear and tear, but the reality was a small, slender woman with assured movements, a bright smile and a readiness to touch and be touched.

'Call me Lotte, dear. Everyone calls me Lotte.'

They sat at the dining table and Kubun brought things to eat and drink. The conversation rested largely with the visitor.

'You think at first you'll never get used to it, but you will, with time.'

'I suppose so.'

'You have your husband, and you may find companionship among the local people—even friendship of a kind, if you're prepared to meet them halfway.'

'Yes, I'm sure.'

'But be careful not to be seduced.'

'Seduced?' Ellen asked.

'Into thinking that the people's lack of civilisation means they are free from our vanities and intrigues.'

Kubun had spilt some tea and was fussing to clean it up. Ellen offered terse advice that went unheeded, leading her to wave him away and complete the job herself. When things settled down Lotte patted Ellen's hand and said that it was hard at first to find the right tone with the local help, but it would come with practice.

'Carl must be in seventh heaven now you're finally here,' Lotte went on between sips of tea. 'But you might find him changed.'

'I haven't noticed any change,' Ellen asserted, wondering as she spoke whether this was entirely true.

Lotte continued. 'In my experience those who spend time in this place either become much more themselves, clinging to every last bit of the identity they bring with them, or they succumb to the new environment and undergo significant change. My husband belongs to the first category. I suspect Carl belongs to the second.'

'Which category do you belong to?' Ellen asked instinctively.

Lotte's answer was indirect. 'We women are more balanced than men, less liable to be overly excited or confused by new impressions and challenges. That's why the men rely so heavily on us. You will inevitably find this with Carl.'

After this initial conversation the subject of Carl temporarily receded into the background. During walks or while sitting in the cool of the evening Lotte told Ellen about her time in

New Guinea, which began before the World War. She and her husband had at first been in the hills behind Finschhafen, almost in sight of the sea, fighting disease and consolidating the work of the Lutheran pioneers. Then they had joined the mission's movement into the eastern highlands, excited by the prospect of bringing the Word of God to people largely untouched by Europeans. There had been a few unfortunate incidents—some prospectors had strayed into the area and used violence that had alienated the natives—but that time had passed and the mission had subsequently been blessed with many converts. Now it had spread further west to this new frontier of high valleys, bounteous gardens and teeming populations.

'The Roman Catholics have come through the mountains from Madang in the north,' Lotte continued. 'Alfred is determined not to be outdone by them. And the Adventists are also showing an interest.'

Ellen did not want to think about this competition for souls, which she thought unseemly. But she found herself telling Lotte the reason for Carl's absence, seeking her assurance that he was not in danger.

'I can't say there is no danger. But for the most part the people restrict their fighting to their own kind.'

'It all seems so primitive, hardly human.'

'Our task is to bring God's Word to these people,' Lotte answered. 'Locating them on the scale of civilisation is not our concern. Sometimes Carl seems not to understand this.'

Ellen resisted the temptation to defend Carl from the charge she did not quite understand. Instead she said, 'Carl told me that only when the highlanders see the Christian message exemplified in the life of the missionaries will they be ready for proper instruction.'

Lotte's next comment closed the conversation. 'It is best, for the people and for ourselves, if we rely on God's Word to speak for itself. We should not push ourselves and our own interpretations to the fore.'

Later the two women walked up the incline behind the house, passing Carl's garden that Lotte only briefly remarked upon before reaching the point where the hill turned sharply upwards into the mountains. Lotte was full of determination, saying that she felt compelled to reach the summit of any mountain that stood in her way. So far she had not been defeated, although she had yet to test herself against Wilhelmsberg to the north. She set off at a brisk pace and Ellen was soon struggling for breath. She fell behind the older woman and about three quarters of the way to the top she had to stop to rest. They agreed to leave the summit for another time.

Six

A small group of figures was winding its way up the hill towards the house. Ellen hoped they would veer off in a different direction, but their progress was undeviating. Lotte was in another part of the house and Ellen called out to her.

As the group drew closer Ellen could see a white man in the lead, a trim figure under a wide-brimmed hat, moving for all the world as if this were his sovereign domain. With him was a small detail of New Guineans with bare chests and legs, their khaki shorts held in place by ammunition belts. Each man had an army cap perched on his tightly woven hair and a rifle slung nonchalantly over his shoulder. Their bodies rippled in the sunlight.

Lotte joined Ellen at the front of the house, wiping her hands on a cloth. 'A police patrol,' she explained. 'I wonder what they want.'

'Hello there.' The white man had taken off his hat, showing fair skin and a sharply receding hairline that belied his relative youth. The man waved his hat back and forth. 'Hello there.'

As they came closer the man spoke to his companions, and they held back as he continued his approach. Lotte called out, 'What do you want, Chas Noble?'

'Well, if it ain't Lotte Fiebiger. And what might you be doing here?'

'That's what I'm asking you.'

'We've had reports of a killing. Too many killings out here lately. We need to clamp down. Show 'em it won't be tolerated.'

'We don't know anything about a killing.'

'And even if you did you wouldn't be telling me, would you Lotte? You'd be wanting to clear it up yourself, or keep it hidden, so you could dole out your own brand of forgiveness.'

The man turned to Ellen. 'Carl's missus, I suppose?' He reached up a hand, which Ellen briefly took. 'Well, I can see why he moved heaven and earth to get you here. But I don't hold with it, a European woman, and one so young, in a frontier place like this.' Noble rotated his hat in his hands. 'But it mightn't be for long.'

'What do you mean by that?' Lotte asked.

For a few moments Lotte and Chas Noble glared at each other. Then Noble said, 'Word is some of Carl's bible boys have been stirring up trouble in the villages round about. The rule is that these boys have to be under the close supervision of a European, which doesn't seem to have been the case. So, we might just close the whole thing down.'

'You can't do that.'

'Sure can do that, Lotte, as you well know. Anyway, where is he?'

'Pastor Starck is away.'

'Gone to clear up the mess, I suppose.'

Lotte did not respond and Noble said in that case he would just have to deal with the local killing by himself. 'With the help of my boys, of course,' he added after a pause, smiling as if amused by what he'd said. He spoke briefly in pidgin to the waiting men, returned his hat to his head, then gave a weak impression of a wave in the direction of the two women. He turned to leave, then stopped and called back to Lotte. 'I suppose your lot might be thinking that the volcano in Rabaul blowing its top is a judgment on the way we Australians are going about things here in New Guinea. But you'd be wrong there. It's just Mother Nature letting off steam, as she does from time to time.' Without waiting for a response Noble headed down the hill, the police contingent following in smart order.

*

Ellen was flustered by the encounter with Chas Noble, and it took her some time to fully regain her composure. Lotte left her in peace during this period. It was only at the midday meal that they discussed what had happened.

'I doubt Noble is too worried about the death of a native. I think he'd heard you'd arrived and decided to come and look you over.'

'I felt he was undressing me with his eyes.' Ellen seemed surprised by her own words, but Lotte took them in her stride.

'You'd do well to keep your distance from that man. He has a reputation for misbehaving with local women, and much else besides.'

Ellen's face reddened.

'Don't look so shocked, dear. They might be whites but

they're also men, and they have their needs. There's quite a bit of it going on, I can tell you.'

*

Kubun had been down to the village, and when he returned he told the women that an arrest had been made and the prisoner taken off to face justice at the government post in the east.

'Whether he's the guilty one or not won't matter to Chas Noble,' Lotte asserted. 'He has his own idea of justice towards the blacks. Let them know who's boss at the beginning by whatever means necessary and save yourself a lot of trouble later on.'

Despite Ellen's adverse impression of Noble she wondered whether prejudice against the Australian administration was colouring Lotte's opinion. Carl had told her that there was still resentment among some of the Germans at the loss of their colony, even after all this time.

'But most of the *kiaps* are not like Noble,' Lotte added. 'They do their best, within their limitations.'

Ellen knew that the word '*kiap*' referred to the Australian patrol officers and that it came from the German word '*Kapitän*'. This thought suggested to her a new topic.

'I can read German and understand simple conversation, but when I speak I make too many mistakes.'

'It's all right, dear. You must devote all your energies to mastering Kâte.' Lotte looked around the empty room. 'You need to surround yourself with children. You'll learn from them without even trying.'

'The people here speak a Wahgi language, which seems extraordinarily difficult. I thought it would make more sense to learn pidgin English, but Carl won't hear of it.'

Lotte stated that Carl was inclined to take extreme positions in matters of language, as in other areas, then asked Ellen if she wanted children of her own. Before Ellen could answer Lotte stated that she had not been able to have children, and this had been a blessing in disguise. She doubted the wisdom of whites bringing children into these foreign and remote places. They either died early from one of the many diseases or grew up lost between opposing worlds.

For several moments Lotte's childlessness filled the space between the two women. Gradually tears formed in Ellen's eyes and Lotte moved beside her and comforted her. She said that there were great sacrifices in the missionary life, but also great rewards.

When Ellen was calm again Lotte asked about her family. Ellen explained that her great grandfather on her father's side had fled religious persecution in Germany and emigrated to South Australia in the 1850s. After a number of false starts he had gone into the wine business. Her grandfather and then her father had followed in his footsteps, building a successful business that had weathered many storms, including the recent Depression.

'And your mother's side?'

'They were English. But when I was growing up we went to the Lutheran church.'

Lotte nodded her approval then moved the conversation back to Carl, asking when and where he and Ellen had met.

'His first parish was in the Barossa Valley. Then he received a call to Adelaide, although he was still quite young. It was there that we met.'

'I can imagine he would have been very hard for a young girl to resist.'

Ellen said that she could have resisted easily enough, if she had wanted to. Carl was the one who claimed to have fallen under a spell.

Courtship

(1933)

One

The rehearsal had run overtime and it was quite dark when Ellen and Britta began their walk back to North Adelaide. The night air was soft, the warmth of the day not fully dissipated. Ellen instinctively put her arm through Britta's. 'What did you say to him?' she asked.

'I told him that I thought his sermons were quite fine and I was urging my friend to come and listen.'

'How did he respond?'

'He thanked me politely. But before he could say more his nibs told us to stop dilly-dallying and to take up our places.'

They walked for several minutes in silence. Then Ellen asked if Britta had undertaken the research she had promised.

'He grew up in the Barossa. He has no brothers or sisters and it was expected that he would take over his parents' farm. His uni studies at first went in that direction, but after his parents died he decided to become a pastor. He studied in Germany then returned to the Barossa parish as an assistant. Not long afterwards he received the call to Adelaide.'

'You're sure he's not married?'

'Apparently there were some flames that burned brightly in his younger days, but none lasted long. At present he lives quite alone in his manse in Klemzig.'

'I won't be able to come to his service,' Ellen said as they stopped in front of her house. 'My mother has forbidden us to have any further contact with the Lutheran church.'

Britta's parting comment as she turned to walk on was that the presence of such an eligible bachelor in the university choir was a clear sign of a desire for female companionship. She would think about how best to make the introduction.

*

Carl stood up as Ellen hurried towards him. He was dressed in a black suit and a high clerical collar, and she felt underdressed in her light skirt, short-sleeved blouse and bare legs apart from short socks and flat shoes. She spoke quickly to hide her embarrassment. 'You got the note, then.'

They were in the botanical gardens, near a pond. It was lunchtime on a still, late summer day under a lightly clouded sky. Ellen sat down on a bench and put her hands in her lap. 'I can imagine what you must think, but Britta insisted this was the best way.'

'I thought you might be the friend,' Carl said as he sat beside Ellen. 'I was hoping so.' Ellen blushed as she took a bundle of wrapped sandwiches and a small thermos flask from the large bag at her side. She began to eat, speaking only when her mouth was entirely empty.

'I wanted to attend one of your services, but my mother has forbidden us to have anything more to do with the Lutheran church, although my father is Lutheran. My mother is English and Unitarian. We go to the Unitarian church in town.'

Carl also had some sandwiches, which he ate slowly. Between mouthfuls he asked Ellen if her mother's opposition was due to political events in Germany. She nodded, then changed the subject. 'I often come here, for the peace and quiet. Do you come here often?'

Carl said he used to visit regularly when he was a student. He especially liked the fact that the gardens had a good representation of Australian natives.

Ellen began to relax. She said confidently, 'One of my forebears was a leading figure in the gardens' early days. He was born in Germany but was an ardent Australian nationalist, especially when it came to plants.'

They sat for a time looking at passers-by. Carl broke the silence to say that his first university course had been in agronomy; he had initially planned to take over his parents' farm and had retained a strong interest in plants. Ellen admitted that she had done some research and knew this.

'What else do you know?'

'You studied theology in Germany then followed a call to the Lutheran parish in the Barossa, where you grew up. You are one of the youngest men to take over the Adelaide parish. And Britta is not the only one to say that your sermons are quite fine.'

'I'm never satisfied with them.'

'Britta says they are a model of lucidity—a series of clear, logical steps from the mundane to the transcendent.' Ellen resumed her normal voice. 'Or something like that. Anyway, I'm sure they're better than what we get from the Unitarians.

The pastor there qualifies everything he says interminably. I doubt he believes anything.'

They skirted the topic of belief and moved to Carl's time in Germany, Ellen carefully bringing the conversation around to the subject of any girlfriends he might have had there. He said that the German girls he had met had fallen into two broad categories: they were either parochial and suspicious of anything foreign or over-sophisticated and superficial. But the men were different. They were patriotic, but they were also very interested in the outside world. They wanted to hear what he thought of Germany, but they were not defensive. And they were passionate about ideas. He could have become friends with many of these young men, but somehow the final step to friendship had never been taken.

After a pause Carl issued a qualification of his statement about German girls. His sister was neither provincial nor superficial. She was open and genuine, and he had found a friend in her. Ellen said in a surprised tone that her research had not uncovered anything about a sister, let alone one in Germany. Carl responded that it was a long story and he would explain one day.

Ellen returned her thermos flask to her bag, arranging some books to make space. *Constitutional Law* was part of the title of one of the books, and Carl asked whether she was studying law.

'You needn't sound so surprised. But if you must know, it's first and foremost to please my mother.'

'Your mother sounds formidable.'

'Yes and no,' Ellen said. 'But now let's sit and enjoy the beautiful day.'

*

Their second meeting in the botanical gardens took place at the end of the same week. Ellen began the conversation by explaining in greater detail why she was studying law. 'My English grandmother campaigned for the right of women to vote, in England then here in South Australia. My mother says the suffragettes won an important battle, but the war is not yet over. Women have to know the law better and use it to their advantage. Therefore, more women should practise law.'

'I see.'

'I'm not sure a man can see.'

Ellen reached out and touched Carl's arm in encouragement. 'It's very unfair to be judged simply on the basis of your sex, but this happens to women constantly.'

For a moment Carl seemed unsure of himself. Then he said that 'war' was hardly the right word for the relation between the sexes.

'A figure of speech. But you haven't asked me if I like studying law. The answer is I'm not sure I have the right disposition. I think I'm better suited to something less dry, more human.'

'But you'll continue?'

'I'm in my second year. I suppose I'll keep going. I don't mind it.'

Carl said that for the moment he was content with his work, but he was not sure it would satisfy him in the longer term. When economic circumstances returned to normal his

Adelaide parishioners would be less in need of him, and it might then be time for a new challenge.

'But you've only just come here,' Ellen said, annoyed by the pleading note she could hear in her voice. 'It's much too early to be thinking of leaving.'

They made small talk for a time, about Britta and her bravado, the choirmaster and his fussiness. They discussed *Israel and Egypt*—Handel's setting of the Exodus story that they were practising in the choir, whether Handel should be thought of as German or English, and how his name should be spelt and pronounced. Then they fell silent. Ellen slipped off her shoes, bent down and massaged her feet through her socks. She said she did not like her feet, which were too narrow and made finding suitable shoes difficult. In fact, her whole body was lanky and ill-proportioned, didn't he think so? He said she was fishing for compliments and she demurred, but her manner indicated that a compliment would be welcome. He said she was a beautiful girl, and she seemed content with that. She leant against him and he put his arm around her.

*

They met usually at lunchtime on Mondays and Fridays, although Carl was sometimes unavoidably detained and came late or not at all. On these latter occasions Ellen did her best to accept that Carl had demands on his time that took precedence over her.

For the most part they would sit and eat their sandwiches

and drink their tea, but sometimes they would walk along the path that wound through the gardens, enjoying the movement and the changing scenery. Carl would talk about individual plants, the origin of their Latin names, their likes and dislikes in terms of soil, moisture and sunlight, and where he had come across them in their natural habitats. Ellen would respond by identifying the people that particular plants reminded her of and explaining the resemblances—shape to stature, foliage to hair, flowers to complexion or eye colour. In this way she acquainted Carl with several of her family and friends.

Occasionally when there was no one else around they would sing out loud their favourite extracts from *Israel and Egypt*, then spend time commenting on the foibles of their fellow choir members. They would hold hands and recite lines of poetry, then gently mock each other's romanticism.

'They know about us at home,' Ellen began one day as they were walking. 'My mother gave me a talking to.'

They continued to walk, smiling automatically at occasional passers-by.

'I can imagine what she said. You must finish your degree, establish your career. No time to think about romance, certainly not with a Lutheran pastor.'

'My mother has her quibbles with Lutheranism, but she thinks the German and British people are racially one. She's antagonistic towards the Nazis because she fears they will drive apart what belongs together.'

'Your mother thinks in racial terms?'

Ellen answered that her mother considered herself modern

and scientific, and she viewed race as a scientific idea. For this reason she had firm beliefs about the Aborigines, who she thought must retain the purity of their blood by refusing to intermarry with whites, while at the same time learning to accommodate the white world.

Carl asked whether it was possible to do both these things and Ellen said that she didn't know. But Carl must not think that her mother was prejudiced against blacks. A half-caste girl was a servant in their home, rescued by her mother from a life of vice and misery. The girl was treated well, she never complained and seemed happy enough. Her name was Flora.

They came to an unoccupied bench and Carl suggested they sit. When they were comfortable he invited Ellen to talk about her religious beliefs.

Ellen asked if this was a test, but Carl just waited. She composed herself. 'I believe in God, of course. How else can we explain our existence and the existence of the world? About Jesus I'm not completely sure. But whether he is the Son of God or just a faultless man, I think we would all do well to follow him.'

She asked if this was sufficient, and Carl replied that for the time being it was.

*

They had sat near the front of the electric tram and watched the suburbs slide effortlessly by, allowing the swaying of the carriage to push them pleasantly back and forth against each other. Now they were at a table in a tea room with a view over the sand and the water. The day was overcast and there were occasional flurries of rain, but Ellen felt exhilarated by the salt smell and the wide vista of the sea, and by the lingering traces of the tram journey.

I told my mother that Britta and I were going to the new picture theatre in town. Britta has already seen the film and told me all about it.'

'Is the deception necessary?' Carl asked.

'It's not really deception. I doubt my mother believed me.'

Ellen dropped her head demurely as the waitress brought their cups of tea and slices of cake and wished them *bon appétit*.

'Mother really mustn't tell me whom I can and cannot fall in love with,' Ellen insisted when the waitress had gone.

A heavy rain shower suddenly blew across the beach, splattering raindrops against the cafe window. The couple sat holding their teacups and looking out at the grey water and the jetty that stood firm against the lapping waves. Carl remarked on a lone figure at the far end of the jetty, surrounded by pieces of fishing equipment and with legs dangling over the side, but Ellen hardly heard what he said.

'Carl?' Tears formed in her eyes and Carl pleaded with her not to cry.

He said, 'Being the wife of a Lutheran pastor will not be easy. There will be suspicion, even hostility, especially now. And who can say to what far-flung field I might be called.'

Ellen said assertively that as long as she had Carl's love she would be equal to any challenge. He held her hand and assured her that she would always have his love.

Carl paid the bill and they went outside into the brisk air. The squall had passed and weak sunlight was breaking through the clouds. Ellen took his arm and they set out along the beach, which was strewn with seagulls, seaweed and pieces of sodden wood. They had the beach largely to themselves and Ellen broke free from Carl's arm, took off her hat and shoes and ran forward with arms flailing and heels kicking to each side. She turned and waved, calling to him to catch her if he could, then watched as he ran effortlessly towards her, a tall figure not in clerical black but in street shoes, long grey trousers and a stylish blue jacket. When he came near he reached for her, but she eluded his grasp and skipped away again, laughing her light laugh.

They repeated this game along the full extent of the beach until exhaustion set in, then began the walk back. Another rain shower threatened and they hurried to shelter under the jetty. Ellen felt hot and sticky and longed to throw off her clothes and plunge into the choppy water. She looked at Carl and imagined his naked body, wondering what it would be like to have him make love to her.

At the jetty she opened her arms in invitation. Carl embraced and kissed her, his lips gentle, almost chaste. Then she laid a restraining hand on his chest. 'That's enough for now,' she whispered, pointing to the dangling legs further along the jetty.

Two

Ellen's parents had asked to meet Carl, and at the designated time he knocked on the door of a large house set in a neat garden. A tall girl of middle teenage years with a clear resemblance to Ellen—the same wide mouth, large eyes and lightly freckled skin—led him into the living room. Ellen was nowhere to be seen, but from somewhere deep inside the house a melody by Handel was being played on a piano.

The couple of the house welcomed Carl briskly and the group arranged itself on comfortable chairs in a well-appointed living room. Shortly afterwards a dark-skinned girl brought in a tea service and placed it carefully on the coffee table. She curtsied neatly then withdrew, closing the door behind her.

'You're much older than Ellen.'

It was the woman who took the lead, speaking while pouring tea. 'In itself this is not an insuperable barrier. But she is still so young, and she has her studies to consider.'

William Winter suggested to his wife that she allow their visitor time to settle, but the woman continued speaking to Carl. 'We have been pleased to hear many positive things about you from our friends and acquaintances. But my concern is that one day you might set off into the wilderness in pursuit of converts among the Aborigines, like your father, whom we know about, dragging Ellen with you. Do you have such an intention?'

'Lou ...'

'I assume Pastor Starck appreciates plain speaking, William.'

Louisa Winter completed her thought. 'From what I can see the missions in our state and in the Northern Territory have brought little advancement to the blacks. They have not prepared them to take their place in the modern world. They have merely helped to create a cohort of half-castes who dilute the race. The Aborigines must retain pride in their race if they are to flourish.'

Carl acknowledged that the missions to the Aborigines might be considered a failure. Perhaps his father had come to think of them as such. But he had nonetheless contributed much to the stock of knowledge about native languages and beliefs, knowledge that would be of great benefit to those who wished to lift up the blacks.

Ellen's mother abruptly moved the discussion to current events in Germany, saying that since Carl had recently spent time there he would have witnessed up close the gestation of what was now happening. Where would it end? And what could he say to demonstrate that he had not himself been infected by the bacillus of National Socialism?

William Winter intervened. 'Pastor Starck can't be held responsible for events in Germany, Louisa. Nor can he be held responsible for his father's wanderings in the desert.' He turned to Carl. 'I'm sure you have no sympathy for the Nazis.'

'When I was in Germany they were not taken seriously. The people around me mocked them and their leader constantly.'

'But what do *you* think?' Louisa Winter asked.

As Carl prepared an answer the living room door opened, the servant girl took a half-step inside and asked softly whether she should bring more tea. Ellen's mother made to dismiss her with a shake of the head but was brought up short when Ellen herself came into the room and said that, since she was the primary subject of the conversation, she should be fully present, not just listening at the door. She sat down next to Carl and took his hand.

William Winter exchanged a questioning look with his wife, then turned to Carl and asked in a ceremonial tone about his intentions towards his daughter. The answer sounded both rehearsed and candid. 'Ellen has opened her heart to me, and I have found myself responding in a way that I hardly thought possible. I would therefore like your permission to make her my wife.'

'I appreciate the sincerity of your feelings,' Louisa Winter interjected immediately. 'But I still have some questions.'

Ellen tightened her hold on Carl's hand and he responded in kind.

'In deference to my husband's heritage we attended the Lutheran church when the children were younger, but I was never comfortable with this, because there are aspects of the doctrine I cannot accept. In particular, I will not have it that each human being is fundamentally flawed from the very beginning, out of the womb. Nor will I have it that our will is insufficient to drag us out of any slough of vice or despond into which we might stray, and that we are solely reliant on God's grace for our salvation. I've tried to impress on Ellen and her sister that our destiny lies in our own hands. I would like to know where you stand.' She added as an afterthought, 'And the doctrine of hell is an abomination, a wicked perversion of the human imagination.'

When Louisa Winter had finished speaking there was a lull. Then she got to her feet and the others followed, standing almost at attention, unsure where to look. Ellen broke the silence by asking her mother for an answer to Carl's question. The woman turned to Carl. 'Before my husband and I can respond to your request we will require a written response to my questions about religious doctrine. We will also require a promise in writing that you will allow Ellen perfect freedom of belief.

'And there is one further thing. We understand that questions remain about the circumstances of your father's death. I would like to know your version of these events. We must be quite sure there is no suspicion of congenital mental weakness in your family.'

Three

They were sitting on their favourite bench in the botanical gardens and Ellen was in a buoyant mood. She said that her father had been impressed; he thought Carl had stood up manfully to her mother's onslaught. They weren't yet home and hosed, but they were in the final straight.

'That's not the impression I got.'

'Mother will want to feel she has done her duty, but she will not stand in the way of my happiness.'

When Ellen's excitement subsided, she asked Carl why he had not told her about his real father.

'I didn't know him well, hardly at all. When I was young he was just a strange man who would visit the Barossa from time to time, say little I could understand then leave again for the north. For a long time I had no idea he was my father.'

Ellen waited and Carl went into detail. 'His name was Herbert Wischner. He arrived in South Australia in the early 1890s, stayed only a short while in Adelaide and the Barossa before heading to the desert and the Aborigines, where he remained until just before his death at the end of the Great War. I was his youngest child, born in the north, as were my two brothers and my sister. My mother died shortly after my birth and the family was dispersed. My siblings were sent to

"

relatives in Germany for their education, but I was considered too young for the journey and instead placed with a childless couple in the Barossa, Peter and Susanna Starck. They were mother and father to me.'

'When did you find out the truth?' Ellen asked.

'Near the end of the Great War my father came here to Adelaide, where I was at boarding school. He asked to speak to me alone, which he had never done before, and he told me he had recently learnt that his two sons had been killed in France, within days of each other. He said that these two sons were my brothers, Paul and Matthias. He said he thought I should know. He gave me a photograph.'

Carl took a creased photograph from his pocket and handed it to Ellen. It showed two boys on the threshold of manhood, in civilian clothing with broad smiles, arms around each other's shoulders.

'At first, I felt nothing, but as time passed I began to mourn my brothers. I would look at the photograph and try to imagine what they had been like, what they would have become, what we would have said to each other when we met.

'I did not see my father again; he died not many weeks later. Only a handful of mourners were at the funeral.'

Carl reached inside a leather case and took out a bundle of old exercise books that he handed to Ellen.

'These are my father's diaries. There are gaps, sometimes of months at a time, but they give a picture of his life in the desert. Please look after them carefully, and do not show them to anyone else.'

*

Ellen read the diaries late at night when everyone else in the house was asleep. She skipped over much of the detail, in particular the long discussions about the translation of biblical concepts into the language of the local Aborigines, focussing instead on the day-to-day achievements and setbacks of Carl's father. She was especially touched by the anticipation with which, after a long period of loneliness, he awaited the arrival of his bride from Germany, and by the love that he developed for her and for the children she gave him. His grief at her death aroused Ellen's pity. But when after several weeks she had finally finished she found herself largely out of sympathy with a man whose persistence in an impossible task had imposed such enormous costs on his family and on himself.

At the next meeting in the botanical gardens she began to discuss her conclusions, but Carl cut her short. For the first time a distance opened between them, and Ellen carried her anguish throughout the rest of the day. Initially she thought that some time apart would be best, but later the next evening she went to visit Carl at his manse, determined to clear the air. She began to speak as soon as she was inside the front door.

'The handwriting was difficult and I didn't understand all the German, but enough to form my own opinion.'

Carl responded in a conciliatory tone. He acknowledged that his father had made few lasting converts among the Aborigines and that at the end he had been quite alone, without colleagues, friends or family. It could easily seem that his life had been in vain. But Ellen should not draw a final conclusion too soon. It was possible that one day his father's work would bear fruit, perhaps in a form they could not at present imagine.

*

Ellen must have fallen asleep because Carl was gently shaking her. She smiled up at him and reached out her arms, but his voice was urgent.

'Get dressed. I have to get you home.'

At first her body refused to move, but when they were finally out in the cool night air she matched Carl's hurried steps through the half-lit streets, over the bridge and along a dark expanse of parkland into North Adelaide. As they approached the house she fumbled in her bag and her pockets, then whispered that she did not have her key.

She opened the front gate carefully and guided Carl along a narrow side path, past a series of squat shrubs. There was a window next to a rose bush and she indicated that this was her bedroom. Carl made a stirrup for her foot, and as he lifted her she reached up and pushed against the squeaking window frame. She held her breath, then gradually relaxed. Carl pushed her higher until she was able to manoeuvre herself through the window. When she was finally inside she turned and reached down a hand to him.

Four

The wedding took place on a sweltering day at the beginning of the following summer. The heat was spread like a thick paste through the church, insinuating itself into every opening. But the wedding guests did not allow the weather to dictate their choice of clothing. The men wore suits, shirts with stiff collars and heavy shining shoes, the women dresses of copious material, long gloves and voluminous hats. Fans were opened and discreetly fluttered, brows were quickly and discreetly mopped, as all the while prayers were spoken and hymns sung, led by selected members of the university choir. Only at the reception, held in one of Adelaide's best hotels, did some of the company adjust their attire to the demands of the heat. Louisa Winter led this movement. The heavy hat was quickly shed and the long hair allowed to fall loose; at one point shoes were slipped off and left resting under a table, abandoned when she hurried off to speak to a friend.

The speeches began with William Winter, who several times had to fight back tears as he spoke. His reluctance to relinquish the stage was evident as he began to repeat himself and to fumble with his hands, as if his daughter would truly be gone from him only when he had stopped speaking. His wife's firm hand on his arm was the eventual signal for him to resume his seat.

Carl's speech was short and to the point, consisting of a simple list of thanks to those who had shaped his life, his deceased parents first and foremost, without elaboration as to whom exactly was meant, followed by a commitment to be the best husband he could possibly be to Ellen.

The best man, a long-term acquaintance of Carl's and pastor of the old township of Hahndorf, related some mildly humorous anecdotes about Carl's youth that received polite laughter. He then reverted to a serious tone, emphasising the reasoned faith that was the guiding principle of Carl's life. He began to explain why faith and reason complemented rather than contradicted each other, then caught himself and apologised for departing from what was appropriate to the occasion. He quickly listed Carl's virtues, honesty and courage the chief among them, then said that, if prevailed upon to mention a shortcoming, he would cite Carl's occasional tendency to excessive self-criticism. But Ellen was the perfect antidote to this problem, and he congratulated him on an astute choice.

A series of toasts was followed by a small band and an invitation to dance. Many of the guests hesitated to oblige, due to the heat or to a suspicion that God or others might not fully approve. But Carl and Ellen were not deterred, and they swirled around the dance floor with ease, with William and Louisa Winter turning at a slower pace in their wake. At one point there was a swapping of partners, then loud applause as Ellen performed a finely balanced pirouette before gliding on in her father's arms. Gradually the music softened and slowed and the dancing became sedate, almost intimate, causing some of the onlookers to look down in embarrassment. The couples finally stood back from each other and reclaimed their original partners.

When the dancing stopped Ellen wiped her neck and throat with a handkerchief and caught her breath. She beckoned to her sister and to Britta Bauer and the trio embraced, laughing and crying.

'It's been a wonderful day,' Ellen said as she extricated herself. Her voice sounded hoarse and someone pressed on her a glass of champagne. There was applause as she drained the glass. 'A perfect day.'

'A perfect couple,' a voice intoned to further applause. Three cheers were called for and heartily given.

'And I have some news,' Ellen continued, taking Carl's hand. Her sister and Britta stood back, bringing the newly married couple into clear relief. The room was suddenly quiet; even the young children who had been running in and out stopped and listened.

'Carl has received a call to the Lutheran mission in the highlands of New Guinea, which are newly discovered. After long discussion and prayer, we have come to the conclusion that this is God's will. So before long we will leave for a new life in a new land. I know you will hold us in your hearts, as we will hold you in ours.'

Exploration

(1937–1939)

One

The man Chas Noble had arrested was not the guilty one, and Carl had set off for the government post in the east to secure his release. Speed was of the essence, and Ellen had reluctantly agreed to stay behind. Carl had promised that he and Aijang would do their best to be back within the week.

After a restless night Ellen dressed herself simply then directed Kubun to fetch the box of medicines that was on the floor in the back bedroom. Kubun did as he was asked, despite his obvious disapproval. 'Pastor Carl says Misis should stay near the house,' he kept saying. But Ellen strode down the hill, quietly determined.

When they reached the village it was largely deserted, with just a few old men slumped about. Ellen sat down on the stool she had carried down from the house and Kubun stood behind her with his chest stuck out in a protective pose, holding an umbrella to shield her from the sun. 'Everyone working in the gardens, Misis,' he said.

Eventually an old woman appeared, a shrivelled thing with flaps of loose skin for breasts. She stood some distance back and called out something in a reedy voice. Ellen asked Kubun to tell the woman that she wanted to see the children with the sores on their bodies.

'Misis stay away from that.'

Ellen pointed to the box on the ground. 'Tell her I have medicine.'

Kubun relented and a short conversation followed. He then explained to Ellen that it was only with Pastor Carl's agreement that the medicine would be accepted.

Ellen continued to sit and after a time a mother appeared, leading a young boy by the hand. Ellen could see festering sores in the creases of the boy's elbows and, when at her request his mother turned him around, behind his knees. She fought back her repugnance and reached out a beckoning hand. The boy held back but the mother pushed him forward, speaking quietly into his ear. Ellen took the boy's hand but kept the rest of his body at a distance, careful to avoid any contact with the sores. She opened the medicine box and prepared an injection, breathing deeply to relax her shaking hands as she filled a syringe with colourless liquid from a vial. She could feel the anticipation of the villagers who had now started to gather round.

The boy accepted the needle in his arm without complaint. When it was over he returned placidly to his mother.

'Kubun, tell the mother that the injection will take several days to work, perhaps longer. She must be patient. In the meantime, no one must touch the sores.'

A handful of other afflicted children were brought forward by their mothers, and when Ellen finally packed the medicines away she was satisfied with her morning's work. On the walk back to the house she explained to Kubun that the sores were the sign of a disease called yaws that was caused by a bacterium, but Kubun showed little interest in this information. He was more concerned about how the people would react if the treatment failed to work, and what Pastor Carl would say when he found out that Misis had been to the village.

*

'Do you know that man, Kubun?' Ellen was sitting on the verandah, pointing into the middle distance. 'I've seen him several times.'

'A no-good man, Misis. Not allowed to marry so he just wanders around.'

'Why is he not allowed to marry?'

'I'll chase him, Misis.'

Kubun started down the hill, calling out and waving his arms. The figure hesitated, then slowly disappeared into the bush.

'Why is he not allowed to marry?' Ellen repeated when Kubun was back.

'No-good man, Misis.'

The topic remained in abeyance until preparations began for the evening meal. Ellen joined Kubun in the kitchen, where she made simple suggestions for improving the meal, which he placidly accepted.

'You're not married, Kubun?'

'Not married, Misis.'

'Too soon to marry?'

'Only warriors allowed to marry, Misis.'

Ellen imagined Kubun's stocky figure arrayed as she

assumed a highland warrior would be arrayed, with exorbitant feathers and garish face paint, a spear or a bow and arrow and a fearsome countenance. She smiled at the incongruity of the image.

Kubun gathered up food scraps that had been put to one side and carefully wrapped them in an old piece of newspaper. 'A warrior must kill a man,' he said quietly. 'Jesus says not to kill.'

'That's right Kubun, thou shalt not kill.'

'I love Jesus, Misis.'

'Of course you do.'

'I like to be baptised, Misis.'

'Then you must speak to Pastor Carl.'

'Pastor Carl always says "not yet". Why does Pastor Carl always say "not yet"?'

For a brief moment Ellen thought of telling Kubun that she herself had not been baptised until quite recently and this had not held her back. Instead, she said that she would ask Pastor Carl when he returned why he always said 'not yet'.

Before Kubun left for the evening the conversation returned to the watching man. This time Kubun said that several girls had shown interest in the man after he had excited them with his dancing. He had been invited to courting ceremonies and there had been marriage proposals, but the man had shown little interest and no one could understand why. They said he must have eaten bad mushrooms and was not right in the head.

'So, you don't need to be a warrior to marry after all?' Ellen asked.

'Sometimes, Misis, not always.'

Two

Carl had been unable to convince the district officer that they had the wrong man. Unless he could produce the one he thought responsible, with a confession or with suitable witnesses, the man whom Chas Noble had arrested would be tried and found guilty. He would be punished harshly, as an example.

Noble and a small contingent of native policemen had come back with Carl. They spent the night in tents near the house, and in the early morning Aijang prepared a big breakfast—fried eggs and bully beef, toast smothered in butter and hot, sweet tea. The police kept to themselves, leaving the two white men together. Noble exuded an air of proprietorship as he lounged at the dining table, taking a familiar tone that irritated Ellen.

'A fine house all right and a nice location, but I wouldn't get too comfortable, Mrs Starck. There's a lot of pacifying yet to be done out here, and we don't need your husband and others like him poking their noses in.'

Carl's demeanour told Ellen not to respond, so she bit her tongue.

After breakfast Carl said he would go to the village alone, but Noble dismissed this out of hand. He said that last time it was only the threat of the rifles that had averted violence.

Carl suggested that the threat of violence was because Noble had taken an innocent man. He would convince the villagers that this man would be returned, and they would give up the guilty one.

'If you get yourself bloody killed down there, mate, whose arse is gunna be on the line? My arse, mate, that's whose.' Noble was jabbing a finger into his own chest. 'Way I see it, we need to show 'em who's boss right from the start. Saves a lot of trouble down the line. And you can forget any idea that you lot are gunna run the show out here, set up some kind of holy state. We're the government and we run the show.'

Carl did not challenge any of Noble's statements. He said simply that the villagers would be more amenable if the patrol was not there.

'Not gunna happen. You point out who you reckon the guilty party is. You get the witnesses to say their piece. Me and my boys make the arrest.'

Despite her antipathy to Noble, Ellen wanted him to prevail in this argument. She said to Carl that it would be safer if the patrol went with him.

'You've got your missus to think about now, mate,' Noble continued, a smile playing at the corners of his mouth. 'Time for heroics is over.'

There were guns in the house, several rifles and a revolver, but Carl did not take any of these with him as he accompanied Noble and the policemen down the hill. Ellen thought of running after him with one of the rifles, but she could not bring herself to touch it.

As the morning wore on Ellen sensed a disturbance rising up from the village, an undercurrent of dispute and violence. At one point she thought she heard gunshots and let out an involuntary cry. Aijang had stayed behind and she asked him if he had heard anything, but he shook his head. She made preparations to go down to the village, but Aijang blocked the way, saying that Pastor Carl had left instructions that she was not to leave the house. 'Pastor Carl knows what to do, Misis,' Aijang assured her.

It was late morning when the arresting party returned to the house. They were in high spirits, chatting and laughing. Even Carl seemed relaxed and at ease with himself.

'Dr Livingstone here sure knows how to sweet talk the *kanakas*,' Chas Noble chortled as Ellen rushed outside to greet Carl. 'Just sits down with 'em and explains things nice and easy in their lingo, tells 'em how things are gunna be, and lo and behold they drop their weapons and deliver up the culprit. Off to the calaboose. Simple as you please.' Noble gestured at the young man they had with them, handcuffed to one of the policemen, eyes cast down to the ground. 'Course I dunno what he said exactly. Threatened 'em all with hellfire and damnation, for all I know.'

Ellen was too taken up with Carl to pay much attention to Noble. But later, when the discussion turned to the return journey with the prisoner, she listened intently. They would have to travel through the original territory of the murdered woman, and Carl urged that this would best be done under cover of darkness, despite the obvious difficulties. Noble said that last time he'd had no trouble, but Carl argued his case and the other man shrugged in acquiescence.

As Carl prepared for the journey Ellen pleaded with him not to go, but he whispered that he would not put it beyond Chas Noble to arrange for an accident to befall the prisoner out in the bush and he could not take the risk. And he was needed to ensure that the innocent man was released and brought back safely; he had given the villagers his word. Ellen was on the point of mentioning the watching man, thinking it might make Carl change his mind, but she maintained her silence.

Three

It was mid-morning and Ellen was at a loss for something to do, but she hesitated to go down to the village. She worried that the injections might not have had time to work or might have proved ineffective, in which case the women would spurn her and she would have nowhere to turn. But then Kubun appeared and said he had heard that the sores of those who had been treated had started to heal. Ellen's feet hardly touched the ground as she went down the hill, despite all the equipment she was carrying. Kubun followed her at a distance, calling out that she should be careful or she would fall.

As soon as they arrived women and children appeared out of huts and surrounding gardens, accompanied by a steady murmur of anticipation. Even some men were there, looking on. Children with sores were quickly pushed forward, but Ellen explained through Kubun that she would first like to see the children who had already received treatment. Passage was made and the children from the first day were brought forward. Ellen could see immediately that the healing was underway, but her satisfaction was marred by the matter-of-fact manner in which the children and their mothers seemed to accept the power of the medicine. They could at least show some gratitude, she thought. And do something about the dirty faces and the runny noses.

After the new batch of patients had been treated Ellen asked Kubun to explain again that the sores could be passed from one person to another, so it was important that they not be touched. And if anyone developed new sores they should come and fetch her immediately.

'Did they understand, Kubun?'

'Maybe, Misis.'

'We don't have an unlimited supply of medicine. Tell them, Kubun.' But the women were already moving away with their children; they were talking among themselves with their backs to her, submerged in their own world.

As Ellen and Kubun were preparing to leave a young female voice intervened. Kubun said something abrupt, but the voice persisted, returning with more urgency after each of Kubun's interventions.

'What is it, Kubun?'

'Nothing, Misis.'

Ellen beckoned the girl to come forward, instinctively holding out a hand. The girl approached and Ellen could not help admiring the open face, the slim, shapely figure and the steady eyes.

'Is she sick? Tell me what she wants.'

'She not want to marry, Misis,' Kubun said reluctantly.

'Why not?'

'The man already got wives.'

Ellen found the girl's hand and pressed it.

'Not your business, Misis,' Kubun said, trying to shepherd the girl away.

The umbrella Kubun had held up for protection was now packed away and Ellen felt the sun press down on her with full force. She also felt that she was under observation, but when she glanced around she could see no one looking in her direction.

The girl started to speak again. The words poured out. She pleaded with her eyes and her hands.

'Tell her she can come with us, Kubun. We'll go to the house and talk about what we should do.'

Kubun provided his final argument. 'Pastor Carl not agree.'

Ellen gestured to the girl and the two of them started to walk out of the village, hand in hand. Kubun followed slowly, glancing back regularly. A small group of villagers, men as well as women, were now standing in the open, silently watching. Ellen maintained the pressure on the hand she was holding and did her best with smiles and gestures to convey encouragement, to herself as well as to her companion.

When they arrived at the house Ellen searched for something suitable to cover the girl's near nakedness, which seemed particularly jarring in this setting. Through their combined efforts a blouse was put on, and there was laughter when the girl was taken to stand in front of a mirror. Ellen waved away Kubun's repeatedly expressed opinion that Pastor Carl would not agree.

Ellen was 'Misis'; the girl seemed to know this, and Ellen was able to establish that her name was 'Kauigl'. She spoke the name several times, but each time the girl's response suggested that her pronunciation had fallen short. Through a process of counting fingers Ellen established that Kauigl was eighteen, but despite her best efforts she was unable to convey her agreement that no woman should be forced to marry a man who had other wives. After this exchange the pair lapsed into an uneasy silence that continued through their shared lunch.

During the afternoon Ellen showed Kauigl where she could sleep. She pointed at different objects around the house, repeating their English names slowly and in return receiving sporadic sounds that suggested words. She found a piece of paper and wrote down groups of letters that she hoped would remind her of what she was hearing, making use of Carl's accents as far as she could remember them.

As darkness fell Ellen and the girl took over the preparation of food from Kubun. Their word play resumed, with items of food, cooking utensils and the processes of cooking providing the subject matter. The atmosphere lightened and there was occasional laughter while samples of food were exchanged and commented on. During the meal the silence returned, but there were smiles and reassuring looks. Kubun hovered for a while, his frustration evident, then went away without a word.

Before the time came to sleep, Kauigl disappeared. Ellen looked everywhere, inside and outside the house, her ears alert for any sound. She glanced discreetly at the latrine, eventually opening the door and shining a torch inside. She crawled through the entrance to Aijang's hut but the smell, the airlessness and the fleas propelled her backwards. She looked down the hill and thought she saw a figure moving out frcm behind a tree. She spoke Kauigl's name but there was no response. 'Are you the watching man?' she called out in a wavering voice. In the beam of torchlight a figure came slowly towards her and she recognised Mbagl. He was armed with a spear and accompanied by a few softly spoken words. When he was near he turned his back to her and raised his spear ready to throw then crouched and made a full circle around her. She thanked him for his protection as best she could.

Back inside the house Ellen began to rationalise Kauigl's disappearance as for the best. But when the girl reappeared with a few nondescript items bundled against her chest Ellen was overcome with relief. She gave Kauigl a nightdress and explained its use, then went away and waited. When she looked in later the girl was sound asleep.

*

The guilty man had been delivered safely to the government post, the innocent villager released and returned home. Carl was well satisfied with his work, but despite Ellen's pleas he was adamant that the girl could not stay.

'She can help me with the language,' Ellen suggested, her voice low, although she knew there was no need for this caution. 'I've already started to write down words.'

'We should interfere as little as possible in their life.'

'But haven't we come to interfere in their life?'

The conversation that followed focused on the wisdom and practicality of dragging the highlanders into the civilised world in one fell swoop. Carl argued that this was neither possible nor desirable. Not all aspects of highland life should be rejected. A distinction should be made between those things that could not be reconciled with Christianity or with civilised behaviour, and those that were less contentious and might even be beneficial.

'And meanwhile this girl is to be married off against her will to a man who already has several wives?'

'The women here seem to come to terms with these arrangements.'

Ellen told Carl that he was talking as a man, just as he had in the botanical gardens. He let this comment pass, then said that sorcery was much more damaging to the highlanders than their marriage customs. 'They think the death of anyone but the very old is the result of malevolence and magic, and they exact revenge. The result is a never-ending spiral of violence.'

Ellen responded that there seemed to be so much wrong with the highland world that she wondered whether progress was possible at all. She admired Carl for what he was trying to achieve, but she feared it would end in frustration and failure.

As she spoke Ellen remembered Carl's father. She chose her words carefully. 'I can hardly comprehend the suffering your father took upon himself and his family in the desert. At least here the land and weather are hospitable and the people stay in one place.' Carl remained silent and Ellen continued. 'It was terribly unfair to your father that whenever the rains came and life was easier the Aborigines abandoned the mission in search of their traditional life, leaving behind everything they had been taught. It must have broken his heart.'

That night the couple made early preparations for bed, but after they lay down neither reached for the other. Carl was soon asleep, but Ellen lay wide awake. Eventually she got up and went to make sure that Kauigl had settled.

*

Early the next morning a handful of village men milled around the front of the house in the cold. Carl went out to them and gently rubbed their shoulders and forearms in greeting. Then he sat on the ground, and the men sat down around him.

Ellen stood watching at the doorway. She saw one of the men look in her direction then turn and say something to Carl. Her response was to pull back quickly and go in search of Kauigl, whom she found standing in the dining room, motionless and seemingly resigned. For a fleeting moment she imagined herself taking the girl by the hand, creeping out through the back door of the house, climbing to the summit of the farthest mountain then descending out of sight into the neighbouring valley. But Carl's appearance put an end to this indulgence.

There was an interchange between Carl and Kauigl, whereupon the girl slowly loosed herself from Ellen and followed Carl out of the house. The waiting men took delivery of her and immediately transported her down the hill. As Ellen watched, one of the men tore the blouse from Kauigl's body and discarded it on the ground. Another man produced a bamboo switch and struck the girl several sharp blows on the backs of her legs.

Four

There was a visitor at the door. At first sight Ellen was not sure that he was a white man, but his clothing, rough and ready though it was, indicated that he was not a highlander. And when he spoke, asking after Carl, it was obvious that he was a countryman of hers.

Her first instinct was to send the man away, saying that Carl was travelling in the west. But the prospect of sharing conversation with another European overrode her nervousness. She invited him inside, then called out to Kubun for food and drink.

A quick survey of the man's body revealed clear signs of deterioration. There were gaps in his teeth and the skin of his hands hung loose. He was heavily bearded, grey infiltrating his original hair colour. He said his name was Ivor Moore, and he knew Carl from before.

'From before?' Ellen asked when they had sat down.

'When Carl first came to New Guinea. Years ago now.'

'Carl came ahead of me to establish himself and set up our home. Time passed and I was about to join him, but then we were told that no more whites were allowed in the highlands. At first I thought it would last only a few months, but it stretched on and on.'

'There were killings. Catholic missionaries, a German and a Yank. After that the powers that be got cold feet. Not enough *kiaps* to patrol the highlands, so they decided to limit the number of whites and their movements. But it wasn't the people's fault. They were just defending themselves.' Ivor's voice trailed off.

Carl had not mentioned Ivor Moore in his letters or since her arrival, but Ellen sensed they were close.

'Where exactly did you meet Carl?' she asked.

'It was in the Upper Ramu to the east. We just got to talking, you know how it is. Sometimes you find someone you can talk to.'

Ivor was eating and drinking slowly. Ellen waited for him to continue.

'I've been in New Guinea a long time. Carl wanted to pick my brains about what makes the locals tick. I told him, you treat them fairly they'll treat you fairly, by and large. But I'm not sure we treat them fairly. We take their gold—that's not so bad, they've got no use for it. But taking their souls? Not sure we have the right to do that.'

'You worked on the goldfields?' Ellen asked, thinking gold an easier subject than souls.

Ivor began to reminisce, a subdued glow to his tone. 'Since Edie Creek in twenty-six. That was quite a thing. Men poured in from down south in their hundreds, blokes from all walks of life. Some cantankerous and others running from something, but most prepared to help out a mate when it mattered. Some made fortunes, some caught their death, some left with nothing or drank away what they had. And a few like me stayed on, searching for the next big strike. Which we never found.'

'The gold's all gone?'

'On the main fields it's all big business now, run by companies from down south. Bloody great dredges flown up in parts in the guts of aeroplanes, if you'll excuse my language. No place for the old hands and the old methods.'

Ellen wondered out loud, 'But don't you miss home?'

Ivor considered this question. 'I reckon the longer I've been away the less I miss it. At first, like most blokes, I planned to be up here a few months, make a bit of capital for a good life back south. But gradually I got used to it here. To begin with it was the other men on the field, the camaraderie. Now it's just me with a few blacks and the elements, searching for some colour in the water. Not too fussed if I don't find any. I make enough to get by.'

'You aren't lonely?' Ellen asked, holding her breath.

'I've got my native help. Good fellas, most of them. And I found I could live with my own company. I even became interested in myself.' There was a chesty laugh. 'And the bush is always changing.'

Ivor took out paper and tobacco and began with obvious concentration to roll a cigarette. Ellen went and spoke to Kubun about making early preparations for the evening meal. When she returned Ivor stood up and stayed standing until she was seated.

'When do you expect Carl?' he asked.

'Any time now.' Ellen instinctively looked towards the front window. 'It's been two weeks already.'

'I might hang around then, if you don't mind. I can camp out the back.'

'We have a spare bedroom. It's a little cramped but there's a bed, a mattress and sheets, a pillow, a pillowcase and blankets.'

Ivor laughed and Ellen joined in. After this they were easier with each other. They related snippets from their childhoods and shared memories of public events, although these were relatively few. Then Ellen found a newspaper she had brought from home and left it with Ivor while she joined Kubun in the kitchen.

She took trouble over the preparations for dinner. She spread a lace-edged tablecloth over the table and put out the good china and cutlery and serviettes in wooden rings. She found some elegant glasses and polished them until they shone. Then she helped Kubun to prepare multiple dishes—soup, meat and vegetables, fruit. At one point she became frustrated with Kubun's lack of agility in moving from one task to another and pushed him to the sidelines, then regretted her abruptness and made space for him to return. When everything was ready she called to Ivor, who was still in the front room, looking down the hill, the newspaper folded in his hand.

The ease they had earlier achieved did not return. Ivor now found difficulty coordinating the movements needed for eating and drinking, his elbows, hands and words seeming to get in each other's way. Ellen apologised that the only alcoholic drink was some old sherry, but Ivor waved this away then changed his mind and said he would not mind a small glass.

'Do you think my husband is taking away the people's souls?'

They had finished eating and the meagre amount of small talk had dried up.

'They got their world and it's all of a piece. If you start chipping away, the whole thing'll come crashing down. And then where'll they be? Like our blacks at home—nowhere.'

'You said this to my husband?'

'We talked about it.'

'And what did he say?'

'Carl listens more than he talks. I like that about him.'

Ellen took this as a rebuke and sat in silence. Ivor went on. 'But he talked about you, Mrs Starck. He talked a lot about you.' The man produced a gap-riddled smile. 'And I can see why.'

Kubun came to clear the things from the table and Ellen shielded herself behind this activity.

'You're probably wondering why I've come,' Ivor said as things settled down. The two of them were sitting with tea in delicate cups and pieces of stale cake on dainty plates. 'I got word my mum is near the end and wants to see me, so I need to head south.'

'I'm very sorry to hear that. But will you come back to New Guinea?'

'I have a wife somewhere down south,' Ivor continued, almost absently. 'And a kid.' He looked down. 'I didn't mean to abandon them. Somehow, they just slipped away.'

'You'll look for them now?' Ellen asked, trying to hide her disapproval.

In place of an answer Ivor said he was tired and needed to lie down. Ellen was quickly on her feet, making sure everything was in order for a comfortable night. As Ivor headed for the bedroom he said he had forgotten to mention that when he was coming up the hill he had seen a young native man watching the house. If he appeared again Ivor would tell him to push off. Ellen replied that she knew the man and he was harmless.

Ellen went to bed to the accompaniment of light snoring from the back bedroom. Sleep eventually came but in the depths of the night she was woken by Ivor Moore shouting indecipherable words in a one-sided argument. She lay awake, listening to the heavy breathing that eventually replaced the shouting, inwardly reproaching Carl for leaving her alone to face a situation like this.

Early the next morning, as Ellen stood enjoying the warmth of the kitchen, she could hear Ivor luxuriating in the shower, singing loudly as he poured water over himself. She recognised the song and sang parts of it to herself, then gave way to a bout of comforting tears that persisted until Ivor came inside, drying his hair and saying that it had taken him a while to get used to the softness of the bed but once asleep he hadn't stirred till morning. When Ellen did not respond Ivor said that Carl needed his head read, going bush and leaving her alone for weeks on end. Sometimes even an intelligent man like Carl could not see what was staring him in the face.

Later in the morning Ivor asked if there was anything he could help with around the house. Ellen thanked him but said that everything was in perfect order. As she watched, Ivor began an inspection, checking the windows and doors for their fit, examining the joins between the walls and the ceiling, checking that there was no sagging of beams, running a hand along surfaces to test for smoothness. At one point he sprang up and down, listening for any sound of weakness in the floor.

'Did you help with the house?' Ellen asked when Ivor was finished.

'Carl did the design and the heavy work, but the finer points of implementation were left to me. I'm a carpenter by trade. Even after all this time I hadn't forgotten what I'd learnt. And my hands were steady enough.' Ivor held his hands out in front of him to demonstrate their steadiness. 'I'd never have thought to put up such a thing for myself. Doesn't seem much point, since I'm never in one place for long. But Carl and me had a fine time building this house, even with all the trouble getting timber flown in from the east. And the galvanised iron for the roof. All paid for out of Carl's pocket.'

When Kubun brought their lunch Ivor asked Ellen where exactly Carl was. She told him that he had gone out west, visiting his New Guinean preachers. He had inherited these evangelists, as he called them, when he first came to the highlands, although the men themselves originally came from the coast. He had brought them with him when he moved to the Wahgi Valley and now they were living with tribes further to the west, learning their language and preparing them to receive the Christian message. The evangelists had been banned by the administration from working unsupervised in the villages after the killing of the missionaries, and while some of the *kiaps* were now turning a blind eye this could change at any moment. So Carl had to spend as much time as possible out in the settlements, making sure there was no trouble.

Ivor tugged at strands of hair that were sticking out over his ears and scratched at his beard. 'I know some of these lowlanders who go out preaching to the bush natives. Maybe they're genuine, maybe not. But some of them get all high and mighty, acting like boss-boys. They need to be taken down a peg or two.'

Ellen bristled at the indirect criticism of Carl.

'Don't be cross with me, Mrs Starck. I've got a lot of time for Carl. As to what he's up to with the people here, maybe it's right and maybe it isn't. I don't pretend to know.'

'I think it's time you called me Ellen. And I'll call you Ivor, if I may.'

'Right enough then, Ellen.'

They exchanged smiles then ate and drank companionably until Ivor broke the silence.

'That boy Aijang still with Carl?'

Ellen offered an inquiring look.

'Definitely has an eye for the main chance, that fella. Needs a tight rein.'

Ellen resisted the temptation to express her doubts about Aijang, saying instead that he seemed very devoted to Carl. She then asked if Ivor knew a *kiap* named Chas Noble. Ivor said that he knew Noble right enough. He was one of those blokes who had no interest in seeing all sides of an issue—better to take one side and push it for all it was worth. If others had a contrary opinion it was up to them to push back, and the strongest position would win. Survival of the fittest, that was Noble's view of life. The other *kiaps* were more moderate; they liked to think of themselves as open-minded. But they all believed one way or another in their civilising mission. That made it hard for them to see the highlanders for who they were.

Ellen said, 'A white woman I met up here told me that we should not be seduced into thinking that the highland world is less complicated than ours.'

'That would've been old Lotte Fiebiger. Lotte likes to think she understands the highlanders better than anyone else. She's been up here a long time, so maybe she does.'

'Is there much to understand?'

'In many ways they're just like us, a mixed bunch with good and bad you can recognise once you understand a bit of the lingo, even before in some cases. But there're lots of things we take for granted that are new to them, and things they do that seem strange to us, quite off-putting some of them, at least to begin with.'

'But you think we should not try to change them?'

Ivor shrugged his shoulders. 'They'll have to learn to deal with us, because we're here and we're not leaving till we get whatever it is we want. But they should be allowed to go at their own pace, decide for themselves what to hang on to and what to get rid of. It's not as if everything we've got is better.' Ivor added, 'If there's any seducing going on it's us seducing them with our wealth and power into thinking they're inferior to us.'

Ellen pointed out that Ivor had said earlier that if the people accepted some of the white ways, they would have to accept them all. Now he was saying they should be allowed to pick and choose. Ivor raised his hands in a gesture of defeat. He did not know the answers, but he was afraid that the whites would make a mess of the highlands, which would be a terrible shame.

The day passed and the night and then another day, and still Carl did not return. Finally, Ivor said he could not wait any longer, but there was one last thing. He had left something with Carl: he knew where it was kept, could he inspect the mattress of her bed? He turned the mattress upside down to reveal a small incision in one corner, and with careful manoeuvring of his fingers he withdrew a battered tobacco tin. 'A few grains to pay for the trip south,' he explained, displaying some modest gold fragments on his palm.

When Ivor had gone Ellen was relieved. She had appreciated his company, but she had begun to suspect that he was on the point of telling her something about Carl that she would rather not know. If he had stayed any longer she would have felt compelled to ask him what it was.

Five

With Carl still away Ellen's days began to take on a rhythm that suited her and her environment. In the early morning, after the mist had evaporated but the air was still cool and fresh, she and Kubun would go to the village where she would ask to see the children who had been treated for sores. With each visit she could see improvement and her confidence grew. She asked the women whether there was other sickness, and gradually the number of her patients swelled. She had only simple treatments to offer—draining abscesses, salving burns and the like—and in many cases no treatment at all, but the women seemed content with what she had to give. There were even tentative signs of gratitude and a slight curiosity about the medicine and its power. Through this process the simplest and most common local words became familiar to her. She repeated them internally and then uttered them out loud, to the amused appreciation of her hearers, but she knew she was still a long way from being able to communicate with any facility. Her frustration at this inability was compounded by an increasing wariness of Kubun's translations, a suspicion that he was not conveying the precise content or tone of what she was saying, either because he was not capable or because he was trying in his own way to protect her.

At first, she had done her best to ignore what she saw as the squalor of the village, but eventually she began to point at the piles of food leavings lying around, the chewed remnants of sugar cane, the excrement of pigs, chickens and dogs with the attendant swarms of flies, recommending that all this be removed and buried. She began demonstrably to clean the running noses of the babies and small children, to examine their heads for lice, to look at their hands and call for water and show the cleaning that should be done in the interests of health before the consumption of food and after visiting the toilet. None of this was received with enthusiasm, but she was determined to persist. All the while she kept her eyes open for Kauigl, but there was no sign of her.

Few men were to be seen during these morning visits, apart from an occasional crumpled shape that lay hardly moving against the wall of a hut. Ellen did not think about where the bulk of the men were; she only faintly registered their absence. The village to her was a place of women and young children, a location of nurture within the limits of highland possibility, and this suited her well. If she thought of the men it was when she looked down the hill from the front of the mission house, and then it was the rough tearing at Kauigl's blouse and the blows to her body that came to Ellen's mind, bringing a tight knot to her stomach.

The older children of the village, while they awaited the arrival of adulthood, were left largely to their own devices. The boys roamed around in groups, testing their growing strength against each other in rough and tumble games, familiarising themselves with miniature versions of the weapons that would later become essential accompaniments of their manhood. A few of the girls hovered at the edges of these games, others wandered around in small groups of age mates, holding hands, talking and laughing, while some chose to stay at the side of their mothers, learning the cultivation of gardens, the rearing of pigs and chickens and the preparation of food or looking after younger brothers and sisters while their mothers worked.

Sometimes on her journeys to and from the village Ellen would be accosted by a band of marauding boys. Usually there would be an initial display of mock aggression that she quickly learnt to dismiss. She would continue to walk and the boys would fall in beside her, chatting animatedly among themselves, demonstrating for her benefit newly acquired skills with their bodies or their weapons before tiring at her lukewarm reaction and racing away back down the hill. At other times a clutch of girls would walk with her, the more forward daring to hold her hand, some lingering at the front of the mission house until she invited them inside.

During the house inspections Ellen would play a record on the phonograph to looks of disbelief, sit and type at the typewriter and read aloud what she had written to bemused silence, or eat an imaginary meal at the dining room table with a knife and fork that was mimicked with giggling laughter. On washing days she would call on Kubun to demonstrate the cycling of clothes through the copper, the rinsing tub and the hand-turned wringer to the clothesline, then she would explain the use of the shower before soaping and washing her hands at the water tank to re-emphasise the importance of bodily hygiene. The finale was usually something sweet to drink and eat in the kitchen. All the while the door to the main bedroom was kept firmly shut, with stern words for any of the visitors who ventured to enter this sanctum.

When the house was quiet again Ellen would discuss the morning with Kubun while he prepared lunch. When she had eaten she would give in to the wave of exhaustion that overtook her, sleeping soundly then waking abruptly to a broad sheet of insect noise that seemed to rise and fall with her breathing. She would get up and wash her face, sit with a book and wait for the heavy gusts of rain that would bring relief from the torpor of the afternoon. Sometimes when Kubun had finished his household tasks he would bend over an exercise book with the stub of a pencil in his hand. He would invariably ask for assistance with troublesome English words and they would work together until it was time to begin preparations for the evening meal. When Kubun was in the kitchen Ellen would sit on the sofa in the living room and look out the window at the blue-green mountains, hoping that today would be the day when Carl returned.

*

One morning when Ellen was in the village the sound of an aeroplane made itself known away in the distance. Heads turned towards the sound and some of the young boys started to run up and down with arms outstretched as wings. Ellen wondered what the people made of this striking evidence of the white man's power, but the upturned faces provided little clue. She asked Kubun to question the women, but he answered for himself, with conviction.

'God gives white men secrets. If you believe in Jesus you will know these secrets.'

'Is that what these women think?'

Kubun shrugged his shoulders.

Ellen asked where the plane was headed and Kubun pointed vaguely towards the west, saying that out there somewhere there might be gold or something else that white men wanted.

When the sound died away and Ellen began to treat the children she realised with some discomfit that she would not be able to explain to them the mystery of flight. Mechanical things had never interested her. But she did have her own intimate experience of flying, coming up from the coast.

*

After a sleepless night of heat and insects, of beating rain and intrusive human noises, Ellen sat exhausted at the edge of a hangar and surveyed the handful of aeroplanes strewn around on the grass. She could hear the pounding of the surf just out of sight, but the salty ocean smell was submerged beneath the vapours of fuel and lubricant.

At least it will be cooler soon, she told herself, picking at the blouse that was already sticking to her skin.

The pilot, Len was his name, was walking towards her.

'Well, Mrs Starck, I must congratulate you on choosing one of the most beautiful places on earth for your first flight.'

Ellen smiled wanly as Len gestured towards the clothing and equipment lying on the ground nearby. Another man wandered over and he and Len helped Ellen into an old leather jacket, a soft helmet, goggles and gloves. She said she must look a sight, but neither of the men took up the invitation to compliment her on her appearance.

She was escorted to the aeroplane where Len stowed the luggage while the other man guided her into the front cockpit. He secured her harness and helped her wriggle her goggles into place, then lifted the flap of her helmet and shouted that Len was one of the best pilots in New Guinea, so she had no need to worry.

Len had explained that they would start out over the ocean then turn inland and fly along the river valley until they came to a break in the mountains to the west. Then it would be up into the highlands, along an upland valley and over more mountains into new valleys. It would take an hour, perhaps a little longer, provided the weather held and the wind did not turn against them.

The engine clattered into life, the propeller started to spin and with little warning they were racing forward, bumping lightly on the low-cut grass then lifting into the air. Ellen braced herself then gradually allowed her body to ease into the swaying and pitching of the machine as it climbed by stages into the sky. She welcomed the cooling air as it rushed past.

There were struts all around her, wings above and below

and a heavily scratched windscreen in front. She could see little of what was ahead but by leaning to the side and looking down she had a clear view of what was passing. The ocean and the coastal settlement, the latter an evanescent thing jotted down haphazardly on the ground, were already disappearing, replaced by long sheets of bending grass and a broad meandering river. There was no sign of human beings or human endeavour, just a tiny moving shadow that confirmed the existence of the aeroplane and reflected its progress.

The plane levelled out and the sound of the engine enveloped Ellen. She found herself listening intently, counting the beats as if she were at the piano. Then the bucking and dipping of the little machine reclaimed her attention. She looked at the dials and gauges on the dashboard, seeking confirmation from the wobbling needles that all was well, but everything was written in a code that she could not decipher.

The engine increased its pitch and they began to climb again, the bumps and lurches coming more often and more abruptly. Soon there were mountains on both sides, closing behind them like a zip being fastened. Then they were in cloud, so thick that Ellen could not see her hands. She recited a short prayer and tried to picture Carl's face and feel his embrace, awaiting her.

When they escaped the cloud the sun shone down on a sweeping valley. The little plane zoomed towards the ground and Ellen could see a smattering of mushroom-shaped huts and areas of land parcelled in a pleasing geometry. She felt a deep sense of affinity with the human presence that these things signified.

Before long they began another ascent. The sides of the valley came closer, the clouds returned and the engine strained, but Ellen now had the utmost confidence in the plane and its pilot. She gave herself up to the movement and to the forces sustaining it.

The next valley was narrow, the hills on either side steep and the valley floor largely occupied by a snaking river. As the plane rushed forward Ellen looked down and saw several human figures almost close enough to touch looking skyward with expectant faces, arms shielding their eyes. The valley floor sloped up ahead and Ellen's stomach lurched as the plane dropped and swayed then seemed to accelerate as its wheels hit the ground. They bounced several times before coming to rest part-way up a slope, at the last moment making a ninety-degree turn. Ellen sat motionless in the stillness, collecting herself and allowing her ears to adjust to the loss of the engine noise. Then a pair of hands reached in and undid her harness, and the audible world returned.

'Misis! Misis!'

Six

Ellen had kept an eye out in the village for Kauigl, but once again there had been no sign of her. When they returned to the house Kubun said that the girl was with her new husband in another village, but when Ellen said she would like to visit, Kubun replied that Kauigl had run away from her husband and was wandering from place to place and from man to man. When Ellen said she did not believe this Kubun finally admitted that the girl was dead. She had hanged herself soon after her marriage.

Ellen accepted this news quietly. She ate her lunch mechanically then went to lie down. She fell into an uneasy sleep from which she awoke with a heavy feeling of loss. She cried for the desperation Kauigl must have felt and castigated herself for her tacit assumption that the native people would be too imbued with instinct, too unreflective and close to nature to do something so unnatural as take their own lives.

She asked Kubun where Kauigl was buried, because she would like to visit the grave. He replied that her relatives had retrieved the body from the vicinity of her husband's village, but he did not know what they had done with it. There was shame among her relatives. In response to further questions Kubun insisted doggedly that Misis should forget about Kauigl.

In the middle of the afternoon a heavy rain shower swept up the valley, lashing out with short-lived fury. When the sun returned the earth began to steam and Ellen went outside, eager for the newly released scents of the bush. She walked some way up the hill then stopped and looked back. The watching man was there, half visible behind a tree. Her first instinct was to ignore him and to continue her ascent, but without being aware of making a decision she found herself turning back and approaching him.

'Why are you always watching me?' she asked in halting speech.

There was no response and Ellen said that he should stop watching her. Her husband would be back soon. The man continued to stand there and Ellen suddenly found herself speaking in English and in summary form, as if explaining her situation to someone who had known her long ago.

'My husband is away so much and I find it very hard without him. I can hardly understand the people or make myself understood. It's as if I'm a child again in a world of children. I think it would be better if I were back among my own kind. But I can't say that to my husband, although he probably suspects.'

Ellen could see that her companion was bewildered by her outburst. She briefly touched his hand and apologised, but the man averted his eyes. She glanced down and her attention was taken by an adornment that was tied around his ankle, which she quickly realised was an item of her underwear. She turned and hurried back to the house, quickly bringing inside the things from the clothesline that was tucked away at the back, although they were still wet from the rain.

94

Seven

'They recruit local men who are young and strong and send them off to plantations on the coast or to the goldfields. They're kept there for years, treated almost like slaves, exposed to diseases to which they have no immunity, herded together without women, subjected to all kinds of degradation. They bring their discontent and their diseases back to their villages.'

Carl was explaining what had caused him to be away for so long. Ellen listened quietly as he continued.

'The highlands are by rights off limits to the labour recruiters. But there are some who defy the law. And some of the *kiaps*, Chas Noble and his ilk, turn a blind eye. The people need to be put on their guard.'

'You should take your concerns to the administration,' Ellen urged.

'Any approach would have to come from the leaders of the mission, but they don't want to rock the boat. The relationship is already fraught.'

Later in the evening Ellen told Carl about Ivor Moore's visit. She did not go into detail, wanting to see how much Carl would volunteer about the relationship.

'Ivor wants to live outside history,' Carl began, 'to be part of nature's rhythms and cycles and nothing more. But deep down he knows he can never succeed.'

Ellen waited but Carl remained silent, so she said, 'He thinks the missions have no right to take the people's souls.'

'I don't think Ivor believes in the soul. Just in a life force that is extinguished when we die or that wanders off somewhere looking for another poor creature to inhabit.'

Aijang was hovering nearby, evading looks from Ellen that suggested he go elsewhere. She asked if there was something he wanted and he responded by hitting his temples with the palm of each hand, rolling his eyes around and saying that the *kanakas* laughed at Ivor Moore because he was soft in the head.

'You allow him too much latitude,' Ellen objected when Aijang had gone. Instead of answering Carl returned the conversation to Ivor.

'He served in the Great War and was wounded several times. He thinks we Europeans have forfeited any right to preach to the rest of the world.'

Ellen remembered Ivor's shouting during the night. She was tempted to say that perhaps it was true that Ivor was not quite right in the head, all alone in the bush with just natives and his memories for company. But she held back, out of respect for what he must have been through in the war, and out of apprehension about how Carl might react.

At bedtime Ellen finally told Carl about Kauigl. It was not her intention to accuse or to blame him, but she could see that he took the girl's death personally. She offered him some physical comfort, but his response was lacklustre.

*

The mission's aeroplane had been badly damaged in a landing accident. Replacement parts had to make the long journey from Germany, and with no air deliveries to the Wahgi Carl and Ellen were in danger of running out of tinned food. As the days passed their supply of trade goods also began to dwindle, and Aijang was required to strike ever harder bargains with the village women who came up the hill with their vegetables and eggs. Ellen started to worry that the women might simply stop coming and that Carl would be forced to replace the experimental plants in the garden with subsistence foods. But then word reached them that a commercial plane had been contracted to deliver supplies, although the precise time had yet to be set. Carl and Aijang made a short visit to the village and when they returned Carl was in a light mood, telling Ellen to prepare herself for a novel experience.

At the landing strip early the next morning Carl and Ellen were greeted by gaudily decorated male bodies, the thudding sound of stamping feet and beating drums and a throng of spectators, mostly women and children. The stomach-turning smell of pig grease hung in a low fog over the ground. Ellen found herself looking to see whether the watching man was among the dancers, but the elaborate ornaments on display—red and yellow bird of paradise plumes in headdress formation, seed pods and animal teeth woven through hair and dangling from noses and ears, pieces of bone through nasal septa—made it difficult to distinguish one face from another. At one point a figure that may have been the watching man separated itself from the group and began a suggestive dance accompanied by piercing bird-like calls that made Ellen's skin tingle. But before she could make a positive identification the figure was reabsorbed into the gyrating mass.

After watching for several minutes Carl edged his way through the onlookers and began to weave in and out of the dancers, as if caught in a maze. He disappeared and for a moment Ellen panicked, fearing that he had been swallowed up by the ground or transformed into a native dancer. She called his name several times into the din then felt foolish as he emerged unscathed, expressing satisfaction with the progress. The landing strip, churned up by recent rain, would soon be smooth enough for the aeroplane to land with ease.

When they got back to the house Ellen asked whether the whole performance was not demeaning to the people, a parody of their customs. Carl assured her that the villagers greatly enjoyed the arrival of an aeroplane, especially one full of supplies that might in some way benefit them. And the dancing had more than the practical purpose of preparing the landing strip; it was also a means of placating the forces that might make mischief with the plane's landing. In reply to Ellen's questioning look Carl said that beliefs of this sort were harmless. With time and more exposure to the European world they would fade away. He added that the aeroplane that would be coming was bigger and heavier than the mission's plane, which made the additional work to smooth out the landing strip a necessary precaution.

The wait for the plane to arrive lasted several days, during which time the contentment of the early weeks returned to Ellen. There were visits to the garden alongside Carl to gauge the health and progress of the plants, and discussions in the village about the vegetables that would be transported back to the coast on the aeroplane. There were language lessons with Carl's dictionary near at hand, and occasional impromptu singing duets that led a small audience to gather out of nowhere around the house with broad smiles and clapping hands. As each day progressed Ellen looked forward with increasing anticipation to the intimacy of the night, and each morning she ran her hand gratefully over the indentation in the sheets left by Carl's body.

One evening the conversation came around again to Ivor Moore. Ellen hoped to hear Carl's considered assessment of what Ivor had said about the souls of the highlanders, but instead he asked whether Ivor had told her how they had met and what had drawn them together.

'He said you were a good listener.'

Carl recounted. 'I'd been in the eastern highlands for almost a year. I'd developed good relations with the local people, learnt their language to a passable level. I'd had some success in protecting them from the worst of the gold miners and the labour recruiters. They seemed ready to hear the Lord's Word— but then some whites were killed.

'They were prospectors, determined to strike it rich at whatever cost. They'd gone into the mountains to the south, wild country where few whites had been before. Word came that there'd been a skirmish and a patrol was sent to investigate. They found the men riddled with arrows, their native boys nowhere to be seen. The men died before they could be brought to the coast.'

'Were they friends of Ivor's?'

'They were friends of nobody, not even of themselves. Ivor knew them and had warned them, but they knew better.

'Even though the killings were in uncontrolled territory the district officer was determined that they not go unpunished. Another patrol was readied, four patrol officers and ten local policemen, all heavily armed. Some of the other prospectors were also involved, including Ivor. I said I would go with them. I feared a bloodbath and thought I might be able to mediate.

'We'd been on the march for more than two days when we came to a deep gorge, with steep rock walls all around us. Suddenly there was a barrage of arrows and our side fired back. I was armed, along with the others; it was a condition of my being allowed to go. I saw a young native man about to let loose an arrow; I raised my rifle and shot. The man seemed surprised, then he fell. At the moment I fired I wanted to kill him. In fact, I did kill him.'

After the initial shock Ellen felt pleasantly calm. She realised she had feared that Ivor had in his possession information about Carl far more damaging than this. Carl had acted in self-defence; he had nothing to reproach himself with.

'I felt I could no longer stay in the eastern highlands,' Carl concluded. 'So when the decision was made to start a new mission outpost in the Wahgi Valley I put my name forward. I arrived here not long before the government introduced new restrictions on movement.'

*

Ellen and Carl were at their separate tasks the next morning when they heard the churning of an engine away in the distance. Carl was quickly on his way to the landing site to ensure that everything was in order and Ellen followed him down the hill, running at such speed that only her continuing momentum kept her from falling. She branched off towards the village, where it was her task and Aijang's to organise the party of men who would carry the consignment of vegetables for the coast and help with the aeroplane's unloading.

The engine noise grew to a crescendo and, as Ellen looked up, it felt as if the plane were right on top of her. It kept on coming, as if wanting to scoop something up from the ground. The village women cried out, cowering with their heads buried in their hands. Even some of the men crouched down and shielded their ears from the sound.

The plane swooped up and away into the light and the engine noise dropped to a less threatening register. Ellen and Aijang quickly assembled a posse of men with their loads of vegetables and led them out of the village. A trail of women and children spread itself out at the rear.

They got to the landing site just in time to see the plane come out of a wide arcing loop and make a swaying and lurching approach. Ellen's stomach moved in sympathy, but the wheels touched the ground almost as one and the machine bumped with little fuss to a stop. The engine shut down and the propeller emerged from the blur, spinning first one way then the other to rest. The resulting quiet seemed to reach out and embrace the onlookers, creating a momentary cone of stillness and silence, before excited voices broke out from all sides.

The pilot was tall and slim and dressed all in white, including his leather helmet. As he stood on the wing of the plane with outstretched arms Ellen felt that she was in the presence of an apparition, and the returning silence among the villagers suggested that they shared this feeling. But the vision could not survive the greeting that the man called out in a broad Australian accent.

Ellen was delighted at the cornucopia stored in the plane's belly. There were crates of tinned meat, enough to last for months, several fifty-pound bags of rice, large bags of flour and packets of tea and coffee as well as copious quantities of trade goods. There were also medicines, packed in an array of neatly labelled boxes.

Carl supervised the unloading of the plane and Ellen stood at his side, impressing on the carriers the value of what was being entrusted to them. Then her attention was caught by a large group of women who had surrounded a young boy and were listening with rapt attention to what he was saying, while the towering figure of the pilot stood on the periphery and watched. Ellen could feel the mixture of awe and scepticism the boy's words were eliciting, and she went and stood next to the pilot and asked for an explanation. As she did so she handed the man several letters for home, asking him to take good care of them. She received a small pile of correspondence in return.

The pilot introduced himself as Lionel Butters and said he had heard a lot about Ellen from his fellow pilot, Len Stroop. Ellen deflected the man's interest by asking about the boy. Butters replied that he had been in the hospital on the coast for quite a stretch with pneumonia. 'I suppose he's telling them what he saw down there, but the lingo's double-dutch to me.'

Ellen tuned into the boy's voice. She began to translate out loud, assuming something of its excited tone. 'The ocean, full of water with salt in it—shells lying on the shore, ready to be picked up like stones—aeroplanes that run along the ground because they have no wings—boats so big that they blot out the horizon.'

'No word about the flight then?' Lionel Butters asked casually. 'We had a bit of a narrow escape. Came close to one of the mountain tops. Probably best he doesn't know that.'

Carl called out that the men were ready to load the aeroplane and Butters excused himself, saying that he had to oversee the process. The whites on the coast would be none too pleased if their highland veggies were bruised or discoloured.

As the loading of the plane proceeded Ellen stood and watched, buoyed by a sense of pride that the highlands had something that was valued by the European world outside.

The boy who was the centre of the attention of the village women had stopped talking and was uncovering something wrapped in a handkerchief. Ellen stood on tiptoe and saw a collection of brightly coloured marbles in a glass jar. The boy turned the jar this way and that, transforming the white light of the sun into blues, greens and reds, smiling broadly as he did so. The display brought forth a renewed round of chatter and excitement.

Eight

'Beth has at long last finished her degree, much to everyone's relief.' Ellen put down the letter she was reading and picked up another. 'And Britta now has a son to go with her daughter.'

Carl was engrossed in his own letter, and when he finally looked up, he asked Ellen to repeat what she had said. Instead of complying she asked about his news.

'It's from my sister, dated last July, so it's taken more than six months to get here.'

Carl passed the letter to Ellen, who briefly examined the tightly covered pages and said that she found the handwriting impossible to read. She returned the letter and asked Carl for a summary.

'The Nazis are increasing their pressure on those pastors still loyal to the Confessing Church to join the German Christians. Pauline's husband has been threatened with imprisonment if he fails to comply. The family is dependent on secret donations that she fears will soon dry up. She asks if there is any money we can send.'

Ellen looked uneasy and Carl responded that, since their current life demanded so little money, they could spare some of what was left from the sale of his parents' farm. Ellen pointed out that they would not live in New Guinea for ever and they should keep something to fall back on when they returned home.

Carl digressed, recounting that in the established missions on the coast and in the eastern highlands regular collections were taken and money sent back to the mission's headquarters in Germany. The preparedness to make such financial contributions, miniscule as they were by European standards, was seen by Alfred Fiebiger and the others as an important sign of their converts' commitment to their new faith. Of course, it would be a long time before anything similar was possible in the Wahgi Valley, even if it were desirable.

Carl fetched a list he had prepared showing expenses both before and after Ellen's arrival, and following further discussion it was agreed that two hundred of the six hundred pounds left in Carl's Adelaide bank account would be sent to his sister.

It was then time for more of Ellen's news. There were painstaking details from her mother about South Australian politics and welcome news that the resurgent anti-German feeling had not affected the family or the business to any great degree. And Beth, flushed with her academic success, was determined to enjoy to the full the summer holiday at the beach with her legion of friends and admirers, few of whom were known to Ellen.

Carl interrupted. 'I remember my first encounter with Beth, the evening of my interrogation by your parents. I felt that she was firmly on my side, and I was grateful for that.'

'Father has added a paragraph to my mother's letter,' Ellen

went on, 'which is typical. He always lets Mother make the running then adds or subtracts at what he considers to be strategic points.'

'What has he added or subtracted?' Carl asked.

'That my mother was delighted to hear about my medical successes, as she calls them, and has been telling everyone. She hopes that when I return home I will take my medical studies further, but she's waiting for the right moment to broach the subject with me.'

'And the subtractions?'

'My mother worries that these successes might encourage me to prolong my time in New Guinea.' After a pause Ellen said, largely to herself, 'As if this were up to me.'

She returned to one of the letters, reading out loud questions her mother had posed. 'Do the New Guineans display more pride in their race than our Aborigines? Is miscegenation countenanced by the administration and is it practised to a significant degree? How extensive will European settlement need to be to civilise New Guinea?'

Carl said that if Ellen's mother visited New Guinea he would take her out with him to meet the people and she could form her own opinion. Ellen pointed out that Carl had not yet allowed his own wife to travel with him, despite her constant requests, and Carl promised he would take her with him on his next trip.

Ellen basked briefly in the prospect of a joint journey, then she asked whether whites would eventually take over New Guinea as they had Australia. Carl replied that, unlike the Australian Aborigines, the New Guineans were settled on their land, and they were present in such numbers that only a full-scale invasion could drive them off. No Australian government would contemplate such a thing, not in the twentieth century. And anyway, Australia's conduct in New Guinea was under the watchful eye of the League of Nations, which would take a dim view of Europeans using violence to displace local people.

Ellen apologised for the naivety of her question. She said that the letters from home had transported her back to a previous world, where the knowledge she had gained in New Guinea did not yet exist. She promised to pay more attention in the future to her own experience and to draw sensible conclusions from it.

Over the course of the next several days Ellen returned to her letters, imagining answers to the more personal questions they posed. To Britta's query whether she was happy in her isolation, she told herself that Carl's love and companionship were sufficient and that she would experience periods of loneliness no matter where she was. To her father's entreaty to inform him immediately if she needed his help in any way, she told herself that it would be a betrayal to share with him her doubts about Carl's mission. To Beth's question how to choose a suitable husband from the crowd of young men pressing their case, she realised that she could not put into words what had drawn her so strongly to Carl. And to her mother's repetition of earlier advice that she not try again for a baby until she returned to Australia, she thought that a child of her own would make all the difference to her highland life.

Nine

Carl explained that, since the mission's plane was still out of service, they would have to travel on foot. They would have to contend with scorpions, rats, leeches and other invasive creatures, and there would be rain and cold as well as the usual heat. Ellen remained insistent. She reminded Carl of his promise, and he acquiesced.

A half a dozen local men had been engaged to act either as carriers, of tents and provisions for the journey, or as guards, bearing rifles that Carl had supplied. The party set out early, leaving Kubun and his aunt in charge of the house and garden. Onyx was also left in their care, Carl deciding that the party would make better time if they avoided the detours that would be required to accommodate the horse.

To begin with the going was easy, down to the valley floor then along the flats adjacent to the river. They crossed to the north side of the valley over a log bridge at a point where the river was narrow and shallow then moved into the lower reaches of the mountains. Mist that muffled sound and limited vision lingered until mid-morning then gave way to a bright day of sharp outlines and clear tones that encouraged brisk movement. They camped in the late afternoon near a stream that rushed away into the depths and was lost to the senses.

Aijang prepared a meal of bully beef, rice and corn, and together the group sat around the fire and ate. The highlanders talked sparingly, perhaps in deference to Ellen's presumed inability to comprehend, but afterwards they conversed and laughed among themselves in loud gusts well into the night. As Carl put up their tent Ellen found herself witness to an intricate display of dancing points of light that she realised must be fireflies, and it took several calls from Carl before she finally crawled into the tent and snuggled up beside him. Despite the continuing noise from outside she was soon asleep.

They started very early the next morning and climbed for several hours into the mountains before descending into a deep gorge. At the bottom of the gorge was a narrow, fast-running stream straddled by a flimsy bridge made of woven vines supporting narrow wooden slats. Carl was the first to cross, testing the structure as he went by stamping on the slats. He called for lengths of vine to be cut from surrounding bushes and he and Aijang balanced precariously as they wound the vine around the existing frame. When the strengthening work was completed, the carriers crossed confidently under Carl's supervision. Then he returned for Ellen, reassuring her that there was no danger provided she remained calm.

After the crossing the party rested briefly then began to climb again. When they finally emerged from tree cover the heat of the sun, now almost directly overhead, was razor-like in its sharpness. The torsos of the highlanders were soon gleaming with sweat, their breathing a series of stertorous gasps.

Ellen stopped to take in the surroundings and her attention

was drawn to the ramshackle remains of a fence interwoven with a stand of stunted trees. A deeper look showed the burnt remnants of several huts and clear evidence of plundered food gardens. Carl and the others waited quietly for Ellen to digest this scene and to catch up to them.

After more climbing the party made a brief stop to eat then continued on into the late afternoon. There were few words as they concentrated on the demands of the climb. The sounds of the mountain—a shrieking bird, a waterfall, faint rustlings of small animals—came and went in Ellen's consciousness, providing welcome distraction from the aching in her limbs and the tightness in her chest. She kept pace with the group, which reached the summit with the last threads of daylight filtering through a heavy mist. A small fire was soon alight, bringing welcome warmth and the inviting prospect of hot food.

The following morning a light wind blew away the mist and the next peak stood clearly visible, but it disappeared as they descended into a new valley and did not reappear until the late afternoon. When they finally reached the summit it was an island surrounded by a whorl of cloud that registered as drops of cool moisture against the skin. The tree trunks, exposed roots and rotting logs all about them carried a thick cover of deep-green moss.

With darkness came the sound of drums, distant at first and faint, then closer and more insistent. Voices yodelled along the ridges and descended into the valley below. The contingent of highlanders conversed among themselves then spoke to Carl, after which he told Ellen that the drums and voices were speaking of their presence, and they would need to keep their wits about them. Before settling down to sleep Carl posted a guard at the edge of the camp, providing him with a few rounds of ammunition that out of caution he had to this point withheld. Several times during the night Ellen was woken by Carl going to check that the guard was still awake at his post.

They had not gone far the next morning when they came across broken tree branches set out in formation across their way. Carl stopped and quietly drew Ellen's attention to an array of sharp bamboo splinters jutting out of the grass on either side of them. Almost immediately an arrow slammed into the ground only a few yards away and quivered to a standstill. The guards brought their rifles to their shoulders, but Carl gestured to them to hold their fire. He called into the surrounding bush then reached slowly into a bag he was carrying and took out some cowrie shells. He squatted and displayed the shells on the ground. He took out a bush knife which he held up, allowing the sunlight to glint on its stocky blade. He positioned the knife across the length of his hand then set it down alongside the shells.

A wiry man equipped with a bow and arrow appeared from the scrub in front of them. He called out and a dozen warriors appeared, bodies painted and ornamented and bristling with weapons. The warriors began to move forward and backward in threatening motions. Carl spoke in their direction, but his words seemed to be of no account. He gestured again at the objects spread out on the ground in front of him.

A rifle shot cracked, one of Carl's guards having lost patience or given in to fear. There was a spitting in the trees above them as the bullet sheared its way through the foliage, but the mountain men were only briefly deterred. They danced their way closer, their chants growing louder.

Carl again signalled to his men to hold their fire. He took several slow steps forward, holding his hands out, turning them to demonstrate their innocence. The hubbub died down. He slowly picked the knife up from the ground then pointed at the bark shield held by one of the aggressors, requesting an exchange, but there was no response. He bent again and picked up one of the warning branches and dismembered it with short sharp movements of the knife. The warriors remained quiet, shifting on their feet. Carl held out the knife again, handle foremost. This time the exchange was made and several of the men gathered around their prize, examining and testing it.

Carl told one of his companions to place the shield against a tree some distance away across clear ground. He instructed the two armed men to fire, each a single bullet, to demonstrate the power of their weapons. The men took aim studiously as Carl counted to three, but the demonstration failed, neither of the bullets finding its target. The warriors scoffed at the ineffectiveness of the weapons and resumed their aggressive display. It was left to Carl to take one of the rifles and to fire several bullets that penetrated the shield before burying themselves deep in the trunk of the supporting tree.

The warriors inspected the shield then gradually withdrew, taking with them the shells from the ground. The shield's owner retrieved it and carried it off, holding it close by his side as if its effectiveness had not been in any way sullied.

Following this incident the trekking was subdued, although from time to time there were brief verbal exchanges among the highlanders, evidently a teasing of those who had failed in their marksmanship. There was more climbing, another peak to scale before they would be within reach of their goal. The party reached the summit and was some way down into the next valley before stopping for the night.

With the arrival of darkness the distant drumming returned and sporadic human cries could be heard in the distance. In the light of the campfire woody vines seemed to hang from trees like the tresses of a woman's hair and in the stillness the fire's smoke hung like a gossamer net. Insects whirred, attracted by the fire, some immolating themselves in the flames.

The group ate at first in near silence, huddled around the fire, but Ellen soon gave in to a compulsion to talk to Carl about what had happened. She said that except for the first few moments she had not been afraid, although she had understood the danger. Instead of fear she had felt confident that this would not be the time and place of her death, that the events taking place were at a remove from her, that even if an arrow had struck her body she would have survived, and not as a hazy spirit but as a creature of flesh and blood. 'It was like a pageant or a play,' she concluded, 'and I was a spectator.'

Carl responded that a mechanism of Ellen's mind had been activated to protect her from reality, but she should make no mistake. The native arrows were dangerous, some tipped with bone or poison; to be struck with their full force would usually mean death. He then said that he had never seen the people of these mountains in such a state of agitation. Something untoward must have happened to provoke them.

Aijang was enmeshed in a vigorous discussion with one of the highlanders, a confident young man who had stood out on the journey through his regular jousting with the others and his desire always to have the last word. Carl joined the discussion, and while Ellen could not understand everything he said his chastising tone was clear. There was resentment in the highlander's response.

'What's he saying, Carl?'

There was a further energetic exchange between Carl and the man. Ellen heard the words 'Adam' and 'Eve' but could not make out their context.

After a lull in the conversation the man began to talk again. This time his tone was more matter-of-fact, the words more distinct. He occasionally looked at Ellen before turning his attention back to Carl or to the fire.

Carl explained without Ellen's prompting. 'It's about their understanding of Christ and his message.'

There was another burst of words from the young man, then silence.

Carl said, 'They think Adam and Eve live somewhere in the sky above Sydney. They've heard of Sydney; it's where the whites come from and where they'll return to when they leave the highlands.'

Carl's expression warned Ellen not to laugh or even to smile. The highlanders sat with bowed heads.

'It's the material things we bring that most impress them.

They want to know where these things come from. Many think they are given to us by our god. They want to know whether he will give them these things too if they accept him.'

Aijang offered a short commentary and the young highlander replied. Carl interjected several times with questions, but the man seemed confident of what he was saying. His tone was increasingly assertive. Carl filled out what Ellen had heard.

'He insists that some of our evangelists are luring people by telling them that if they accept Christ they will learn the secret of the white man's wealth. They'll become rich and powerful and will be able to expel the whites.'

Ellen found herself explaining to the circle of watching faces that there was no truth in this story. Religion had nothing to do with material things. And there was only one God, the same God for the white man and the black.

The men looked silently at the ground and Ellen asked Carl if they had understood. He said that her meaning had been clear.

Some tea had been prepared and Carl passed Ellen a cup. The company gradually slipped away and left them alone, with Aijang squatting just out of easy earshot.

Carl spoke softly. 'Sometimes they appear to understand, but they are at constant danger of falling back into the pagan world. It's more comfortable for them there, surrounded by familiar things, even if many of these things are malevolent.'

There was a round of laughter from the highlanders, the teasing apparently not yet run its course. Carl stirred the fire. It crackled and flared briefly before settling back to a muted smoulder. He reached for an ember and nursed it in the palm of his hand for several seconds, seemingly oblivious to the pain it must be causing, before Ellen shouted at him and slapped the ember away. She bathed the burnt hand in water from a flask and found some ointment to smear on it. When she asked what had possessed him to do such a thing, Carl just shook his head.

Ten

There were free-standing shrubs and vines traced around trellises. There were beds of roses, red croton, orchids, rhododendrons, poinsettias, dahlias and other annuals and perennials that even Carl was at a loss to name. Often the colours were on the point of clashing, but then a new shade or shape would entice the eye onwards. Butterflies glided in and out on exquisite wings, causing the atmosphere to shimmer, while off to one side an aviary sparkled and squawked in the sunlight.

The house that emerged from this display was of well-cut timber with a corrugated iron roof, a brick chimney and a wide verandah with sturdy railings encased in clematis. It stood with its garden on a large piece of slightly raised land that offered uninterrupted views of the surrounding mountains. There were other buildings scattered around that Carl said belonged to the government post. The missionaries from the coast, Artur Schmidt and Peter Weiss from the Huon Peninsula to the east and Luke Sommer from Madang in the north, would stay in one of these buildings, along with Sven Jonsson, who came from the highlands but well to the west of Carl's mission house, out towards Mount Hagen. Carl and Ellen would have the use of the second bedroom in the Fiebigers' house.

'You never mentioned there was another Lutheran mission further out than us,' Ellen said.

'Sven Jonsson came from Madang along a newly discovered route into the highlands and then went further west. His connections remain largely with Madang.'

'Does he have a wife and family?'

Carl shook his head. 'Sven is quite alone out there, as far as other Europeans are concerned. He seems to like it that way.'

Ellen tried to visualise this man in his loneliness, but she could not see past Carl. She searched his face for any sign that he had read her thoughts, but he was speaking normally, detailing the routes the missionaries would have taken to reach the meeting. 'Sven would have gone north-east across the mountains down to Madang, from where he and Luke would have taken the supply boat that does regular trips around the coast. In Lae they would have joined forces with Artur and Peter for the hike into the highlands. Luke, Sven and Artur are used to walking long distances so they should be none the worse for wear. Peter I'm not sure about. He isn't long in New Guinea.'

When the company came together for dinner on the first evening they were greeted by a fine spread on a large table in the Fiebigers' dining room—vegetables and meat both local and foreign, crockery and cutlery of good quality. The English spoken was often idiosyncratic but easily understandable, the atmosphere congenially European and cultivated.

Ellen worked with Lotte and the local help to ensure that none of the men went short of good things to eat and drink.

She said little but listened closely to the conversation, which was full of numbers—of attendance at services, of baptisms, of young men from the district studying to prepare themselves to take the Word of God to their fellow natives. All the hard work of the pioneers, all their sacrifices, were now bearing abundant fruit. There was so much to thank God for.

'Sven and Carl, how are you coping with the continuing restrictions on the work of your evangelists?' Alfred Fiebiger sat back and waited.

Sven Jonsson said that he limited his evangelists to a tight area that he kept under constant supervision. There had been no trouble with the *kiaps*, who were anyway scarce on the ground in his far-flung place. Attention then turned to Carl, who acknowledged that his evangelists had been involved in an unfortunate incident, but this had been quickly brought under control.

'We heard about this,' Alfred interjected. 'If there is a repeat the administration will come down hard. They might even reintroduce the restrictions that have been eased here in the east.'

Carl responded that he was constantly visiting his evangelists and as a result spent little time at the mission house. His wife had been required to fend for herself for long periods of time, although she was only recently arrived.

'You could take her with you,' Lotte said.

Ellen felt a flush of embarrassment at being the centre of attention. She was grateful for the next intervention.

'I think we'd all agree that we should leave Carl and his wife to arrange their domestic affairs as they see fit.'

Ellen was instantly attracted to the voice. It was American, she was sure of that, slow and slightly drawn-out but warm and comfortable. She glanced at Luke Sommer then looked away.

Alfred returned the conversation to the challenges facing the mission. 'The Roman Catholics are less reliant on evangelists than we are and therefore less affected by the government restrictions. And now the Adventists are expanding. We must not allow ourselves to be upstaged.'

Again, Luke intervened. 'Carl and Sven are the ones on the front line, Alfred. I think we should let them decide the pace.'

'We don't have so much time now,' Alfred countered. 'The Catholics have all the might of Rome behind them, and the government will favour the Seven Days because they're all Australians. We cannot rest on our laurels.'

Lotte deflected attention from questions of mission policy by asking Peter Weiss about his wife and Artur Schmidt about his sister. How were they coping with the language, the heat on the coast and the loneliness? Lotte assured the men that she would come to visit again as soon as she could find the time.

Lotte turned to Luke. 'And your fiancée, Luke? Is there any news?'

'Thank you for asking, Lotte. As a matter of fact I've just had a letter. Hilda says her preparations are well underway, but to get everything finalised and then with the trip itself we're looking at another six months.' Luke added, in a subdued tone, 'Her father understands but her mother is full steam against it. Doesn't want her only daughter travelling halfway round the world to die of fever among infidels. I guess I don't blame her.'

'I'm sure the delay will make the reunion with your fiancée, when it does come, all the more joyous.' Ellen blushed as she voiced this sentiment.

'That's the way I'm trying to think about it,' Luke said warmly. 'And it gives me time to get everything prepared. Get the house built, set up nice, and a garden. Along the lines of Lotte's, but not quite so grand.' He laughed easily.

Carl entered the conversation. 'Your fiancée won't want to leave her departure too long. The way things are going there'll be another war in Europe. Who knows what that would mean, even for us in this forgotten corner of the world.'

Alfred Fiebiger and Artur Schmidt said almost as one that it would not come to war. Alfred continued alone. 'If Germany's rightful demands are met there will be no reason for more conflict.'

Luke pointed out that, whatever the rights and wrongs, another European war would certainly not help the administration and the missions to convince the New Guineans to stop their incessant fighting. Carl agreed, adding that another white man's war would only confirm what many of the highlanders already suspected—that the whites were human beings not so different from them.

*

Ellen and Lotte spent the morning together while the men held their meeting. At first the conversation was stilted, but gradually the words began to flow. Ellen spoke about the experiences she had gathered in her short time in New Guinea and her confidence grew as she recounted her successes. She gave particular attention to her healing work, which in itself was enough to justify her presence in the highlands. She said that with the new supplies of medicine that had recently come there was no end to the amount of good she could do.

They stopped walking and sat down on a bench that was stretched out under a broad shade tree. Lotte took Ellen's hand. They sat quietly together, observing the slow moving, slowly warming morning. The flower garden was in partial view and Ellen could see figures on all fours working there, several raising their hands in silent greeting. Without warning a pair of small children raced up to Lotte and nestled against her, then flew away with shouts of achievement.

'It's really very beautiful here,' Ellen acknowledged.

Lotte said that the beauty of the place was God's way of compensating her for the sacrifices of the missionary life. Ellen's healing work was also compensation, for all her sacrifices.

Ellen began to cry softly and Lotte put an arm around her, saying that in the early days she had often cried and found it a pleasant release. But over time she had learnt to save her tears for moments of special misfortune, which had come often enough. Young missionaries had died well before their time or had been forced by sickness to abandon the field and return to Germany. Converts had renounced the faith and reverted to their pagan ways, encouraging others to join them in resisting the mission. Such things were the proper subject of tears.

Lotte next asked if Ellen had found any companionship among the local people, and Ellen replied that the extraordinary difficulty of their language made this impossible. Lotte suggested that language difficulties could always be overcome if you had the right intentions, but you needed to tread a fine line between reaching out to the people and maintaining justified pride in your own race. Race was something given by God, and pride in race was respect for God's creation. The highlanders must be encouraged to retain pride in their race. 'But I'm sure you understand this,' Lotte concluded.

In the distance a line of shackled men could be seen shuffling along under the eye of a contingent of local policemen. Several members of the line were obviously unhappy with their treatment and were complaining with provocative gestures. A policeman made as if to strike one of the men with the butt of his rifle and his comrades stepped back and levelled their weapons with clear intent. The line grumbled and resumed its movement.

'The administration has started the construction of a new road,' Lotte explained, 'which is greatly needed to open up the country. We cannot rely on aeroplanes forever. They must be replaced by motor vehicles. Good roads will lead to a prosperous future. They will help us to spread the Gospel, and the people to expand their world.'

Ellen asked about the jail at the government post and Lotte said it was called the calaboose. 'Some of the local men don't seem to mind it. There's no stigma attached to imprisonment, and useful contacts can be made. If someone is in trouble in his village he can come here and be out of harm's way. Many take the opportunity to learn pidgin English, which is becoming more and more popular, despite our best efforts.'

Ellen said she hoped the prisoners were well treated, to which Lotte replied that every now and then the native guards lost their composure, beating the prisoners or even urinating on them while they lay defenceless on the ground. She said she had brought this up with the district officer but had been told to mind her own business.

*

There was small talk around the dinner table, but the dispute about the pace of things in the Wahgi Valley soon resurfaced.

'We all know the competition is pushing ahead. If we don't act, we'll miss out.' Alfred Fiebiger looked around the table for support.

Carl explained his position, seemingly for Ellen's benefit. 'I've reminded Alfred that our mission's approach since the early days has been to take time to learn the local language and way of life. We need to instil in the people a sense of their own unity, then win over a majority to the idea of Christ, particularly those in authority. Only then should we start with individual baptisms.'

Alfred countered briskly that times were different; a race for souls that had not existed before could not now be ignored. 'And we'd agreed to concentrate on a small selection of languages so as not to expend all our energies learning every last one of the local tongues. Now you've decided to use one of the Wahgi languages.'

Artur Schmidt said that these matters had been thoroughly discussed during the day. It was now up to the mission's leaders in Germany to resolve the matter.

'America and Australia will also need to be consulted,' Carl interjected.

Luke Sommer introduced a new topic. 'We're also not in complete accord on the conditions that should be placed on the people before they can be baptised. A particularly difficult question is whether we should continue to insist that those with multiple wives give up all but one. The wives who are turned out often have nowhere to go.'

Ellen was unable to stay silent. 'It is an intolerable injustice to a woman to require her to live as one of several wives. Such a practice cannot be condoned.'

Before Luke or any of the others could respond Carl stated that the missions should interfere as little as possible in local customs.

'You always go too far, Carl,' Alfred interjected. 'Next you will say we should excuse the eating of human flesh.'

'We should focus on sorcery,' Carl said. 'That is the source of everything that holds the people back.'

Lotte called for the help to come and clear the table. Then she made for a piano that was tucked away at the far end of the room and began to play. The men followed her, with the exception of Luke, who stood next to Ellen and said that he would not allow his singing voice to spoil the evening. The two listened as the piano stopped and started before settling on a classical German song.

'But please don't hold back on my account, Mrs Starck,' Luke said when the song was finished.

'Ellen, please.' She was surprised at how easily the smile that followed came to her face and at how pleasant it felt. 'I do like to sing, but tonight I think I'll just watch.'

The music began again and Luke said in an undertone, accompanied by a relaxed smile that carried no demands, 'I'll wager you've never seen anything like Lotte's garden. I call it the Garden of Eden.' Ellen replied with a finger to her lips and Luke waited until the song concluded before finishing his thought. 'I suggested to Lotte and Alfred that they use the new coloured photographs to advertise the mission to the world. I think it would make a tremendous splash. They say it would be too expensive, but I suspect they think it would give the wrong impression.'

During the next song Ellen found herself glancing back and forth between Luke and Carl, comparing the former's blond openness to the latter's darker, more angular features. The song had finished and Luke had spoken one or two sentences before Ellen was able to refocus her mind. 'The best of German culture,' she repeated, hoping she'd heard correctly.

Luke continued. 'But despite our Lutheran faith I'm American and I dare say you're Australian.'

Ellen was on the point of saying that while she was certainly Australian she was only partially Lutheran, but instead she said,

'And here we are, shipwrecked amongst people I can hardly understand and don't particularly like.'

As soon as the words were out Ellen regretted them, but Luke assured her that she would soon find things to like about New Guinea and its people, just as Carl had.

'And what is it that Carl likes?'

Luke hesitated, but Ellen pressed him.

'The challenge it represents. To understand the people; to help them to understand us. To bring them to Jesus without doing unnecessary violence to their way of life.'

'You think Carl is in danger of taking the side of the New Guineans?'

'We're all on the side of the New Guineans. In our own way.'

A change in the room's atmosphere suggested to Ellen that her conversation with Luke was attracting the attention of the others, so she spoke in an undertone. 'But Carl has chosen the wrong way?'

'Perhaps he wants to know more than is necessary, more than is even possible, for an outsider.'

While Ellen considered a defence Luke said that Carl was a fine man who would make a great contribution to the mission and to New Guinea. She had every reason to be proud of him.

*

As night surrounded the house Ellen and Carl lay in bed and talked. Carl said he suspected that what the highlanders had told them on the trek was true. Some of his evangelists were using false promises to attract the people to Christ, appealing to the materialism that was so prominent in highland culture.

'The people don't understand how our wealth is produced. Even the few who venture down to the coast see only the finished goods and the ships in which they're transported. They think everything is made in Sydney according to instructions delivered by our god then transported by ship to the coast and by aeroplane to the highlands.'

Ellen was pleasantly tired and in the mood for intimacy. Hearing Carl's mind at work at such close quarters was a deeply sensuous experience for her, perhaps even more sensuous than love making, which they usually conducted without words. She pressed herself against him and encouraged him to continue.

'New Guineans don't understand nature and its laws,' he said. 'Before we bring them to God we must teach them about nature.'

'Nature,' Ellen murmured dreamily, letting her fingers play across Carl's chest.

He took her hand. 'We humans are part of nature but separate from it at the same time. That's why we're so hard to satisfy.'

A series of argumentative shouts away in the distance disturbed the quiet. Ellen sat up and Carl said that it was probably the calaboose—prisoners arguing among themselves or with the guards. They would soon get tired of it. As if on cue the shouting stopped but it soon started again, louder and more hostile than before, until an unmistakably white voice put an end to it.

Ellen lay back down and Carl returned to the topic of nature. 'We have learnt that there is nothing in nature that is in principle outside the reach of our senses and our reason. But for the New Guineans nature is full of capricious spirits with minds of their own. These spirits can sometimes be manipulated to serve human interests, but only by those with special knowledge. Sorcerers and the like.'

Ellen wanted the conversation to continue but she also wanted a less abstract topic, so she asked about Artur Schmidt's sister and Peter Weiss's wife. Carl said that Artur's wife had died not long ago, worn out by the isolation and the malaria, and his sister had come from Germany to keep house for him. Peter's wife was also a new arrival, having followed her husband who had only recently graduated from the seminary in Bavaria. All Carl knew of these women was that they belonged to a long line of wives and sisters who had sacrificed themselves to the missionary dreams of their menfolk. He hoped that Clara Schmidt and Mathilde Weiss would eventually escape their coastal enclave and discover a fuller life in the outside world.

Ellen waited for Carl to acknowledge the sacrifices she was making on his behalf, to elaborate on what he had said to the others about leaving her alone so much, but he remained silent. She thought briefly about bringing up his birth mother, her desert life of privation and her ultimate sacrifice, but instead she mentioned what Lotte had told her about pride in race. She then said that earlier in the day she had stolen a look into Alfred Fiebiger's work room and seen Nazi paraphernalia on his desk and a photograph of Adolf Hitler on the wall.

Carl spoke to the ceiling. 'The district officer asked me about support for the Nazis among our German colleagues. He wants to know if there are more like Alfred. I told him I don't think so, but I doubt he believes me.'

*

The next day several white men were rushing in and out of the district office, shouting orders to each other and to a squad of native policemen. Lotte looked out from her front verandah and suggested to Ellen that they go and find out what all the fuss was about.

Ellen feared that Chas Noble might be somewhere in the vicinity, so she followed Lotte only at a distance. But as they approached the government buildings she noticed that some of the whites looked to be even younger than she was, hardly into their twenties, and she felt curious about them. She was also curious about the much older man who had come out to meet Lotte. She inched a little closer but did not commit herself to joining Lotte's conversation. Instead, she stood still and looked into the middle distance, hoping to make herself inconspicuous.

All of a sudden two of the young whites were standing almost within arm's reach. They had taken off their broad-brimmed hats and were smiling. One of them asked jauntily if he could be of any assistance. 'You seemed a bit lost, standing here and looking around. So Fio and I thought we should see if we could be of help.'

'I'm perfectly well, thank you.'

Ellen immediately regretted the aloofness in her voice, so she tried again. 'I'm sorry, I was miles away. I'm here with Lotte.' She gestured in the direction of Lotte and the older man, who were deep in conversation.

'You're with the mission, I suppose?'

'My husband is, yes.'

There was a knowing look on one of the faces, a hint of disappointment on the other.

'I told Fio there'd be a husband, but he refused to take my word for it.'

'Leo Fiocchini,' the second of the young men said, holding out his hand to Ellen. 'And this is Keith Dawes, who talks too much.' The two men jostled each other.

'My name is Ellen Starck. My husband and I are in the Wahgi Valley. We've come here for a meeting of our Lutheran missionaries.'

'Germans then,' Keith Dawes said, not disguising his disapproval.

'My husband and I are from South Australia and Pastor Sommer is from America. I think Pastor Jonsson is from Sweden.'

Dawes remained unimpressed. 'We've been told to keep a close eye on you lot. There are doubts about your loyalties.'

A voice called out from the building, berating the young men for engaging in idle chatter when there was so much to be done. Dawes abruptly turned and walked away with an airy wave of his hand, but Leo hesitated. The conversation became softer.

'Don't mind Keith, he's just acting big. It's our first time in the highlands. We're only a few months in New Guinea.'

Ellen put her hand on Leo's sleeve. 'Shouldn't you go?'

'You must be the only white woman in the Wahgi Valley.'

'I suppose so.'

'I think it's mighty brave of you. It's hard enough for us men, but for a woman.'

'I have my husband.'

'He's a lucky man, that's all I can say.' Leo blushed and Ellen looked down.

'Anyway, you should be careful,' Leo went on. 'I'm not really supposed to say, but there's a white man somewhere in the mountains who has gone rogue and is shooting blacks for no good reason. We have to go and find him. He might bring the people out against us, or even start shooting whites.'

Before Ellen could tell Leo about her own recent experience with aggressive highlanders Lotte appeared, took her firmly by the arm and led her back towards the house. When they slowed their pace Lotte said, 'You need to watch yourself with these young *kiaps*. Some lose their bearings at the sight of a white woman, especially one who isn't old and worn out like me.'

Ellen looked around but Leo Fiocchini had gone. She turned back to Lotte and asked about the older man she had been talking to.

'He's one of the most experienced government men up here and sees this territory as his kingdom. The other *kiaps* answer to him, the gold miners look to him for favours, and he thinks he understands the people better than they understand themselves. He has delusions of grandeur.'

Ellen found the idea of the highland population forming a kingdom in the mind of a white man hard to accept. Without doubt the landscape was imposing—the ranging mountains and deep long valleys with their profusion of plant life, everything brought into sharp relief by bright air regularly washed cleaned by teeming rain. But it should be obvious to anyone that the human inhabitants did not do justice to their surroundings.

'What's his name?' she asked.

'Reg Thompson.'

'The discussion seemed very serious.'

'He says he wants to improve relations between our mission and the government. Some of the *kiaps* don't trust us. Chas Noble and his kind are convinced we're scheming to get our colony back. There's even a rumour that the Führer wants to resettle Germany's Jews here. Reg says he's prepared to give us the benefit of the doubt. If we accommodate the government's requirements he'll put a stop to the hostility.'

'What are the requirements?'

'There's a long list, which is constantly growing.'

Ellen waited and Lotte elaborated. 'Accept the government as the primary authority everywhere in the highlands. Negotiate fairly with the people for any new land we need. Leave the timber alone—there's a shortage down in the valleys. Not take sides or try to arbitrate in tribal disputes. Not compete with the other confessions for converts. Stay out of uncontrolled areas.'

Ellen said that none of this seemed exceptional, but Lotte responded with irritation. 'Please don't take offence dear, because we like you and Carl, but we have grown tired of the egotism and arrogance of the Australian administrators. They always think they know best.'

The two women reached the house and turned to survey the view. Lotte said, 'We Lutherans were the first in the highlands, before the government and before the other churches, even before the gold miners. God has entrusted the souls in this place to our care. We will continue to assert our priority, despite the government's hostility.'

When Lotte spoke again her voice was shorn of all emotion. 'Reg Thompson told me that a madman is on the loose in the mountains nearby, killing blacks. Apparently he's a German. A patrol will be sent.'

*

Several women, their eyes bound with strips of bark, crept into the clearing at the centre of the circle and the chattering and laughter of the onlookers died away. As the women moved they collided with each other and fell to the ground then got quickly to their feet and continued the movement, before stopping in unison and cupping their hands behind their ears. At first nothing was audible, then the air began to hum. The women strained their heads towards the source of the sound. They held hands and moved in its direction, but the sound receded. Then on the far side of the circle a quartet of men appeared, blowing into long bamboo flutes. They twisted and turned before disappearing into the audience, the sound following them.

An elaborately ornamented man burst into view. He crouched, then jumped, then stood stock still. He gestured to the audience and some of the women onlookers turned their backs; others covered their eyes with their hands and lowered their heads. The quartet of flute players reappeared in full voice. The blindfolded women rushed in their direction, but again they stumbled and fell. The flute players formed a circle around the fallen women, playing at high volume.

Another man entered the clearing. He was tall, lithe and unadorned, dressed simply in a long *lap-lap*. He held a small crucifix in front of his face. The flute players jumped back in apparent shock and fear, letting their instruments fall to the ground. The tall man approached the blindfolded women. He bent down and ceremoniously untied their blindfolds then led them to the collection of fallen instruments, holding the crucifix aloft. The women positioned the instruments at an angle against the ground then broke them into pieces with several sharp movements of their bare feet. They piled the pieces together and lit matches until a fire began. As the fire took hold there were audible intakes of breath from the onlookers.

The tall man started to speak. He pointed to the fire and lifted the crucifix above his head. The words poured out of him, transfixing the audience. Then he stopped his sermon. He took a cloth bag from his pocket and emptied its contents on the ground. There were clumps of hair, clippings from fingernails and pieces of what might have been dried excrement. He pushed these things into a pile with his foot, picked them up and returned them to the bag that he then threw into the flames.

The fire flared up briefly before dying down and petering out. A silence spread among the watchers and held, as if suspended over a cliff, before collapsing in sounds of excited speech.

After a short hiatus a narrow passage formed itself through the crowd. The whites who had been watching the play made their way through the passage to the small mission church, followed by a stream of highlanders. When the pushing and shoving was finished the vast majority found themselves outside the church, but their determination to participate was undiminished. Hymns were sung with so much intensity that the air became almost too hot to breathe, and when Alfred Fiebiger spoke from the makeshift pulpit his words were taken up and passed on by the congregation with such enthusiasm that they seemed to fill the entire valley.

*

At the dining table Alfred was accepting the congratulations on the souls he had imbued with such fervour for God. He said proudly that among the new converts were members of clans that had been enemies for as long as anyone could remember. And the older men, who had for so long rejected the Christian message and turned their backs on the converts among the young, were now giving up the ways of their ancestors and joining the fold.

Alfred asked Ellen if she had understood the message of the play but began to explain before she could reply. 'The flutes belong to the secret life of the men. They must not be shown to women and children, on pain of death. By allowing women to see the flutes and by breaking them into pieces, the play demonstrates that the people have put aside these superstitious beliefs.'

'The hair and the other things that were burnt?' Ellen asked.

'Bodily leavings are used by sorcerers to harm those from whom they come. The burning shows that the people have turned their backs on magic.'

Ellen waited for Carl to join the conversation, but he remained silent, so she asked Alfred for the gist of his sermon.

'I said that Christianity does not belong to the white man. To be saved the people do not need to become just like whites. They need only to believe and trust in Jesus as the Son of God.'

Ellen found herself wondering out loud why God had waited so long to make Himself known to the people of New Guinea. She said it surely could not be true that the New Guineans who had lived and died before the missions came were damned for all eternity. Artur suggested that the natives' forebears must have committed some special sin that had caused God to neglect them, while Luke said that the only explanation that made sense to him was that the New Guineans of the past had not been ready to receive God's Word. Alfred headed off further speculation by saying that it was impossible to know why the Incarnation had happened when and where it did, and they should simply be grateful that this greatest of all gifts had been given to humanity at all.

As the group sat in silence one of Lotte's servants rushed in and announced that there had been a breakout from the calaboose. With most of the *kiaps* now away on patrol the house might be attacked.

Alfred and Lotte called their staff together and told them to take up positions outside. They should demonstrate in their bearing their faith in Jesus and he would protect them from any harm. Carl instructed his men to join the guard, but he took their rifles, keeping one for himself and handing the other to Aijang. The Fiebigers also armed themselves and distributed pistols to the other missionaries. A tense time of watching and waiting followed before word came that the escapees had fled the area. The weapons were put aside and normal life resumed.

Eleven

For several weeks after their return from the east Carl spent his days in the nearby village or in other settlements to the west and south that lay within a few hours' walk. Ellen often accompanied him on these journeys, striding out in the loose-fitting pants, sturdy boots, long-sleeved shirt and wide-brimmed hat that had become her regular attire. While Carl sought out the leading men Ellen treated the illnesses that lay within her competence and the reach of her medicines. She engaged in rudimentary conversations commensurate with her command of the language, gravitating to those few women she found congenial. None of these relationships approached friendship, but her interest in the lives of the women grew, and she looked forward to visiting them again.

On the journey home Carl would recount what his informants had said, about friendships and enmities in their clans, battlelines with neighbouring tribes, and their perception of whites. He said it took time to make the locals understand that not all whites were the same, bent on exploitation of the land and the people. Ellen responded that she was only beginning to understand that the New Guineans themselves were not all the same.

Carl continued. 'The *kiaps* encourage small hamlets to amalgamate into large settlements, for ease of administration.

They designate one or two men as the representatives of each village, and they deal primarily with these men. But often the men they appoint are not the true leaders, which leads to discord and a distorted view of the highland world.

'In each clan and sub-clan there are currents and undercurrents of power and influence, of debts and recriminations. Long-standing feuds and recent quarrels, almost impenetrable to an outsider. That's why the work goes so slowly.'

Ellen cautioned Carl not to become too close to one man or one clan and he assured her that he was careful in the allocation of his time and attention, taking in as much of local life as possible. But when Ellen occasionally mentioned items of information that she had learnt from her discussions with the women—about the violence or unfaithfulness of a husband, disputes between old and new wives, the industriousness or laziness of girls approaching the age of marriage—Carl would remain silent, and she would sense his realisation and frustration that the highland women lived in a world that was doubly opaque to him.

On the paths between villages they would often meet separate groups of men and women on the move. The women would invariably be accompanied by pigs, carried in arms or led by a piece of bush rope tied to a foreleg. The men would be armed with spears or bows, and if the encounter took place in a stretch of tall kunai grass or in dense woodland Ellen would be anxious until it became clear that the men's intentions were peaceful. Sometimes Carl recognised a man he knew and a short conversation would take place, interspersed with reciprocal touching and sometimes with laughter. As they walked on Carl would explain who the man was, how they had met and what his hopes were for the relationship.

Inevitable bands of prepubescent boys would also regularly accost them and provide an escort for a section of the journey. They would run and talk at such a rate that Ellen could only gesture in response, and even Carl was often compelled to call on Aijang to interpret. If Onyx was with them the boys would examine her from all angles and touch her cautiously, unable to hide their amazement at her size and strength and offering the wildest speculations about her place in the animal world. The amusement provided by the boys would quickly pale, and when they had gone Ellen would relax and allow herself to enjoy the pleasant tiredness of her body and the rhythm of the walk. She would feel no resentment when Carl turned away from her to discuss with Aijang the tasks to be completed before the end of the day.

If the journey was relatively long and they were still not home by late afternoon Aijang would set off ahead in order to have the evening meal ready on their return. Ellen and Carl could then talk and touch more freely. Ellen would sometimes ask Carl to kiss her, and on occasions they would use the privacy provided by a stand of trees or a patch of thick undergrowth to indulge more fully their desire for each other. A half hour's walk from the house was a well-protected grove with soft ground where they often stopped. Carl once asked Ellen if she could imagine making love there, but she replied that the possibility of being disturbed, by humans, animals or insects, made it unsuitable.

In the evening they would sit together and read by the light of kerosene lamps, Carl one of his heavy reference books, Ellen a textbook on tropical diseases or, if she was too tired, a novel or a magazine. Carl would get up at intervals to select a new record and rewind the gramophone. On the few occasions when an aeroplane was due they would be consumed by the last-minute composition of letters, sitting opposite each other at the dining table, Ellen wondering what Carl was telling his sister, she herself doing her best to be informative without divulging anything that might cause her family or friends undue worry. A more regular diversion was provided by the two-way radio on which the mission was allocated a scheduled time several evenings each week and whose etiquette, with its call-signs and words used as punctuation marks, Ellen had quickly come to master and even to enjoy. Carl usually stayed with his books, but Ellen never missed the opportunity to hear new stories from the missionary world and sometimes from the world beyond. Often it was just Lotte Fiebiger, Clara Schmidt and Mathilde Weiss and Ellen would need all her concentration to understand the German conversation, wondering what the other women were holding back because of her. But when Luke Sommer took part, the conversation would be in English and Ellen would delight in her effortless command of the language and in the reassuring view of things that Luke conveyed. She would ask him about progress with the house and garden he was constructing for his fiancée, and when he had finished she would assure him that any woman would be thrilled to live in the place he had described.

A point of unease remained Mbagl's regular nightly visits, when Ellen would be reduced to the role of spectator as Carl and his visitor smoked and talked. Occasionally Carl would fetch something from his desk, a sketched map or his dictionary or even one of his technical books. He would search for a particular page, show it to Mbagl and the pace and density of their speech would increase for a time before falling back again to the bare bones of communication. Ellen would sit quietly during this time, witness to an intimacy she could not share but unwilling to leave Carl and the man alone.

When Mbagl had gone Ellen would be overcome with exhaustion, but her passion for Carl would keep her from sleep. In the darkness and silence she would imagine the grove on the journey back to the mission house, feel the leafy earth under her body, smell the fresh scents of the bush and enjoy the thrill of possible discovery. At these brief moments there was no place on earth she would rather have been than her highland home.

Twelve

For the next journey they travelled light, without Onyx and without Ellen's medical supplies, Carl and Aijang carrying small rucksacks of food and drink. Mbagl was with them, having been convinced by Carl to witness the demonstration he was planning. The target village was four hours' walk away and they left at dawn so that they would arrive well before midday. Carl walked beside Mbagl and Ellen left the pair to their companionship, which was largely wordless. Occasionally Mbagl spoke and Carl explained to Ellen that a boundary had been crossed and the territory they were now in was foreign to Mbagl in a way that was difficult for whites to understand, although the language spoken was little different.

When they came near their destination they were met by a trio of local men armed with spears and protected by shields. Mbagl hung back and Carl led a brief exchange full of expressive arm movements. After a lull there was more discussion and gesticulation before the whole contingent set off into the mountains to the south. There was little talk as they climbed higher and higher.

At the top of a rise a spate of threatening voices was followed by a series of arrows slamming into nearby trees. The party stopped and the native members called out their defiance.

There were answering calls then a dozen or so warriors appeared from the surrounding bush, barring the way. The exchange between the two groups of highlanders quickly grew in intensity and Ellen feared there would be violence. She tried to draw Carl back, but he loosened his arm from her hand and began to speak. He told those blocking the way that he would prove they had nothing to fear. They could stay well back and observe. They would be in no danger.

One of the warriors scoffed at Mbagl's lack of a weapon and his subservience to a white man. Another screamed at Carl and had to be restrained by his fellows. A third man spoke more moderately, but the message was the same. Carl was courting danger not only for himself but for them, their women and children, and they would not allow it. But Carl was not deterred and Ellen listened with a mixture of admiration and apprehension as he questioned the manhood of the warriors, telling them they were no better than children who were scared of their own shadows.

There was more loud talk and threatening gestures before one by one the armed men stood aside to allow a narrow passage. Several voices shouted that a woman could not pass, but under Carl's guidance Ellen found a way through. The stares of the warriors burned into her back as she walked on.

After another half an hour the group approached a ravine bounded by sheer limestone cliffs that almost blocked out the sky. Ellen could sense the accompanying men becoming more hesitant. Carl asked the men for precise directions and as they answered they fell further back. Mbagl showed clear signs of nervousness and even Aijang needed Carl's urging to keep up.

Near the far end of the ravine an indentation in the rock face several yards above the ground marked the entrance to a cave. Carl pointed to a pair of projecting rocks and said the climb would not be difficult. He opened his rucksack and took out a length of rope, tied a large loop in one end and after several tries succeeded in lassoing one of the protruding rocks. Ellen held her breath as Carl tested the rope then made the climb. He disappeared into the cave but was soon outside again, calling down that it was small, hardly big enough to stand up in and contained nothing of interest, just a few bats hanging from the ceiling and some animal bones.

When Carl was back on the ground he and Aijang emptied their rucksacks and set out a picnic lunch on a blanket. Mbagl was nowhere to be seen and Aijang said he did not know where he was. The group ate and drank for a time in silence then Carl instructed Aijang to fetch the villagers who had accompanied them so that they could see there was nothing to fear.

As soon as Aijang had gone there was a whistling noise high above followed by a protracted shriek that mimicked a bird cry. The air began to whistle and vibrate and there was eerie laughter, modulating around a rising and falling whirring tone that led Ellen to cover her ears with her hands. It was several minutes before the cacophony ended.

Carl stood up and looked as high as possible towards the tops of the cliffs. He said that he could not see anything, but the source of the din was undoubtedly up there somewhere.

He was sure the whirring sound was made by a bullroarer, a wooden device that was swung in vigorous circles at the end of a cord, while the other sounds were probably the product of contorted human voices. If the people thought he would mistake this display for the anger of disturbed spirits they would be disappointed.

Ellen could not free herself from the feeling that they were unnecessarily tempting fate. She wanted to leave but Carl asked her for patience. It was important that the local people saw they had nothing to fear from the cave. Hopefully one of them would be prepared to climb the rope and look inside.

When the three guides finally appeared none was prepared to climb up to the cave, but they were all in a relaxed mood, talking and joking. One of them even replicated the whistling and laughing from the earlier display, catching Carl's eye and smiling broadly.

Finally, one of the men agreed to climb up to the cave, and when he re-emerged he tossed the animal skeletons down to the ground. His companions took turns in handling them until they began to fall apart then threw individual bones against the cliff face until nothing was left but tiny fragments. Ellen was unnerved by this behaviour, but Carl seemed quite relaxed, even offering the men some leftover food. As they ate he asked them to spread the word about what they had seen. The cave was harmless; there were no spirits of any kind living there.

The warriors who had tried to block their path earlier in the day now appeared and milled around, their previous hostility replaced by joviality. From the pieces of conversation Ellen could follow they were claiming that they had never believed in the evil cave spirits. It was just a story that it suited them to propagate. Carl asked them to elaborate but contradictory explanations were given and retracted until the conversation petered out.

Carl next asked the men to go and fetch their women; they too should see that there was nothing here to fear. The men refused, stating emphatically that this was no place for women. Carl pointed at Ellen but was told that because she was his wife and a white woman they could make an exception. Carl's response that there always seemed to be convenient exceptions to their rules was met with a stony silence.

The whistling and laughter from earlier began again, at first in the distance but quickly coming closer before reaching a crescendo. After a brief lull the air suddenly began to pulsate, buffeting bodies and stretching eardrums. Some of the men fell to the ground and covered their heads with their hands, while others swayed or turned in circles and groaned. Then a torrent of stones, some as large as a clenched fist, began to fall from the sky, forcing the whole group to scatter for shelter.

The performance was over as quickly as it began. Both groups of highlanders departed without a word and Carl went back into the ravine, dismissing Ellen's warning of a possible further attack. He freed the rope he had used for climbing, examined the stones that lay on the ground then packed the picnic things into the rucksacks. When he returned he explained that the place was probably an initiation site where boys on the brink of manhood were brought to confront the spirits of the cave. That would explain the ban on women.

The piece of theatre they had witnessed was the work of traditionalists wanting to preserve the terror of the place.

'Those stones could have caused terrible injury,' Ellen warned.

'They all fell close to the foot of the cliff. They weren't intended to cause harm.'

Carl added that theatre and performance were an essential part of highland life; you could not understand the highlanders if you did not understand this. But he acknowledged that at times the theatre spilt over into reality. He had witnessed the physical suffering inflicted on boys during their initiation, smelt the sickly metallic smell of the blood they had shed to demonstrate the end of childhood, and it had turned his stomach.

As they set off on the return journey Aijang urged Carl and Ellen to hurry; the afternoon was already well underway and they had many hours' travel ahead of them. For the next period there was little talk, just the awkward descent of slippery paths full of sharp turns and exposed tree roots. At an indeterminate spot Mbagl rejoined the group and walked silently beside Carl, giving no indication of what had caused him to disappear. Ellen had several moments where she was assailed by the memory of the stones falling from the sky, and she was relieved when they reached the bottom of the mountain and turned towards the east.

They walked for a time in an easy rhythm, then without explanation Mbagl increased his speed until he was almost running. Carl called out to him, but he kept up his pace and before long he was out of sight. Carl dispatched Aijang to catch up to him and make sure he reached his home village in safety.

As she watched this scene Ellen could see the sun hovering well above the horizon, but she knew from experience that at any moment it would fall suddenly like a dead weight, plunging everything into darkness. She suggested to Carl that they walk more quickly, but he seemed content with their current pace, which encouraged conversation.

'The story about the cave and its spirits might be just a useful fiction,' Carl admitted. 'I'm not sure about many of the things the highlanders profess to believe. Sometimes they tell me things just to test my credulity. But I hope that at least some are using me to help them separate truth from myth.'

'Mbagl?' Ellen asked.

'Like all of his people Mbagl has only a vague idea of what we whites know and what our intentions are, but he fears that his world will not be able to resist us. He wants my word that not all the beliefs and values he has lived by will be swept away, that he will be able to live alongside me and other whites as an equal. I reassure him as best I can, but he's not convinced.'

Ellen mentioned Ivor Moore's comment about the souls of the natives, to which Carl replied testily that Ivor was just a spectator who made things easy for himself. The highland world needed change and change was in any case inevitable. It all came down to what was changed and how fast, and who controlled the process.

Ellen decided this was a good time to tell Carl that Luke Sommer thought he was allowing distractions to divert him from his mission. Carl responded that he knew what Luke thought, and he did not doubt that the others shared his view or were even more critical. But their understanding of the mission was too narrow. Unlike his colleagues he was searching for a form of Christianity that would sink deep roots into highland culture, remaking it from within. It was inevitable that this would take time. But when the change did come it would be profound, embracing all aspects of local life, and it would be irreversible.

Ellen said she could not bring herself to like the highlanders and their culture. With the exception of a few of the younger ones, the women were too uninterested in things outside their narrow world to be attractive to her, while the children were dirty and spoilt. She could not forgive the men for their treatment of Kauigl or for the way they lorded it over the women generally, and their strutting and posturing when challenged was laughable. Carl replied that he could understand her frustrations, but it would become easier with time. The key was mastery of the language, which required much more than simple translation to and from English. You needed to think in the local language. He still had a long way to go himself.

As they walked on Ellen could not help but remember Carl's father, whose command of the language of the South Australian Aborigines, which culminated in the compilation of a dictionary and a translation of the New Testament, had not brought him success in his mission. She glanced at Carl striding beside her and made a fervent wish that he would be spared his father's fate.

Thirteen

Ellen was becoming increasingly familiar with death, of tiny babies and malnourished infants and of women who did not survive childbirth. The keening sounds of mourning began to haunt her dreams, and a residue of loss shadowed her throughout each day. She threw her energy into encouraging the women to delay giving their daughters in marriage and to increase the time between their own pregnancies, explaining over and over the benefits these measures would bring, but her words were met either with incomprehension or an exhortation to speak to the men. She enlisted Carl's help with the latter task, and he promised to do what he could.

The newly arrived medicines had given her a period of renewed confidence, but increasingly she found herself confronted with illnesses that were beyond her competence and the power of the medicines to treat. And she was particularly discomfited by a severe case of yaws that had stubbornly refused to respond to the injections, leaving ugly distortions on the face of the sufferer, a young girl called Waiya. In the wake of these failures she could sense some of the older women beginning to slip away from her. She raised the prospect of a visit by a European doctor from Lae or Madang or treatment in a white hospital on the coast, but this had little impact. Carl said that she needed to limit expectations, both her own and those of the villagers. She supposed he was right, but feelings of impotence and unfairness plagued her.

Over the following weeks she stayed closer to the mission house, with the garden taking up increasing amounts of her time. She would go there in the early morning before the heat of the day took hold and stay for several hours. She enjoyed tending the plants and gauging their progress, relaxing in their lack of demands on her.

She was surprised one morning when Yere instigated a conversation. They were kneeling not far from each other, each working with a weeding stick. Ellen had been lost in thought, remembering Carl explaining that if the highlanders had not copied their settled agriculture from elsewhere, which given the remoteness and inaccessibility of the highlands was unlikely, they must have devised it themselves. At the time Ellen had not given this much thought, but now she realised how remarkable it was. She wondered who the first cultivators had been, what had moved them to take this momentous step, and what the people had done for food before they had their gardens. As far as she could tell there were few edible wild animals to hunt or wild foods to gather, apart from lizards and perhaps some birds and berries, and an occasional wallaby.

'Pastor Carl should pay more,' Yere began.

'Pay more?'

'For our work in the garden. And for Kubun's work in the house when Pastor Carl is away.'

Ellen did not answer and the woman stated that Kubun had

found a girl who was prepared to marry him, but her family was demanding a high bride price. Kubun was not a sought-after match. Because of his unattractive looks he had never been invited to courting ceremonies, and now his insistence that his wife become a Christian had limited the field. His only chance was to provide a bride price well in excess of what others were offering and make the payment without waiting for the birth of a child.

Ellen replied that Kubun had told her that only warriors could marry and that to be a warrior you had to have killed a man. Yere scoffed at this story. She said there were few warriors left now, and if the whites had their way there would soon be none. The young men would be enticed away to work on the coast. They would bring disease when they returned, they would talk in a language no one understood and refuse to raise children with local girls. They would be good for nothing. Like the man who was constantly watching Misis, a no-good man wasting his life in search of impossible things.

To deflect from the watching man Ellen asked if life was better before the Europeans came, and Yere admitted that the whites had brought some good things. She liked working in Pastor Carl's garden with the new plants; she liked being near the mission house, which was the most beautiful house she had ever seen, and she liked watching Pastor Carl as he moved up and down the hill with his horse. But she did not like the arrogant *kiap* who came to the village and shouted orders in a language no one understood. Nor did she like the old white man who came to the mission house when Pastor Carl was away, although Kubun had assured her that he slept alone.

'What about me?' Ellen asked her. 'Do you like me?'

'You should not allow Pastor Carl to travel away by himself so much. And you should give him a child.'

Ellen asked Yere if she had children, but instead of answering the woman complained that if Kubun got married she would have to share the house with his wife and she did not want to do that. Kubun would give all his time to his wife and forget about her. He might even force her to live somewhere else, and she would be alone.

Ellen was tired out by the talk and the increasing heat. She started to make preparations to return to the house, but Yere held her back. She asked if Pastor Carl had other wives in the place he came from and showed relief when Ellen said he did not. Then Yere said that when she was young she had been married but had been beaten by her husband's other wives and had run away. Her father had not wanted to return the marriage payment that had been given for her and had forced her to go back to her husband, but the man's wives had continued to mistreat her and her husband had decided to give her to another man. This man had quickly grown tired of her and had passed her on to a relative who was anxious for a son, but Yere had been unable to conceive and the man had discarded her. Through no fault of her own she had acquired the reputation of a wandering woman, a harlot, and her father had refused to take her back. She had lived for many years as an outcast until Pastor Carl had given her his protection and allowed her to work in his garden. She was grateful to Pastor Carl, but now he should pay more so that she could live independently and Kubun could secure a wife.

*

Several young village women were outside the mission house calling out Ellen's name, asking why she did not come to the village anymore. They were going to swim in the river and she should come too. She allowed herself to be talked into accompanying them but said she doubted she would swim; the water would be too cold.

As the group walked Ellen was assailed by questions about why Pastor Carl was away from the mission house so much and why she had still not produced a child. She answered that Pastor Carl was away doing God's work and that a child would come in good time. In response to speculation about how often she and Pastor Carl lay together as man and wife she answered confidently that she and Pastor Carl were very satisfied with their married life.

'What about the village man who watches you? Would you like to lie with him?'

'This man would make an excellent husband for one of you,' Ellen replied. 'But I can't say who would be best suited to him or how best to win his favour.'

The women replied dismissively that there was plenty of time for them to think about marriage. In the meantime, they would exercise their right to sample what the young men from neighbouring settlements had to offer as givers of love.

The group had gone well past the village and climbed through sweltering pitpit up a steep incline. Alongside them a creek had taken pause on its journey down to the river, forming a swirling pool many yards in diameter. The women quickly removed what little clothing they were wearing and plunged into the water, beckoning to Ellen to follow them. The bright sunlight and enthusiastic atmosphere encouraged her to dip a hand into the water, but the sharp cold confirmed her decision not to swim, although she had taken the precaution of wearing a swimming costume underneath her clothes.

The pool must have been deep at its centre because several of the women disappeared under the water and did not reappear for several seconds. Ellen wondered whether they were performing for her, but they seemed largely caught up in themselves. Then gradually they came together in a chorus of appeals for her to join them. She responded with an exaggerated shiver, but the chorus continued until she began to undress.

As she entered the water she hugged herself to resist the cold. She was taken aback by the paleness of her skin, her upper arms and thighs striking her as otherworldly in their whiteness. She stood half in and half out of the water, not knowing what to do next, when several of the women approached and began to finger the material of her swimming costume. They lifted the shoulders straps and let them slap back against her body to cries of amazement and delight, then conducted similar experiments with other parts of the costume.

One by one the women returned to their own pursuits until only the girl who had asked about the watching man remained. Without speaking the girl carefully loosened the straps of Ellen's costume from her shoulders, then gently peeled the material down Ellen's body until her breasts were free. The girl cupped the breasts in her hands then bent and kissed each nipple in turn. Ellen told her she should stop but she made no effort to force her. The girl straightened herself and offered her breasts to Ellen, who responded by letting her hands take the soft weight and her fingers touch the firm nipples.

After this exchange Ellen immersed herself in the water and swam until she grew tired. By the side of the pool she allowed the sun to warm her body then dried herself and put on her clothes. Her companions were already out of the water and ready to leave, but Ellen said she would stay a little longer. They gave her directions back to the mission house.

As she continued to sit Ellen remembered her recent conversation with Yere. She imagined being forced to share Carl with another woman or several other women and told herself that she would die before accepting such a thing. She resolved to use the remainder of her time in the highlands to convince as many of the village women as possible that their subservience to men was not inevitable.

She had not listened to the directions she had been given by the swimmers, instead trusting her body to lead her back the way she had come. But when the pitpit started to rise above her head she lost her bearings. She stopped and slowed her breathing, but the stalks seemed to close in around her, cutting off the air. She stood on tiptoe and tried to clear a path of sight, but to no avail. She called out, but the reedy sounds seemed caught within the constricted space around her. She feared she would dissolve in the heat and light of the sun.

'Misis.'

The watching man was steadying her arms as they flailed around. She let herself be calmed, resisting a temptation to rest her head on the man's chest. She stepped back and reasserted herself, insisting that she had recovered from her brief loss of control. When she was out in the open she was mortified to realise how meagre and unthreatening the pitpit looked from the outside.

She turned to thank her rescuer, but he had already started to walk ahead. She realised that he would have seen her in the pool, and she felt her face begin to flush.

Fourteen

Carl had returned with a nasty gash in his thigh and a fever. Ellen cleaned the wound, applied an antiseptic liquid and a sterilised dressing. She gave him a powder for the pain and sat next to him on the bed, wiping his face with a damp cloth as he slept. When he woke and needed the toilet she could not take his weight and was forced to fetch Aijang, who showed strength and adeptness in manoeuvring Carl out and back again. She acquiesced in Carl's suggestion that Aijang sleep in the house, to help him in the night.

The following morning a stream of villagers came up the hill. At first it was just the men, who waited outside until Carl hobbled out to talk to them. Then the women came, bringing their children, until it seemed that the whole village had relocated to the mission house. An easy chair was set out at the front and Carl sat propped up against cushions under a baggy hat, watching as the villagers milled around, the women feeding their children with food they had brought, the men talking in small groups and occasionally approaching Carl, seeking his assurance that he was well and providing advice on how to protect himself from injury in the future.

Ellen had not seen the men of the village together in this way before; she realised that she did not even know most of their names. She tried to imagine what had led them to pay their respects to Carl in such a public way. Was it part of the love of theatre that he had talked about, or a disguised competition for his favour? She found herself forming critical opinions about character and motivation from individual gestures and words then formulating responses that would show she had seen through them. This kept her occupied for a time, but eventually her fantasy faltered.

When watching the women it gradually became clear which men they belonged to and where they stood in the hierarchy of wives. Some of the women jockeyed obviously for position, others sought to convey an impression of unconcern, while a few put their resentments about present or past mistreatment blatantly on show. Ellen adopted the guise of the perfect hostess, interacting with the women as if the tensions between them and with their menfolk were invisible to her. This role was not unfamiliar from her Adelaide life, and she felt that she performed it well.

In the middle of the day the villagers collected their possessions and their children and went back down the hill, taking with them an elevated speech of gratitude from Carl and leaving behind trampled grass, scraps of discarded food and a knotted atmosphere of hopes furthered or thwarted.

After nightfall Mbagl came alone. Ellen escorted him to the bedroom where he bent over Carl, holding his hand and rubbing his arms and shoulders. Ellen fetched a chair and offered it to Mbagl but he sat on the floor instead. Over Ellen's protests Carl pushed himself out of the bed and slid down next to his visitor. Ellen repositioned the chair and sat down herself, sensing as she did so that her presence was burdensome to both men.

The conversation was in low tones with long periods of silence. Then Mbagl suddenly became animated, clearly giving Carl a dressing down. Carl appeared to have nothing to offer in his defence, meekly accepting the other man's criticisms. Mbagl ended his tirade and waited, then he began to laugh, a deep, resonant laugh that caught Ellen by surprise. Soon Carl was laughing too, an uninhibited laugh that Ellen could not remember having heard before. Before the laughter could also infect her she left the room.

When Mbagl was leaving he took Ellen aside and said, repeating himself several times to ensure he was understood, that Carl was too fond of taking unnecessary risks. If he were not careful something very bad might happen.

In the subsequent days Carl's pain eased and he became more mobile. Ellen inspected the wound regularly and was relieved that there was no sign of infection. She asked several times about the circumstances of the attack and eventually Carl said that he was not without fault in what had happened; he needed to learn to control his temper better, even in the face of egregious provocation. He said he hoped that news of the incident would not reach the government post, because his adversaries there would use it to make trouble for him and the mission.

Fifteen

'Misis, look!' Kubun was standing in the garden, pointing into the distance, a pair of heavy binoculars he had taken to borrowing from Carl propped against his eyes.

Ellen was admiring a plant that was displaying new growth, removing with a sharp stick a few recalcitrant weeds. She stood, shielded her eyes from the sun and saw a series of fixed points stretched out in a line across the brow of a distant hill. She reached a hand for the binoculars and found that with their aid the points resolved themselves into moving human forms, a few Europeans recognisable by their clothing, the rest native policemen and carriers. A pair of dogs seemed to be vying with each other for a place at the head of the line. She tried to count the number of figures but gave up as the line spilled beyond the circle of her vision.

'What's a patrol doing here now?' she asked out loud, heading as she spoke in the direction of the house.

Carl was on the verandah and Ellen helped him to stand before handing him the binoculars. After a short look he concluded that it was not an ordinary patrol; it was too large, he estimated forty or more men, and there was too much equipment.

'They might pass us by,' Ellen said hopefully, 'if they keep to the ridge.'

Carl raised the binoculars again. Then he called to Aijang to help him, saying the villagers needed to be warned. Ellen objected that surely the patrol did not represent a serious threat, and anyway he was in no state to leave the house.

'They need to be warned,' Carl repeated.

The trip down the hill was difficult. Carl was still unsure on his feet and on several occasions Aijang needed all his strength to stop him from stumbling on the sharp slope. Ellen did her best to help him regain his balance when he overcompensated after a near fall, the expression on his face suggesting that the pain was a test that was not entirely unwelcome.

As they approached the village a vocal group of men streamed out to meet them. Carl offered reassurance, saying they would not be attacked, at least not in the way they feared. The visitors would want food, but they would be prepared to pay. He said they would offer shells, trinkets and ornaments, small pieces of brightly coloured cloth, things that would beguile at first but which would quickly lose their appeal. The villagers should instead demand useful things such as salt and tobacco.

Before Carl had finished many of the women had already headed off towards their gardens, and some of the men went with them. Carl found a comfortable place to sit and asked Ellen to move out of hearing distance. He addressed the mostly older men who had remained.

'You will need to keep a close eye on your wives and daughters. Some of those who are coming will want women to satisfy their urges.'

The men began to talk among themselves. Some stood in a

way that suggested they were prepared to fight, while others were reserved and thoughtful. Carl continued. 'These men may carry disease. If your wives get this disease they will pass it on to you when you have sex. Then your male organ will wither and die.'

Some of the men laughed outright while others shifted uncomfortably. Some put their hands to their crotches, making sure that everything was intact. They waited for Carl to continue.

'If your daughters get this disease they will not be able to have babies. You will not have grandchildren to delight you, to look after you and listen to your stories when you grow old.'

All traces of laughter among the men had now gone. Their heads were bowed; their feet padded aimlessly on the ground.

'You must protect your wives and daughters from these men, even from the whites. They too can carry disease.'

Some of the women had already returned with mounds of vegetables—beans, watercress, cucumbers, bamboo shoots— and *bilums* full of sweet potato. Carl instructed some other women who were observing to go into the bush and collect large amounts of the vine that could be plaited into rope.

The line of approaching men had come down from the mountain and had for the time being disappeared from view in the folds of the foothills. Supported by Aijang, Carl went with a few of the villagers to mark out a boundary around the settlement, which had no clearly defined perimeter of its own. He indicated trees and bushes that could be used as supports for the rope and explained that guards should be placed at regular intervals with orders to allow no one to cross in either direction. His instructions were accepted in silence.

During this time Ellen was surrounded by a horde of entreating children, but her attention was drawn to the girl from the river, who was standing alone beside a hut. Ellen smiled and the girl smiled back, cupping her bare breasts in her hands as she did so, leading Ellen to turn and attempt to shield the children from the sight. But they seemed indifferent, apart from a pair of older boys who assured each other that when they were men they would not waste their time on such easily available females. Ellen found welcome distraction by admonishing a precocious boy who was announcing that the approaching men were eaters of human flesh. 'There are white men there as well,' she reassured the younger children. 'They would never allow such a thing.'

The first part of the rope was completed, a length of about thirty yards. Aijang tested it for strength and Carl directed a small party of men to stretch it tightly around trees, with strands at knee and chest height. More rope was produced and installed and soon the entire village was enclosed, with the exception of a narrow path leading to the vegetable gardens.

Before long sounds from the encroaching patrol drifted in on a light breeze. Dogs barked and words could be made out, pidgin English followed by shouts in a rudimentary form of the local language emphasising that the speakers' intentions were peaceful and there was no need for concern.

As the line came fully into view Ellen could see that it comprised, in addition to a handful of whites in wide-brimmed hats, shorts, long socks and billowing shirts, a contingent of a dozen or so New Guinea policemen, smartly dressed in khaki shorts and peaked caps and armed with rifles. There was also a larger contingent of thirty or more baggage carriers, wearing *lap-laps* and shouldering substantial rucksacks packed to the brim.

When the line reached the boundary rope Chas Noble was the first to speak. 'Carl Starck, of course you'd be here. But what's the meaning of this?' Noble lifted the top strand of the rope and made to step inside, but Carl gestured to him to stop. 'You stay on your side, we'll stay on our side.'

'Our side, is it?' Noble thought for a moment, then said in an elevated voice, 'Want to keep all the women for yourself? And you with that pretty young wife.'

A second white man, shorter than average with a barrel chest, told Chas to keep a civil tongue in his head. Then the man approached Carl and held out his hand. 'Gordon Davenport, in charge of this endeavour.'

The two men shook hands and stood appraising each other. Carl said, 'The villagers have food to sell, for a fair price. But the women and girls are off limits. Please instruct your men not to cross this line.'

Davenport said that the rope was not necessary; in fact, it was a bit of an insult. His men knew how to behave themselves.

The village women brought their vegetables to the vicinity of the rope and displayed them in piles on the ground, while Chas Noble organised some of the line's New Guineans to take charge of the bartering. He instructed the men to pay attention to freshness and not to be too generous in their payments, quipping that shells didn't grow on trees. He reminded them that they had a long way to go, much further than they had ever gone in their lives, and that their supply of trade goods was not unlimited.

The trading was vigorous and it was not long before all the vegetables had changed hands. The villagers pored over the trinkets they had received in exchange, broad smiles demonstrating their satisfaction. Some of the women indicated that they could bring more vegetables, but this offer was ignored.

More and more of the patrol's members pressed forward against the boundary rope, full of laughter and chatter. Aijang offered Ellen a precis of what they were saying. 'Highlanders they bush *kanakas*. Never seen the sea, don't know about money, scared of magic. That's what they saying, Misis.' Aijang added, 'These lowlanders think they pretty big fellas.'

A wailing sound went up from one of the village women and she suddenly rushed forward and grabbed one of the line members. The man jerked away in disgust and the woman fell to her knees. Then another woman began to wail, she too lunging towards one of the visitors. Several village women held her back. They spoke soothing words to her, stroking her arms and her hair. Gradually the wailing of both women gave way to a quiet sobbing. The men from the patrol went back to their laughing and chatting, teasing those who had received the unwanted attention.

'They think their dead sons have come back from the sky,' Carl explained to Ellen. 'They want to reclaim them.'

Ellen looked at the two women slumped on the ground. She knew they deserved her sympathy, but their shapeless figures aroused only aversion.

Chas Noble rejoined the white group in good spirits. The vegetables that had been secured would keep them going for several days, and the cost in shell and other trade goods had been very reasonable. If they could get some fresh pig meat they could be content with their afternoon's work. He looked inquiringly at Carl but got no reply.

Gordon Davenport took the opportunity to introduce the European members of the party, which he described as an expedition rather than a patrol. Alongside himself as leader were Chas Noble and Dick Lacey—they already knew Chas, and Dick was also experienced in the highlands—and two young *kiaps* who had not been long in the country but had already proved their worth. At this point Keith Dawes and Leo Fiocchini stepped forward. Ellen had been vaguely aware of their presence in the background, but now she gave them her full attention. Davenport explained their achievement.

'These two young fellows were instrumental in bringing to account a white man who had gone rogue and murdered several blacks.'

'The right place at the right time,' Keith Dawes said with easy humility. Leo Fiocchini nodded his agreement, looking blankly at Ellen.

Davenport continued with his account of the incident. 'The man was heavily armed and completely deranged. It was of the utmost importance that he be quickly brought under control.

The response of these young men speaks volumes for their maturity and courage. It also speaks well of the training they received before being sent to the field.'

Carl excused himself and walked several yards unaided to give instructions to some of the local men. When he rejoined the group he asked Davenport for explicit assurances that the members of the patrol, white and black, would not step over the boundary rope; nor should they try to entice any of the village women to cross in the other direction. When the assurances had been given Carl invited the white contingent to follow him up the hill to the house. Davenport said they would come after they had set up camp.

Sixteen

At the table in the dining room Gordon Davenport was full of the expedition. It would travel through country untouched by the white man and would therefore be one of the last expeditions of its kind anywhere in the world. It would forge a thin line from which enlightenment would spread to the people of this dark land. It was an honour and a privilege to be entrusted with the task of leading such a venture.

Davenport continued in a less exalted tone, directly addressing Carl. 'Chas has been filling me in on some of your doings. I'm sure you understand that it's the government's job to open up new lands, to build roads and establish law and order. Once that's done you missionaries can follow. We don't want you pushing ahead. And you need to keep a tight rein on your evangelists.'

'The gold miners should come after us,' Noble interrupted. 'Before the God-botherers we should give the gold miners a go. There might be another bonanza up here for all we know. The missions would just get in the way.'

There was only tea and some biscuits from a tin as refreshments. Noble asked if there was something stronger than tea to drink and more substantial than stale biscuits to eat, but he was waved away by Davenport, who returned his attention to Carl.

'Maybe Chas is exaggerating, but different missions competing against each other, taking sides in local disputes. We can't have that.'

'We don't take sides,' Carl responded.

'That's not what I heard,' Noble retorted. 'I hear you copped a spear as a result of not minding your own business.' Noble smirked at Carl. 'You've been trying to hide it, but you've been tottering around like you've got a hot poker up ya bum.'

Davenport asked Carl what had happened. There was a cool undercurrent to the surface friendliness.

'It was the labour recruiters,' Carl responded. 'I encouraged the villagers to send them away. Some agreed and some didn't, and the recruiters refused to withdraw. When I tried to arbitrate there was a confrontation. A spear was thrown and I was struck in the leg.'

'But the highlands are out of bounds to labour recruiters,' Davenport stated, turning to Noble for confirmation.

Noble said that was the letter of the law. There might be one or two recruiters out and about but the natives they took on were only sent to other parts of the highlands, mainly to the gold mines, not to plantations on the coast. He then turned his attention to Carl, saying that the highlands couldn't be kept off limits for ever. The men needed to be given a chance to earn, to do something apart from fighting each other.

'Labour recruiters have no place in the highlands,' Carl responded.

Noble snorted that this holier-than-thou attitude got on his wick. As if the missions were not dragging the natives into a foreign world, one of dogmatic beliefs and outdated morals that did them no good—not to speak of scaring the hell out of them by promising a big fire when they died if they didn't shape up.

Ellen entered the conversation, saying that at least the missionaries lived among the people and took the trouble to learn their languages and understand their ways. They did not just breeze in and out like the *kiaps*, relying on their guns and their white skins to see them through.

'I'd say we do a bit more than breeze in and out, Mrs Starck. We stop the blacks fighting each other at the drop of a hat. We caution the men against beating their wives, and we teach them a language they can use to find their way in the world outside their own tribe. We expand their horizons.'

Davenport added census-taking to the list of crucial activities carried out by the *kiaps*. It wasn't so long ago that no one knew that the highlands had any inhabitants at all and now it seemed there were tens of thousands, if not more. If the authorities down south got clear evidence of the extent of the highland population they might open the purse strings a bit more.

Davenport's remarks gave rise to a general discussion about Canberra's penny-pinching policy towards its mandated territory, which could not all be put down to the Depression. The result was that the administration had to finance its activities from within. If it weren't for the taxes on gold it would be completely bankrupt. As it was it provided only a bare minimum of services. Carl asked why in that case the authorities did not do more to assist the work of the missions, which came at little financial cost. Davenport admitted that many in the administration were unsympathetic to religion and wanted to minimise its influence on the people. The more the missions went their own way and refused to abide by the administration's rules, the more power those opposed to religion would have.

'Do you count yourself among these opponents?' Carl asked.

Davenport replied that as far as he was concerned giving the highlanders a new religion stood pretty low on the list of things needed to improve their lives.

'Don't forget the German angle, Gordon,' Noble urged. 'Lutherans and Catholics full of Huns, using native languages we don't understand to stir up the blacks against us, likely as not.'

Carl asked if there was any evidence of subversive activity, more than just a picture or two of Adolf Hitler on a wall. Davenport responded that it was hard to find concrete evidence, but the suspicion was not unreasonable.

Noble returned to the theme of Carl's injury. 'I'd like to know exactly where this fracas of yours took place. For all we know you were in an area where you'd no right to be.'

Before Carl could answer Gordon Davenport called time on the discussion. He said he was sure that, if Carl had ventured into an off-limits area it would have been unintentional and he would not do so again. He would also ensure that his evangelists were subjected to proper supervision. Carl's response was a curt nod.

Ellen stood up and began to clear away the tea things. Leo Fiocchini hurried to help her, and the two of them spent the next few minutes ferrying cups and plates to the kitchen and stacking them ready for Aijang to wash. Dawes and Lacey, both of whom had been largely silent to this point, came to life, whispering to each other, grinning and gesturing in Leo's direction.

The conversation around the table took as a new theme the route that the expedition planned to follow and the contingencies needed if assumptions about the quantities of food that could be purchased along the way proved to be wrong. Davenport was eager to hear Carl's impressions of the land and the people. There had been reconnaissance by aeroplane, Carl may have seen the planes flying overhead, but only so much could be learnt from the air.

Carl's reply was interrupted almost before it began by Noble, who seemed intent on continuing an ongoing argument with Davenport. 'The line's too big, like I said. Makes us too dependent on local food. Increases the risk of some of our people getting out of hand, stirring up trouble with the locals.'

'We need a certain size to deter attacks,' Davenport responded.

Noble turned to Carl. 'You've been to Hagen and beyond, even though it's well outside your territory. How lively are the blacks out there? Any man-eaters among them?'

There was an outburst of jesting among the *kiaps* about the toughness of Noble's sinewy flesh, but the humour was forced. Everyone waited for Carl's reply.

'The highlanders who eat human flesh do so because they think they can in this way assimilate the spirit of those whose flesh they consume.'

There was more nervous laughter from Dawes and Lacey, but no commentary.

'Or to assert dominance over those defeated in battle. Or because they want to ensure that the dead do not suffer the indignity of being eaten by pigs or dogs, or of just rotting away.'

'And you think they wouldn't care two hoots about my spirit or my dignity. So, all up I'm not worth eating? Well, that's fair enough, I wouldn't want to eat them either.' Noble looked around for approval of his retort.

Carl ended the discussion by saying that, despite the talk, he had not seen any firm evidence of cannibalism among the tribes further west. He often found that members of one tribe would accuse their neighbours of eating human flesh to emphasise to the Europeans their own superior virtue. 'They learn very quickly to tell us what they think we want to hear.'

*

Ellen had something to tell Carl and she could hardly wait until the visitors had headed down the hill. She asked Aijang to leave them alone.

'It came from Leo Fiocchini.'

'He seems to have taken quite a shine to you. You need to be careful. Some of these *kiaps* think the rules of civilised behaviour don't apply out here.'

Ellen concentrated on what she had to tell Carl. 'The man they were chasing, the one who was shooting the blacks. When they found him he was sick with fever. He was in no position to resist, but Keith Dawes panicked and shot him dead.'

'Has Fiocchini told anyone else about this?'

'He says Reg Thompson knows but has done nothing.'

Carl said that the wheels turned slowly in such cases, but he trusted Thompson to report the incident. What might happen further up the line of responsibility he couldn't say. 'I've heard a few things about Gordon Davenport. Apparently he's close to the high-ups in the administration, which might explain him being put at the head of this expedition. From what he said it looks like Fiocchini's information hasn't penetrated that far, or if it has it's been ignored.'

Ellen wondered aloud whether the fact that the outlaw was German might have played a role in his death, but Carl said it was more likely that the young *kiap* had simply panicked. Despite what Davenport had said about training, inexperienced young men were often sent into dangerous situations with little idea how to handle themselves. And some of them were undoubtedly trigger happy.

Seventeen

As the light faded Carl's purposeful footsteps indicated his intention to leave the house. He collected some camping equipment then went to rouse Aijang. As the two men started to descend the hill Ellen rushed to join them, directing a narrow beam of torchlight on the ground in front of their feet and helping to take Carl's weight. Carl said he could manage, but he leant heavily on her.

When they reached the village small fires were glowing and the smell of smoke and cooked food was everywhere. There was soft talk from the vicinity of each of the fires, interrupted by occasional excited shouts from a child, an adult voice issuing an instruction, the barking of a dog or the grubbing of a pig. Carl exchanged a few words with each family group as he passed and Ellen followed his lead. Several times the pair stopped briefly to grip a proffered hand.

'Would you take some food with us, Pastor Carl? Misis too?'

Carl expressed his thanks and kept moving, leaving Ellen to explain that they had no time tonight, but in the future they would eat together.

A small contingent of children began to form around Ellen, calling shyly or cheekily to her, getting under her feet, holding onto her hand, her shirt or her trousers. She named those she recognised, telling them they should return to their parents or they would miss their dinner. Some of the children performed acrobatic acts to impress her, cartwheels, handstands and somersaults. Finally, she stood still and clapped her hands together several times like a schoolteacher, then found her sternest voice to shoo the children away.

She caught up to Carl at the far boundary line, where he was talking to one of the guards. In the middle distance a shimmer of firelight from the expedition's camp burnished the sky and voices from the camp and the village intermingled peacefully.

Carl selected a sheltered spot a little back from the perimeter to wait. Ellen snuggled against him for warmth and began to doze but she was disturbed when Aijang appeared, weighed down with the camping equipment. The two men pitched the tent, then Aijang disappeared into the night.

Ellen slept fitfully. She woke and listened to Carl's soft breathing then sank back into sleep. She woke again and reached for Carl, this time in vain. She squeezed her eyes closed, then opened them and looked out through the flap of the tent. The darkness seemed impenetrable. She wrapped a blanket around her shoulders and crawled outside.

Her first instinct was to call to whoever was there to show themselves. The steadiness of her voice gave her courage and she stood her ground as the night pressed in around her, the rushing of the air loud in her ears. Her eyes adjusted to the darkness and revealed a jumble of shadows, but she realised that they were just bushes, not the bush demons that the people sometimes talked about. She listened carefully, made out a distant pool of murmuring voices and walked in bare feet in their direction. With perfect timing the moon came out from behind a cloud, bathing the scene in a wash of soft light.

When she came nearer she could make out several local men standing at the perimeter rope, talking intensely with members of the expedition. Objects were being offered and appraised, terms discussed. In the background a collection of young women stood encircled by a second group of local men. Carl was standing on the outskirts of this group, hemmed in by a pair of villagers, talking agitatedly to Mbagl. Aijang was watching from nearby.

The negotiations soon came to a close and the women were shepherded across the boundary, where they were paired off with expedition members and led away. Some of the women seemed resigned to their fate, while others looked back as if hoping for rescue. Ellen recognised the girl from the swimming hole and she instinctively called out to her. The girl broke loose from the man accompanying her and ran towards Ellen, but her path was barred and she was wrestled to the ground. Ellen called for Carl to intervene and he castigated the villagers, shouting they would never find favour with God if they sold their wives and daughters like this. The men concealed their spoils and stood with bowed heads, leaving the girl from the river free to slip away into the night.

When Carl's agitation had subsided, he instructed Aijang to retrieve their tent. He and Ellen then made their way back to the mission house, hardly speaking.

*

Before dawn the next morning Ellen was woken by the incongruous sound of a bugle, its notes rolling up the hill in discrete groups of threes and fours. She got out of bed and found a message from Carl saying he had gone to make sure that the expedition left without further trouble.

When Ellen arrived at the camp site tents were being dismantled and distributed among the carriers, along with the food that had been purchased from the village and the supplies and equipment that were part of the original provisioning. An Australian flag that had been drooping from a makeshift flagpole was being ceremoniously taken down and packed away. There was no sign of the village women from the night before.

With little ado the line swung into motion, Davenport and Noble at the front with the two dogs, Lacey, Dawes and Fiocchini at the rear. Before long the line was strung out along the bottom of the valley, parallel to the gently sparkling river. Initially the line's motion could be clearly discerned, but as the figures grew smaller they seemed to slow to the point where they became fixed features of the landscape. It came as a surprise to Ellen when, having turned to speak to Carl, she looked back to the horizon and the line had disappeared.

The locals who had come to watch, mostly men and boys, speculated about the reception that the expedition would receive further west. The consensus was that the white men and their native underlings could not expect the benign welcome they had received in this village. The tribes to the west were ferocious; some were even eaters of human flesh. They would react violently to any intrusion into their territory. Ellen thought she saw in the faces of the men shame at the passivity of their own response to the expedition and a resolution to make up in some way for their weakness.

183

Eighteen

Carl met a village delegation at the front of the house. He was soon back inside, explaining to Ellen that several young boys had disappeared unbeknown to their parents, almost certainly gone after the expedition. Some of the local men wanted to set off to bring the boys back, by force if necessary. Carl had told them that he would pursue the expedition himself and convince the boys to return. There would be no need for violence.

Preparations for the journey were made quickly, Carl waving aside Ellen's concerns about the capacity of his body to withstand the rigours of the trip. Within the hour he set off with Aijang and Onyx. He walked the horse down the hill, turning several times to wave to Ellen until he was out of sight.

Ellen went back inside the house and busied herself tidying things away. Kubun appeared and prepared lunch, and for the first time she invited him to eat with her. The pair sat opposite each other at the table, speaking only occasionally. Every few minutes Kubun sprang to his feet and asked Ellen if he could bring her something, but she told him she could easily fetch anything she needed herself. Kubun sat down gingerly, ready to spring back to his feet if need be.

'Did you want to go with the expedition?' Ellen asked him.

'I don't like those *kiaps*, Misis, or the policemen from the coast. But I would like to go with Pastor Carl some time.'

'I will ask him.'

'Thank you, Misis.'

'I asked Pastor Carl about baptism, why he always says "not yet". His answer was long.'

'Thank you, Misis. Sometimes Pastor Carl says things that are long. But I like to listen when he talks.'

Ellen remembered her conversation with Kubun's aunt and she asked about the bride price. Kubun said that Pastor Carl had agreed to increase the payments and he would soon have what was needed. He had talked again to the girl and she had given her word that she would wait for him. He would like the wedding to be in the village church, and he would like Pastor Carl to baptise him and his new wife at the same time.

'You won't forget your aunt when you're married, will you Kubun?'

Kubun said that his aunt was his only close relative and he would look after her, even though she had a sharp tongue and thought mainly of herself. Once before he had found a girl prepared to marry him, but his aunt had spread the rumour that he was unreliable and a poor worker; the girl had married someone else. He was concerned that even now his aunt might do something to jeopardise his marriage.

Ellen was about to give a bland assurance that Kubun's aunt would never do such a thing, but she checked herself. Instead, she told him that if he felt this girl was the right one he should marry her as soon as possible. Life did not offer many opportunities for happiness and those that did exist should be grasped with both hands. When she had finished speaking she replayed the words in her mind, grimacing at how old she sounded.

*

During Carl's absence Ellen did her best to convince herself that it would be wrong to let the trading episode define her view of the local people. Not everyone had been involved, probably only a small minority, and it was the men who were primarily at fault. She tried to engage with the women as though nothing untoward had happened, but there was a wariness in their behaviour towards her. They pushed their children forward to receive injections or other treatment and then quickly withdrew, without eye contact and without waiting to test her on her language and laugh at her mistakes. When Ellen asked whether any new sickness had appeared they pointed to the young girl whose yaws had not been cured by the injections and whose face now carried a large welt that puckered her mouth and contorted her left cheek. There were unanswerable demands to know why the medicine that had worked so well for the others had not worked in this case. The girl herself showed no obvious bitterness about her condition and she appeared to be fully accepted by her peers, but Ellen feared what the disfigurement might mean when the girl grew older. She resolved to explore whether there were any possible treatments in the outside world that might benefit her.

Ellen calculated that Carl should be back within three or four days, even allowing significant time for him to convince the village boys to return. She made plans for a special meal to mark his homecoming and she told Kubun to keep a look out as she busied herself with baking. Kubun returned to say that the watching man was there again; he was closer to the house than he'd ever been before.

Carl was not back at the end of the fourth day and Ellen cried herself to sleep. She woke the next morning unrefreshed and forced herself to go down to the village, where she asked whether anything had been seen or heard of the missing boys. She was met with blank faces from some and recriminations from others, and she retreated back up the hill. She ate several slices of the cake she had baked for Carl and invited Kubun to help himself. She put a large slice on a plate and took it out to the watching man, then stood next to him as he studiously ate.

Later in the afternoon the watching man appeared at the door of the house with a collection of wildflowers in his hand. He took a step forward and held them out. Ellen thanked him and took the flowers. She went back inside as quietly as she could, but Kubun was waiting for her. He said that Pastor Carl would not agree. She replied that it had nothing to do with Pastor Carl, or with him.

Nineteen

Carl had still not returned and Ellen told herself that he had given in to the temptation to join the expedition himself. She could see him at the front of the line with Gordon Davenport, planning the route and enthusing over the prospect of new lands and new people while stressing the importance of maintaining tight discipline—or in friendly conversation with Leo Fiocchini and Keith Dawes, asking what had brought them to New Guinea and what they hoped to take away—or sparring with Chas Noble, telling him that his aggression masked a deep insecurity about his assumed superiority as a white man. 'If you meet the people halfway, try to understand them better, you might find contentment, instead of the debilitating anger you carry around.' She could even hear Noble's reply. 'Way I see it, mate, you're the one who's angry, 'cos they're not buying what you're selling.'

She quickly dismissed all this as wild imaginings. Carl would not have joined the expedition with no forewarning and no instructions as to what she should do during his absence. Instead, there must have been an accident. He had fallen from Onyx and reinjured his leg and was lying helpless in the bush while Aijang sought help. Or he had met resistance from members of the expedition who would not relinquish the village boys and in the ensuing struggle he had taken another spear to his body. Or a sickness that had been lurking inside him had risen to the surface.

At the edge of these thoughts was the memory of passages in the diaries of Carl's father in which he had despaired about the value of his work and his life. Ellen had not seen anything resembling despair in Carl, but in recent months there had been moments of abstracted silence that may have corresponded to low moods and doubts. She wondered whether she had done enough to convince him in these moments that she was fully by his side.

*

Ellen was in the garden and did not see Ivor Moore walking up the hill, nor did she hear his soft tapping on the door. Kubun had to come and alert her to his presence. She walked down to the house with a hint of hope in her step.

'You're back from down south,' Ellen said, gesturing for Ivor to go into the house. He took off his hat as he crossed the threshold, then stood and waited for Ellen to give further directions. He asked if Carl was there, and Ellen said that he was away in the west but should return soon. She prepared some tea while Ivor watched. He helped her to carry the things to the front room, where they sat with the cups balanced on their knees.

'You never told me which part of Australia you're from,' Ellen began. 'I assumed it was Sydney, I don't know why. I saw Sydney briefly, on the journey up. The harbour is beautiful.'

Ivor said he was not from Sydney but from a little town north of Melbourne. It was not much of a place, just a few houses straddled along a handful of streets, a post office, a church and a scratchy old pub. Dry as a bone and hot as hell in the summer, cold as charity in winter. When he was a boy he could not wait to leave and eventually he had escaped to Melbourne. It had been better there, all the distractions of a big city, but it was no paradise. Some good times but lots of grind. Then he had heard about gold in New Guinea.

'Carl said you were in the Great War.'

'Done my best to forget that, Mrs Starck.'

'Carl's two brothers died in France. They were fighting for Germany.'

Ivor took his time before replying. 'I came to hate the Hun because he killed my mates. Then I realised he must have felt the same about me. We were both right and both wrong.'

'It must have been terrible.'

'That's not even the half of it, Mrs Starck.'

Ellen reminded Ivor that they were on first-name terms. Then she asked if he had arrived home in time to see his mother.

'I never went south. I was all ready to go but I just couldn't seem to take the final step. Then I got word that my mum had passed away.'

'I'm so sorry. But your wife and child?'

'I doubt they'd have too much interest in me. Not after all this time.'

Ellen stood up and went to the door of the kitchen. She had

something to say to Kubun, but when she came to speak she had forgotten what it was. She returned to the table and sat down.

'You say Carl's out west, then?' Ivor asked. 'How far out might that be?'

Ellen waited for the tears that welled up inside her to recede. 'I'm sure you've heard of Gordon Davenport's expedition. Some local boys followed it without their parents' knowledge. Carl has gone to bring them back.'

Ivor fiddled with his fingers as Ellen described the disruption that the expedition had brought to the village. She said that Carl saw it as his responsibility to protect the people from this threat. He would not be told that this was impossible for one man, even for an army of men.

'That sounds like Carl all right,' Ivor acknowledged.

They sat for a time without speaking, then Ivor said offhandedly that he might have seen Carl.

'What do you mean?' Ellen asked.

'I might have seen him,' Ivor repeated.

Ellen's breathing came in fits and starts. She demanded that Ivor explain what he meant.

'There's a river that comes down from the mountains. It doesn't have a white fella name yet and the local name won't mean anything to you. I was camping there, doing some panning round and about, though I didn't really hold out much hope. But it's a beautiful place, wild and untouched, with the clearest air you could wish for. I had a few natives to keep me company. We had plenty of supplies. I was content.

'Then one morning a couple of days back there was a body

in the river, carried on the current. Sometimes after a big fight you see bodies washing down a river to God knows where; you just watch them go by, think a bit about your own mortality then get back to whatever it was you were doing. But someone yelled out that it was a white man, so I waded in to try to catch it. The current was fast and the water deep and it got past me, but I got a fair look. I'm sorry Mrs Starck, but I think it was Carl.'

Ellen shook her head and stood up. She said that the expedition had gone along the bottom of the valley so Carl would not have been in the mountains. Whatever Ivor had seen it could not have been her husband. 'Carl's a very strong swimmer. If he'd fallen into the water it would have been easy for him to swim to safety, even with his injury.'

'I'm sorry, Mrs Starck.'

Ellen asked about the clothing the figure in the water had been wearing. Ivor thought for a moment before saying that he did not remember any clothing; the body might have been naked. Ellen said this was clear evidence that what Ivor had seen must have been the body of a highlander.

*

When Ellen was again ready for conversation Ivor mentioned that the expedition might be equipped with a radio. She went immediately to the back bedroom where she put on the headset and began to fiddle with the dials, and before long she was in contact with the mission station in Madang. Luke Sommer was not available, but she explained to her interlocutor that she needed to contact the Davenport expedition urgently.

As they waited Ivor asked if there was anything he could do but Ellen shook her head. She went back every half hour to the radio but the voice on the other end called for patience. She lay on her bed but felt burdened by her body. She walked up the hill then started to run back down, giving her body free rein until her legs could no longer keep up with her trunk and she stumbled and fell. She lay in pain, curled up in a ball, until Ivor found her and brought her inside, where he tended her cuts and bruises.

After a short rest Ellen went back to the radio. This time Luke Sommer's voice told her that contact had been made with the expedition and Gordon Davenport would be available to speak to her at dawn the next day. She accepted blankly Luke's assurance that everything would turn out well and she asked about his fiancée. Whatever Luke said in reply made no impression on her.

In the morning her stomach was wrung out with nerves and lack of sleep. She could hardly bear to listen to Davenport. 'Carl tried to convince the village boys to return with him, but the prospect of a great adventure was too appealing and they refused. He kept on at me but I told him I would only give them up to their families. Eventually he accepted this and turned back east. That was several days ago.'

'He should have been back well before now,' Ellen said mechanically.

'He probably got waylaid, Mrs Starck, by his missionary

work. From what I've heard he's an accomplished bushman, and he has his cook-boy with him. I expect he'll turn up.'

During the course of the day Ellen tried to imagine life without Carl. It would be an emptiness without end, a featureless desert. The only relief from this thought was the realisation that now she would be able to leave New Guinea and return home.

Loss

(1939-1941)

One

When Ellen saw Aijang and Onyx approaching the house she curled up on the floor and sobbed violently, the sounds she made coming from a place inside her that she had not known existed. Ivor Moore eventually got her to bed, where she fell into an exhausted sleep. When she woke she asked Aijang to tell her what had happened.

'Pastor Carl went off by himself and didn't come back. I looked for him but only found Onyx. Some local villagers helped me search more, up in the mountains. We called out Pastor Carl's name as loud as we could but there was no answer, just echoes. So I came back here.'

'Did Pastor Carl say anything before he left you?'

'Nothing special, Misis.'

'Nothing about me?'

'Just to stay with you, Misis, if anything happened to him. He always said that.'

Ellen gradually realised that Ivor was no longer in the house and asked Aijang if he knew where he was. '*Masta* Ivor gone to look for Pastor Carl. He said if Pastor Carl is anywhere around he'll find him.'

In the days that followed Ellen started desultory preparations for leaving the highlands. She told Kubun that

Aijang would look after her now and he should focus on his upcoming marriage. She asked Yere to continue to work in the garden until its future was decided. She packed Carl's books and papers, reading a few lines here and there, trying to take in the meaning. She wondered what to do with Carl's clothes and accepted Aijang's offer to look after them. Then she waited for the repaired mission plane that would bring Lotte Fiebiger, who had agreed to come and keep her company until she was finally ready to leave.

*

When Lotte arrived she did not question Ellen's right to her tears, and she contributed a good portion of her own. Ellen could see that the tears were genuine, and for this she was grateful. When it was time to talk Lotte took the lead. 'Reg Thompson says all the *kiaps* to the west are on the lookout. There has been talk of sightings in some of the villages, but these have all dissolved on further inquiry. The *kiaps* will keep looking. Sven Jonsson and his evangelists are also on the alert, in case Carl got that far.'

Ellen accepted these assurances without comment. Then she said that she would stay in the highlands until Carl's body was found. Lotte responded that it was possible, even likely, that this would never happen. The body could have been washed down the river to the Papuan coast and then out to sea, where it might be lost forever.

'If villagers saw the body of a white man they would retrieve it and take it to a government post,' Ellen said, but Lotte replied that it was best not to think about what might happen in such circumstances.

*

Aijang said that the people were asking for something of Pastor Carl's to help them remember him. He would give them some of Pastor Carl's clothes, if that was all right. Ellen agreed without thinking. She invited Aijang to sit and asked if he knew why Pastor Carl had gone off by himself.

'Sometimes Pastor Carl would go off like that, but I never worried. He knew his way in the bush.' Aijang added that there had been no change to these absences from the time before Misis came to the time after, so they probably had nothing to do with local women.

Through a suppressed blush Ellen invited Aijang to go back to the time when he had started to work for Pastor Carl.

'I didn't think much about him, Misis, to begin with. Later on, I saw he was different from the others. But he always treated me good. I got no complaints.'

Ellen asked in what way Pastor Carl was different.

'He wasn't so sure about his white skin. Or my white name.'

'What name was that?'

'Zachariah, Misis. That's what they called me.'

Ellen asked about Aijang's birthplace and his childhood, and he spoke of a village on the coast not far from one of the early places of the Lutheran mission. He had got used to whites quickly enough, their energy and their bossiness, but when he had first seen them staring quietly at a book he had no idea what they were doing. He had been sent to a mission school and had learnt to read and write in his own language. Now he could even read some English, and before long he would be able to read a newspaper. Then he would be ready to start on one of Pastor Carl's thick books, which contained enough knowledge to last a lifetime.

'But don't you want to live with your own kind, among your own people?'

'Nothing much for me back in the village, Misis. No books.' Aijang laughed then said that he would like to go to Australia, maybe when Misis went back.

'Is there somewhere in particular you'd like to go?'

'Sydney, Misis. I've seen pictures and I'd like to go there. Ride around in cars and climb to the top of the tall buildings. Some of the bush *kanakas* think God lives in Sydney, but that's rubbish. Those fellas know nothing.'

'Don't you want to get married, have your own family?'

'Plenty of girls round about, Misis. I don't need to choose just one.'

Ellen tried to keep the primness out of her voice. 'Didn't Pastor Carl tell you that was sinful?'

'Pastor Carl never talked to me too much about religion, not after the early days. He just asked me about the people up here and their ceremonies, what they thought, what they said among themselves and what they meant. He kept asking all the time about that.'

Ellen warned Aijang that, apart from anything else, sleeping with many different women might make him sick.

'If I get sick I'll ask you for medicine, Misis.'

*

During these exchanges it became clear to Ellen that Lotte Fiebiger and Aijang were uncomfortable in each other's presence. More than once Lotte implied that Ellen should be careful what she said to Aijang or in his hearing, and that she should not believe everything he told her. Then one evening when Aijang was busy elsewhere Lotte remarked that the boy was mixed up in the trouble that had befallen Carl in the east.

'Alfred and I felt Carl was becoming too close to one of the local clans, taking their side in disputes. We discovered that Aijang had developed a relationship with a girl of the clan and was encouraging Carl to favour them. Alfred had to be quite forceful in bringing Carl into line.'

Ellen reacted wearily to this revelation, but Lotte went further. She said that she and Alfred had suspected Carl of taking part in local rituals, although thankfully not the more abhorrent ones, from some misguided belief that this would bring him closer to the people. He had also helped to stage a dance festival, contributing rice and making a speech. Again, Alfred had found it necessary to intervene.

Ellen said she did not understand why Lotte was telling her this now. Lotte responded that it might help to explain Carl's disappearance; he might have become too close to the people and fallen victim to one of the clan disputes that regularly flared up. Ellen shook her head at this speculation, and the two women spent the rest of the evening quietly at odds with each other.

Before going to bed Ellen went outside and stood on the verandah, holding a shawl tightly around her shoulders for warmth. She silently asked Carl where he was, why he had left her and what he expected of her now that he was gone. She said that he had no right simply to go away and not come back.

The next day Kubun came with his wife-to-be, a woman well into her twenties but with an affected shyness that Ellen found irritating. Kubun thanked Ellen effusively for the things she had given him for the bride price and pronounced himself the happiest man alive. He assured Ellen that his aunt would continue to look after the garden, in honour of Pastor Carl, and asked if he could work in the house for the man who would come as a replacement. He listed the accomplishments that would make him a good candidate, in particular his knowledge of English, and he asked Ellen to intercede on his behalf. He ended by saying that he would like to take over Aijang's hut. He would extend it so it was suitable for himself and his wife, and for the children who would come.

'Aijang is still here,' Ellen replied curtly. 'And Pastor Carl's replacement will make his own arrangements.'

Kubun was unperturbed. He said, 'We've heard the new pastor will come from America. Where's America, Misis?'

Ellen's mood softened, and she busied herself opening several of the packed boxes of Carl's things until she found a National Geographic magazine with a map of the world. She displayed this on the table, pointing in turn to South Australia, England and Germany, explaining to Kubun the significance of these places for her and Pastor Carl. Then she ran her finger over the full extent of America and traced the voyages of discovery across the Atlantic. She pointed to New Guinea and indicated the approximate position of the Wahgi Valley then sketched possible routes that the first highland settlers might have taken. She highlighted the substantial stretches of ocean these people would have had to cross to reach New Guinea from their lands of origin and concluded, fully realising the fact for the first time herself, that they must have been exceptional sailors.

When she had finished Ellen handed Kubun the magazine to keep but he refused to accept, saying that the villagers would ask him to explain its contents and would scoff at his inevitable failure. She replied that ignorance was nothing to be ashamed of; the important thing was to recognise ignorance and replace it with knowledge. Kubun said with a show of respect that Misis sounded just like Pastor Carl when she talked like that.

Two

Lotte called out that more villagers had come but she would send them away. They should know by now to leave Ellen in peace.

A young woman and a small boy, neither of whom Ellen recognised, were waiting at the front of the house, while several yards away a pair of native men squatted on their haunches and watched. Without speaking the woman placed her hands on the shoulders of the boy and pushed him forward. Ellen quickly appraised the boy's face and skin, but she could see no sign of disease, although there were some marks that may have been the remnants of bruising.

'Is he sick?'

The woman gave no indication that she understood. She removed the net bag that had been draped from her forehead down her back and placed it on the ground, next to a miniature version of the net bag that the boy had been carrying.

'You're not from nearby?'

The woman replied in a language that meant nothing to Ellen. She called Aijang to assist but after a brief exchange he said that, while he understood some of the woman's words, he could make no sense of what she was saying.

Ellen returned her attention to the boy, who was naked,

except for a dirty grass skirt that draped down at the front and back. She turned him around and examined him more closely and saw clear evidence of injury—partially healed scars and the remains of burns on the backs of his arms and legs. The skin of the buttocks was marked by weals, while the penis showed signs of a badly performed circumcision.

'Who did this?' Ellen asked the woman, as she did so observing her more closely. She saw symmetrical facial features, tightly coiled and vibrant hair, and shapely breasts. But there were also signs on her body of abuse, discolouration of the skin and swelling on the upper arms and thighs.

The hint of shame in the woman's eyes caused Ellen to refrain from asking further about the injuries to herself and the boy. Instead, she took the woman's hands and gently rubbed them, saying in English that no woman should have to endure what she had endured. She wished she could help, but she was about to leave New Guinea and return to her own country. She made an eating gesture and the woman responded positively. Ellen indicated that she should bring her son into the house. She decided against extending the invitation to the squatting men.

Lotte was quick to make her irritation plain, telling Ellen that she needed to learn where to draw the line when it came to the local people. Even at this late stage and with all that had happened, she should not lose perspective.

The mother and child ate greedily as Lotte and Ellen watched. The boy constantly tried to get down from the chair on which he had been put, but his mother restrained him. She spoke to him, words of admonishment or encouragement, and Lotte said something in response. The woman reacted immediately and soon she and Lotte were in earnest dialogue. Lotte broke off the conversation to tell Ellen that the woman came from the eastern highlands, and she had some acquaintance with her language.

The conversation resumed, the young woman pointing several times at the boy. Ellen felt that a connection was being made to her, but she could not imagine what it might be. Lotte drank some of the tea that had gone cold in her cup, then she took Ellen's hand.

'At first, I thought I'd misunderstood so I asked her again, but there was no mistake. She insists that this boy is Carl's son.'

*

When Ellen had first examined the boy she had focussed on the evidence of maltreatment, paying no attention to his complexion or his features. But now she could see that he was lighter than a typical highland child. His eyes were a shade of green, his skin on the golden side of brown and his nose relatively narrow and long.

'I told her to go,' Lotte continued, 'but she refuses.'

'What does she want?' Ellen managed to ask.

Lotte turned back to the young woman. Several sentences passed back and forth, during which Ellen could not take her eyes off the boy.

'She's found someone who will take her as a sole wife, freeing her from her current position where she is the youngest of many.

But the man refuses to take the child, so she has brought him here, to Carl.'

'You told her about Carl?'

'She doesn't believe me. She says she will wait until he returns.'

Ellen insisted that Carl would never have been unfaithful to her, let alone with a highland woman. She was sorry for the woman and child; she could see they had suffered, but she could not help them.

The child wriggled again on his chair and his mother stood up and led him outside, away from the house. When they returned they sat on the verandah, propped up against the house wall.

Lotte told Ellen that the woman had come to extort wealth and should not be rewarded. She would soon tire of waiting and take herself and her child back to where they came from. She was handsome for a native woman and would make her way in the highland world, even with the encumbrance of a white man's child, which was not so unusual.

When darkness set in Ellen took some food to the mother and child. Later she brought blankets to soften the hard surface of the verandah and to protect against the chill. She could not resist touching the child's head as he lay sleeping against his mother.

As she turned to go inside she heard Mbagl's voice assuring her that she had nothing to fear from the foreign men who had come with the woman and child. He would keep watch over the house until the men had gone.

*

When Ellen opened the door to the verandah the next morning Lotte was already there, comforting the boy. Ellen saw immediately that his mother and the accompanying men had gone, and she realised that she was not surprised.

'What should we do?' she asked distantly.

Lotte said that when she went back home, which would be soon because she was urgently needed there, she would take the boy. She would find new parents for him among their converts and he would be brought up a Christian.

In the course of the morning, as Lotte packed her few things together, Ellen asked if it were feasible to find the boy's father and convince him to take responsibility for his child. Lotte waved away this idea, saying that most white men would not admit to sexual relations with a local woman, and those who would admit to such a thing would accept no responsibility for the product of their sin. The boy would find his way in the highland world, the only possible life for him.

'Couldn't you take him, Lotte?'

'Alfred and I are too old to look after a child, let alone one like this.'

When his mother had been there the boy had listened intently but hardly spoken. Now he found his voice, which he directed at Lotte. When there was a pause she told Ellen that he wanted to know when his father would come and what he would look like.

Ellen held out her arms to the boy, but he gave her a puzzled look and she let her arms fall. She prepared some simple food and encouraged him to eat. She looked again for signs of Carl, then admonished herself for doing so.

Later in the day engine noise announced the arrival of the mission's plane. Lotte urged Ellen to accompany her, but Ellen said there was still time for word to come of what had happened to Carl. She would stay a little longer, and the child would stay with her.

Lotte cautioned that the more time Ellen spent with the boy the more difficult it would be for her to give him up. In her confused state she should be careful not to do anything that might jeopardise her future. It was well known that Australians were prejudiced against their own blacks. What would they make of this half-caste, if she were to return to Australia with him? After delivering this message Lotte set off down the hill, calling back as she went that the boy's name was Aino.

Ellen immediately set about reorganising the house. With Aijang's help she moved the mattress from the single bed to the main bedroom, indicating to Aino that he was to sleep there. She inspected the kitchen and told Aijang to put out of reach anything that the boy might break or injure himself with. She took Aino out to the latrine and did her best to explain its use, then followed the same procedure with the shower.

Back inside the house Ellen searched in the wardrobe for something she could use as clothing for the boy. She had no sewing skills so the best she could do was to take a pair of short pants that she had packed hastily and never worn and reduce the waist size by means of safety pins. Aino stood passively as the pants were adjusted to his body, but as soon as Ellen left him for a moment he discarded them on the floor. She accepted that the problem of clothing would have to be left for another time.

For the remainder of the day Aino followed Ellen around the house, at regular intervals breaking into a monologue. Aijang knew enough of the boy's language to decipher the recurring theme. Since Aino's father was not there he wanted to return to his mother and his village. They should leave at once.

Later that night, after Aino had finally fallen asleep, Ellen went to the radio. She was hoping for Luke Sommer's calm voice talking of everyday things, but instead Luke told her that Hitler's armies had marched into Poland and that France and Britain, and by extension Australia, were now at war with Germany. If as was likely the authorities required Ellen to return to Australia, the mission plane would be available to take her from the highlands to the coast.

Three

At the front of the mission house Mbagl pointed to the watching man, who was standing some distance away, and informed Ellen that he had found her a new husband. Ellen acknowledged the man and listened as Mbagl warned that it was unnatural for a woman in the prime of life to remain unmarried. He would have offered himself, but he already had several wives, and he knew this made him ineligible in her eyes. But the man he had chosen had never married, although several girls had offered themselves, and this man was prepared to accept the boy who had been mysteriously left at the mission house by his mother. Mbagl ended by saying that if Ellen wanted to marry a white man she would have to go in search of him, and the people wanted her to stay.

Ellen avoided the invitation to talk about Aino, who she could feel tucked away behind her. Instead, she said that it was too early to think about marrying again, since she was not yet certain that Pastor Carl was dead. In any event she could not accept Mbagl's proposal, because it was against nature for white and black people to marry each other.

Mbagl shrugged and said he would like to have something of Pastor Carl's to remember him by. Ellen took him into the house and pointed at the cardboard boxes that contained Carl's things. Mbagl said that pieces of Pastor Carl's clothing had started to appear on the bodies of village men, and he suspected that the cook-boy had been trading these items to the men for their daughters' favours. If he found proof he would punish the boy.

Mbagl used a long fingernail to break the seal on the first of the cardboard boxes then carefully removed its contents. There was a box camera with several rolls of film, a pair of binoculars in a solid leather case, a two-storeyed wooden pencil case with a sliding lid containing a fountain pen, pencils of various colours, a pair of worn-down erasers, a protractor and a pencil sharpener. Mbagl put each item on the floor and Ellen explained its use. When she came to the fountain pen she found a bottle of ink, filled the pen then wrote several letters of the alphabet on a piece of paper in her neat script. She offered the pen to Mbagl for him to try, but he shook his head.

The next box contained some old photographs in a large envelope, and Ellen talked briefly about the people who were featured. The two young men were Carl's brothers who had died in a big fight in a faraway place. Ellen had never met them, although she would have liked to. She had also never met the woman in the heavy black dress standing in front of a rough hut on a barren piece of land. This woman was Carl's mother, who had died not long after his birth. The elderly couple who were squinting into the light in front of a cottage with a neat flower garden were the parents Carl had grown up with. They were also long dead.

There was a large photograph of herself and Carl that Ellen tried to pass over, but Mbagl insisted on an explanation. It had been taken on their wedding day and it showed Carl sitting upright on a high-backed chair in a suit, waistcoat and tie, a flower in his buttonhole and a pair of gloves in one hand. Ellen was standing beside him in a flowing white dress with puffed sleeves and a long white veil, holding a garland of flowers. One hand was resting on Carl's shoulder. Both faces were serious, but Ellen insisted that if you looked hard enough you could see beneath the surface clear signs of happiness.

Ellen invited Mbagl to keep the photograph, knowing there would be other copies when she returned home. She watched as he rolled it into a cylinder and slipped it beneath the bark girdle that he wore around his waist.

The final photograph in this collection was of the head and torso of a fatigued man with sallow skin and sparse grey hair, dressed in a dark coat buttoned all the way up to the throat. The man was staring into something beyond the camera. Ellen told Mbagl that this man was Pastor Carl's true father. He had lived most of his life in the Australian desert, where he had been tested beyond the limits of human endurance.

Mbagl asked what a desert was and Ellen said she had never been to the desert herself, but she had experienced desert air when on regular occasions it had blown through her home town of Adelaide. This air was of such merciless heat and dryness that there could be no doubt that it came from a place devoid of water. As she spoke she took a piece of soft paper from Carl's things that she unwrapped to display a pair of heart-shaped stones. She said that these stones came from the desert where the local people used them to make rain. But Pastor Carl would never have believed that a pair of stones could help to bring relief to such a place. The stones were just to remind him of his father.

Mbagl insisted that a place without water was impossible, and Ellen said that every now and then rain did come to the desert; she had learnt this from writings Carl's father had left. She then translated a remembered passage from Herbert Wischner's diaries. 'The rains slanted down from the sky in great sheets of water, accompanied by searing flashes of lighting and booming claps of thunder. Creeks sprang from the ground and birds arrived in enormous shrieking clouds. Almost overnight there was green all around and wildflowers of exquisite colour. The beauty was totally unexpected, almost overwhelming.'

As she spoke she felt the words of the language coming to her with unprecedented ease, so she continued. 'Pastor Carl's father would swim in a lake that formed after the rains, in the night when everyone else was sleeping. Sometimes there was moonlight, at other times a deep darkness that hid even his own body from him. When he swam he felt that he was alone with the fullness of God's creation. He was at peace.'

The recitation left Ellen flushed with Herbert Wischner's moment of transcendence, but Mbagl seemed unaffected. He said that he would like to see the rest of Pastor Carl's things.

The next box contained objects of highland origin carefully packed and annotated, among them a small bamboo cooking pot, a stone mortar and pestle, a necklace of dogs' teeth, a headdress of fine feathers and a piece of jewellery bone. Mbagl fingered these items then picked up a pot of ochre used to colour the skin. Ellen explained that Pastor Carl had collected these things to help him understand the spirit of the people. He had kept them to study when he went back to his own country. He would have taken good care of them.

They moved on to a block of photographs secured tightly with a rubber band that Ellen showed Mbagl how to remove. The photos depicted local villages from several angles, at different times of day and in different weathers, sometimes with human or animal figures in the background, at other times deserted. There were detailed shots of human faces, looking up in surprise, turning away suddenly or grinning behind partially upraised hands. There were close-ups of young men and women with legs intertwined and noses pressed against each other. There were secretly captured expressions of concentration, laughter or distraction, and several explorations of the lesions caused by yaws, before and after treatment, and of the deformities in bone and tissue that the disease could cause.

Mbagl went through the photographs several times, marvelling out loud at how revealing they were, sometimes laughing at an awkward face or gesture. Then he lingered over a series of photos showing a strongly built man of early middle age with a full beard, a wide forehead, high cheekbones and uneven teeth. He reached his hand to his hair and after a moment's rummaging produced a cylinder of paper which he unfolded and held out to Ellen. It was a photograph showing Mbagl's full figure in the adornment and pose of a warrior. He said Pastor Carl had given it to him as a keepsake and that it captured his likeness much better than the photographs she was showing him, which he handed back to her.

The remaining boxes contained Carl's books and magazines. Mbagl selected a heavy book that featured pictures of aeroplanes amongst reams of words. He nursed the book in his lap and Ellen said he was welcome to keep it. He began to turn the pages and Ellen joined him in examining the pictures, translating as she did so pieces of explanatory text. She sensed in Mbagl a mixture of wonder and diffidence and she said that there was nothing special about what she was doing. All that was necessary to learn to read and write was proper instruction and a determination not to give up.

As Mbagl made to leave Ellen held him back and asked if he knew what had happened to Pastor Carl. He said that maybe Pastor Carl had got into a fight or had an accident. But Misis should not worry. He was sure that Pastor Carl had not taken his own life; only women and no-good men did that.

*

Ellen found an old primer and sat down to translate one of the stories into the local language. With the help of Carl's dictionary she completed a rough version of *Jack and the Beanstalk* that she read aloud to Aijang, whose suggested improvements she incorporated. Aino's understanding of the language was still sketchy, but he nonetheless sat spellbound as she read, giving her confidence in her plan.

The next visit to the village saw Ellen surrounded by a group of children as she read out loud, concentrating hard on her enunciation. Several of the mothers who had also gathered around interrupted Ellen to explain that their ancestors had sprung from the ground like beans in some unspecified past, but the women's delight at the coincidence was gradually replaced by perplexity and anxiety as the plot unfolded. A group of marauding boys tried to distract the listeners by mimicking actions from the story, climbing trees and calling out with menace, but eventually they grew tired of this and either joined the circle of listeners or found something else to do. When the reading was finished Ellen was called on to explain the white man's fascination with gold. She mentioned its scarcity, its attractive colour and its resistance to corrosion. Some of the onlookers spat on the ground to indicate their dismissive view of the explanation, but Ellen nonetheless considered the reading a success. Later that same afternoon she began work on a new translation.

Over subsequent weeks the fairy tales continued to prove popular with the young children, and Ellen decided to supplement the readings with more advanced work for the older ones. She prepared sheets of paper with letters of the alphabet and Carl's accents and began the work of explaining the relationships between the distinctive shapes and particular sounds, before organising the letters into words and demonstrating the astonishing results. The few pencils she had were shared among the children so they could try their hand. She also made cards with numbers and tried with their aid and a collection of small beads to teach simple arithmetic. Her efforts to devise new ways to hold the interest of the children proved draining, as did the propensity of her pupils to absent themselves from her classes without any explanation. And there was the constant frustration of the regular requests, particularly from the older boys and some of the men, to teach them pidgin, which she dismissed by saying that Pastor Carl had not considered pidgin a proper language, and that anyway she did not speak it. Several times she was on the point of giving up, but there was just enough resonance from a small number of loyal pupils, almost all prepubescent girls, to keep her going. Waiya was a prominent member of this group, showing a sharpness of mind and a determination to learn that greatly encouraged Ellen—although she sometimes wondered whether her wish to see some light in the girl's future meant that she attributed more promise to her than was warranted.

While her medical supplies lasted Ellen continued her health clinics, alternating these with her teaching. A regular routine developed in which she spent each morning in the village, and she felt for the first time in her life that she had a proper job, albeit one without remuneration, although she was presented with sweet potatoes and vegetables from the gardens from time to time without the need for payment. She brought Aino with her and kept a close eye on him as he mixed with the local children, initially hoping for his success then fearing that it might become too complete. But Aino never seemed to stray too far into the orbit of the villagers, and Ellen increasingly allowed him the freedom to pick and choose between her world and theirs.

Sometimes in the afternoons Ellen would take Aino to the river where she would hold his hands as he kicked the water into a foaming mass before practising his arm movements and his breathing then splashing out briefly on his own. Occasionally young women would come to swim and there would be shouted conversations about goings on in the village, invariably about marriages planned, broken or resumed. Ellen dismissed questions about her intentions towards the man chosen for her by Mbagl, saying that she would probably never marry again. She encouraged the women to resist any pressure to hurry into marriage. They would never be as free as they were now.

On the walk back to the house after one such conversation Ellen told Aino not to pay any attention to the women's talk. If she did ever marry again it would be to a white man like his father. She said that she knew his father and promised that one day soon she would explain all about him.

Four

Many of the Lutheran missionaries in New Guinea had been sent to internment camps in Australia and Luke Sommer had taken over responsibility for all the Lutheran mission stations in the Territory of New Guinea. In regular radio conversations Ellen urged him to visit the Wahgi Valley but he told her that, with no prospect of a replacement for Carl until after the war, the mission in such an out-of-the-way place could not be kept up. Ellen persisted, arguing that Carl's evangelists deserved to hear their fate from the mission's leader, and Luke agreed to come when he could.

When one morning sometime later Luke finally arrived Ellen was waiting for him at the landing strip. She shook his hand, thanked him effusively for coming and led him on the journey to the house, talking freely to mask her nerves.

'When I first arrived here they carried me on a chair as if I were royalty. I felt very foolish.'

'I'm sure you looked quite fine.'

'The journey to the highlands was my first aeroplane flight and my stomach was very unsure of itself. I needed the toilet.'

When Ellen drew breath Luke apologised for taking so long to visit. He explained that it had been difficult to get the administration's approval. The authorities were becoming increasingly worried that war would come to the Pacific and that New Guinea would be targeted.

Ellen strode out and Luke, who was carrying a heavy rucksack, struggled to keep up. In response Ellen walked more slowly and talked less frequently. She could feel Luke breathing in the sharp mountain air and the natural beauty, and she felt a moment of pride. She asked whether America had scenes of splendour to compare with this and Luke said not so much the Great Plains where he came from, but America was a big country with lots of variety.

Ellen had instructed Aijang to keep Aino out of sight when she arrived with Pastor Luke but when they reached the house Aino was waiting near the front door, dressed neatly in shorts and a shirt that were part of a consignment of boys' clothes that had come unbidden from Mathilde Weiss on the coast. Despite Luke's attempt to conceal it, the shock of recognition on his face as soon as he saw the boy was unmistakable.

'At first I didn't see it,' Ellen said, 'but now I can't see past it.'

When Luke had washed and eaten they were ready to talk. Ellen began the conversation with a question about Luke's fiancée, which he answered by saying that her plans to come to New Guinea had been put definitively to one side. They would wait for the conclusion of the war before deciding what to do.

Mention of the war led to a discussion of news from Europe, where Germany was carrying all before it. Luke said that France had been invaded and Britain would soon be left alone to confront Hitler. Unless America intervened the war would soon be over, and then the part of New Guinea that had formerly been a German colony would in all likelihood revert to German control. The prospect weighed on their mood.

'Carl had two brothers who died fighting for Germany in the Great War,' Ellen said to resume the conversation. 'Did he tell you?'

'Carl never spoke to me about his family.'

'His father was a missionary in the Australian desert, but Carl grew up in another family. He even took their name.'

'I knew none of that.'

'His father failed in his mission, and it was rumoured that as a result he took his own life. Now I fear that Carl has done the same, perhaps for the same reason.'

Luke said Ellen should put any thought of Carl being a failure as a missionary out of her mind. His work in the highlands had only just begun, and who was to say what impact he might have had in the long term. And Ellen should not torture herself with thoughts about how Carl might have died.

Ellen justified bringing up the subject of Carl's death by saying that Luke was the only person she could talk to about it—with the exception of an old gold miner who showed up out of the blue from time to time. She trusted Luke not to share her fears with anyone, not even his fiancée when they were finally together. 'And now you must tell me about her.'

Luke took his time. 'When I was at the seminary I would go regularly with a group of fellow students to the house of one of our professors on Sunday afternoons. We would talk about good and evil, time and eternity, the perennial questions, hoping all the while that our host's daughter would appear when we paused for food and drink. One of our number described us aptly as a wholesome bunch with good morals, as befitted students of theology, but one not immune to the attractions of earthly beauty when presented to us.'

'She must be very pretty.'

'Every young man who came within Hilda's orbit felt compelled to shine brightly to demonstrate his worthiness, but the effort invariably proved too much and one by one they fell away. For a period of years I stayed quietly in the background and eventually my chance came. No one was more surprised than me when I was chosen.'

Ellen said that she was not at all surprised that Hilda had chosen Luke. Then to avoid embarrassment she asked what else he and his friends had discussed on their Sunday afternoons.

'We talked about reason and religious faith, our professor insisting that it is a mistake to think of these faculties of mind as being at odds. He said this is demonstrated by the United States, which combines intellect and faith like nowhere else and is for this reason the greatest country on earth.' Luke added that Americans were by and large very patriotic. The Australians he had met seemed more sceptical of their country, but this might just be for show.

'Our founding was very different from yours,' Ellen said. 'More in sin than grace. Although my state of South Australia was an exception in this respect.'

Luke passed over this last reference. He said solemnly that America had committed the sin of slavery, in his view an original sin for which proper penance needed to be done.

'Is that why you came to New Guinea?' Ellen asked.

'The economic depression was in full swing when I took my first parish, in my home state of Nebraska. The parishioners were almost exclusively of German and Scandinavian stock, submissive to God but suspicious of enthusiasm, yet over time I could feel them warm to the eagerness of youth that I brought. Then the economic situation began to improve, and I felt the people start to tire of me, so I looked for other opportunities. A call came from the mission in New Guinea, and despite knowing nothing about the country I suspected that it would favour enthusiasm. So I threw my hat into the ring.'

Aino demanded Ellen's attention and she busied herself with him for several minutes. Luke tried to insert himself into the scene, holding out his hand to the boy and asking him questions about his name and age, but Aino refused to be drawn. Ellen sent him off to find Aijang, who would have something for him to eat.

'You won't mind me asking,' Luke said, 'but what are your plans for the boy?'

Ellen picked invisible pieces of lint from her trousers and let them fall to the floor. 'I lost a baby,' she said eventually. 'Carl had already left for New Guinea when I found out I was expecting. When I miscarried I could not bring myself to tell him by letter, and after I arrived here the right moment never seemed to come.'

'I'm very sorry.'

Ellen said she would show Luke where he was to sleep. As she stood up she asked whether he would like to have something of Carl's as a memento, perhaps one of his books. Luke thanked her but said that he did not know Carl well enough for that. He had liked Carl and felt drawn to him, but their relationship had never taken the final step to friendship.

*

Early the next morning Luke left with Aijang on a journey to Carl's evangelists in the west. They took Onyx with them, Luke saying that the horse would enjoy the exercise. Ellen could see in Onyx's willingness to be led a recognition of experience and trustworthiness in her new master. She hoped that the evangelists and the highlanders whom Luke would meet would show the same perceptiveness.

As soon as Luke had gone Aino asked whether this man was his father and, if so, why he was going away. Ellen was delighted by Aino's capacity to think such a complex thought and express it in English, and she hugged him hard. She told him that Pastor Luke was not his father, but he was a good man whom they would both benefit greatly from having known. She went on, 'Your father was a missionary like Pastor Luke. His name was Pastor Carl. One day he went off into the bush, as he often did, but this time he did not come back. Everyone says he must have been killed in an accident. I suppose that is what happened.'

Aino said nothing and Ellen assured him that his father would have loved him, just as she loved him. It was right that he had come to her because he had a white father and therefore belonged in the white world. She would take him to that world soon; he would be amazed by the things he found there.

That night when Aino was asleep Ellen imagined her return to Adelaide. She would be able to explain about Carl easily enough by saying that he had fallen victim to a terrible, although unspecified, accident. The people at home had a primitive view of New Guinea and would accept this without question. The only danger would be her own need to share her innermost fears about Carl's death with someone, although she was not sure who this might be. To explain about Aino would be more difficult, but she would manage. He was a half-caste child who had been rejected by his mother and was unacknowledged by his white father. It would be impossible for him to find a place in the highland world, so she was searching in Adelaide for a suitable family for him. She would be exacting in her process of selection; the right couple would never be found and by default Aino would remain with her. Her mother would be the biggest obstacle, but Ellen felt sure that she would soon come to love Aino, despite her racial views. And if anyone intimated that they saw signs of Carl in the boy she would dismiss this idea with blithe confidence.

*

Luke brought back from his journey a miniature bow and arrow and a ball made of soft bark, and he demonstrated their use to Aino. The boy soon overcame his shyness and before long the pair was engrossed in a boisterous game. When the game began to pall Luke produced a coin that he held between his fingers then made disappear into thin air

226

and return again. Aino demanded that the trick be repeated, gravitating between delight at the illusion and distress at his inability to understand it. Luke calmed him by saying that one day he would show him how to perform this trick himself.

Ellen put Aino to bed early and she and Luke had the evening to themselves. Ellen asked about the trip and Luke reported that the evangelists had reacted stoically to the news that there would be no immediate replacement for Carl, although it was clear that his death had shaken them. They had told him that Carl had sometimes done rash things against their advice, but they had always assumed that Jesus would protect him from harm. His death must have some kind of meaning, but they could not work out what it was. The bush people by contrast were convinced that Carl was still alive somewhere in the sky. They expected him to return soon, leading a line of their ancestors. Such a line had visited them not long ago, but their ancestors must have forgotten their birthplace because they had continued further to the west. Before long they would surely remember where they came from and return, and Carl would be with them.

Ellen and Luke took this opportunity to discuss the Davenport expedition, but they had little to say that was new. The enterprise had been hailed as a great success. Despite sporadic aggression from the untouched tribes encountered along the way there had been little loss of life or injury on either side, and the groundwork had been laid for the remaining unchartered parts of New Guinea to be opened to civilisation.

Later when Ellen was cleaning up in the kitchen she heard

Luke's side of a hushed conversation on the two-way radio. When Luke reappeared he said that France had capitulated and England now stood alone. The English would resist bravely, but sooner or later their will would break and Hitler would be victorious.

'I like and respect the Fiebigers and our other German missionaries,' Luke concluded. 'But I could not stay in New Guinea if it returned to German control. It would feel like a betrayal of my country, although we are not yet in the war.'

Five

Ellen had ignored the appeals of government officials over the radio for her to leave the highlands, and the peremptory official letter that followed had been put to one side. But now a patrol had arrived to lay down the law, although at first Chas Noble seemed more intent on rubbing salt in her wounds.

'Right careless of Carl. And him such a fine bushman and all. Makes a man wonder.'

There was another white man there, much older and less sure of himself, and Noble introduced him as Murray Saunders. Noble invited himself and Saunders into the house, leaving the handful of accompanying New Guineans to mill around outside. Noble caught sight of Aino and scrutinised him before turning back to Ellen.

'I know about the boy. Told the mother where she could find Carl. How was I to know he wouldn't be around when she came?' Noble paused, then added, 'Pastor Carl Starck, who would have thought it?'

Ellen steered Aino away and told Aijang to look after him, while Noble assumed a posture of authority. 'Orders are that all the women are to go back to Australia, unless they're performing a vital function. Can't see you falling into that category, Mrs Starck.'

'I distribute medicines to the people, and I teach the children to read and write.'

Noble said he did not think Ellen's dabbling at nursing and schoolmistressing would impress the powers that be in Lae. And he was not sure she was safe, out here all by herself. Of course, that could be easily fixed.

Ellen said she would give the patrol some food and drink and then they should leave.

'No need to take so haughty,' Noble remonstrated. 'I may not have the same education as Carl, but I've read a few books in my time. I'm every bit the man that Carl was, and then some.'

Aino had returned to Ellen's side and Noble said he was even prepared to take on the kid, which showed how broadminded he was.

'What gives you the right to speak to me in this way?' The butterflies in Ellen's stomach caused her words to come out in a weak staccato.

'No crime in asking, Mrs Starck,' Noble said, his bravado tapering off. He took an envelope from his pocket and held it up, saying that Ellen must come from an influential family because there was political pressure from down south to make sure she was escorted out of the highlands safe and sound and put on a ship back to Australia. Noble returned the letter to his pocket. 'Nothing about the kid, though. I bet they don't know about him.'

Aijang had prepared a large bowl of rice and an assortment of vegetables and there was plenty of tea. All this was taken to the verandah, where the members of the patrol were invited to eat. Chas Noble and Murray Saunders sauntered outside to join them but Noble was soon back inside, eager to talk.

'The native woman came to me with quite a story about Carl. Least I could do was let her know where to find the father of her child. Even if I had my doubts.'

'What do you mean?' Ellen asked.

'Prone to hanging around whites, that one. Might even have done a bit of hanging around with me.'

'How dare you!' Ellen had turned pale. She was shaking.

Aijang approached Nobel with his hands raised in a boxer's pose. 'You bugger off,' he blurted out. 'You fuck off.'

Noble took a step back in mock fright. 'Calm down, sonny. Mrs Starck here'll be right pissed off with you, foul mouth you've got. And if you talk to me like that again I'll give you such a thrashing you won't stand up for a week.'

Ellen stood between the two men with her arms outstretched and her heart thumping. She was rescued by Murray Saunders, who came in from outside asking what all the fuss was about. Noble stepped back and announced that the patrol would camp outside for the night. In the morning there would need to be a serious talk about Mrs Starck's future in the highlands.

Ellen retreated to her bedroom, but she was pursued by Noble's words. She fully believed that Aino was Carl's child; after an initial period of denial she had wanted to believe this, because of the claim it gave her to Aino. She thought Noble must have sensed her need and was intent on making mischief.

When Aijang brought the evening meal Ellen told him that she never again wanted to hear the language he had used with the *kiap*, which was demeaning to both speaker and listener. Aijang defended himself by saying that Pastor Carl had used this sort of language when arguing with other whites. Usually Pastor Carl was calm, but sometimes he got angry. 'He used to tell those whites what was what, Misis, like nobody's business.'

*

Ivor Moore appeared at the front of the house early the next morning, and Ellen greeted him warmly. They were interrupted by Chas Noble, who appeared on the verandah and called out a lazy greeting to Ivor. 'Hardly recognised ya, mate. Thin as a whippet and grey as an old singlet.'

'I recognised you sure enough,' Ivor responded, 'especially that scratchy, wheedling voice.' Noble reacted with a mirthless laugh.

Ivor demanded to know if Noble had come just to pester Mrs Starck or if there was something useful he was doing. Ellen answered first, telling Ivor that the patrol had come to escort her out of the highlands, but she was still not ready to go.

Murray Saunders had come outside and Ivor spoke to him as well as to Noble. 'I'll have you know that Mrs Starck has friends out here, me foremost among them. And among the local people she's well respected, as the widow of Pastor Starck and in her own right.'

'Not sure your friendship counts for much, mate,' Noble scoffed. 'Doubt anyone remembers you back in civilisation. Or if they do, you're just another gold miner gone native.'

Saunders intervened with a summary comment on gold miners. 'They were a motley crew, those blokes. My missus used to say to lock up everything, daughters as well as property, till they'd moved on. But there aren't many left now, at least not of the old sort.'

Ivor shrugged these comments aside. Ellen invited him into the house and the other men followed. Remnants of breakfast still lay on the table and Ellen asked Aijang to make fresh tea. She encouraged Ivor to eat.

The discussion was at first about the war. Noble said that Hitler had been stopped in his tracks by the RAF, some Aussie pilots had been involved and hats off to them. An invasion of Britain was off the table, at least for the time being. But when it came to this part of the world, while it was still quiet you couldn't trust the Japs. More likely than not they'd get involved, but if they tried it on in New Guinea they'd get more than they bargained for.

'You're proving your mettle by bullying a defenceless woman,' Ivor said drily.

'We're checking the airstrips round about that might be used if the Japs come, or pieces of land that might be used for airstrips. Some of the sing-sing grounds might be just the thing. Our business with Mrs Starck is just by the by.'

Ivor Moore and Chas Noble busied themselves increasingly with each other and Ellen listened to Murray Saunders, who seemed more than happy to talk about himself. He said that he was a copra planter from the coast and had been in New Guinea for nearly twenty years, stretching back nearly to the last war. The coast was bearable, there was a middling white population and he had made a decent life for himself and his family, although his wife and daughters were now out of harm's way in Queensland and he missed them mightily. He said he could not understand what would keep a lone white woman in an isolated place like the Wahgi Valley. The highland climate was a big improvement on the heat and humidity of the coast right enough, and the highland gardens were a fine display of human ingenuity. But a white woman in this place without a husband, where the loneliness must be interminable? That was hard to fathom.

Ellen replied that even when her husband was alive he would travel for long periods, so she was used to being by herself with no one but natives for company.

The conversation faded away and Ellen turned her attention to Ivor and Noble, who were talking about the Davenport expedition. Leo Fiocchini's name came up and Ellen asked how he was faring. Noble gave her a sideways smirk, and through a blush she said that Leo's attentions had reflected nothing but politeness.

'Very polite is young Fio. Maybe that's what attracted Gordon. Thought the sun shone out of his arse.' Noble added, not entirely to himself, 'Maybe Gordon had more than a passing interest in Fio's arse.'

Saunders suppressed a laugh while Ivor told Noble not to forget that there was a lady present. Noble went on. 'There was a fracas early on in the expedition with some of the locals and Gordon put the blame on me. After that Fio would sit with

Gordon every night, discussing plans as he wrote in his journal. It undermined my authority with the line.'

'And now they've sent you to bring in a defenceless woman,' Ivor taunted. 'To put you properly in your place.'

Noble acknowledged that the task he was engaged in was a humiliating one. He said it was no skin off his nose if Mrs Ellen Starck spent the rest of her days in the highlands, building memorials to her husband and playing mother to the boy who might be his son. She was welcome to the highlands and the highlanders were welcome to her. He was done with the New Guinea service. When he got back from this patrol he would apply to join the army or the air force, where there was real work to be done.

Saunders reminded Noble that Reg Thompson had politicians from down south and the Territory's administrator on his back. He would be ropeable if they returned without Ellen. Noble responded that Reg was probably thinking along the same lines as he was. Time had come to leave New Guinea and join the war.

*

Aijang appeared leading Onyx and ready for travel, his few possessions in a knapsack. He told Ellen he could see she was getting on all right without Pastor Carl so he would go with the patrol in the hope of experiencing a white man's war. Since she had no use for Onyx he would take the horse with him.

Ellen insisted that Onyx belonged to the mission and must stay behind, then she was at a loss for what more to say. Ivor came to her aid by declaring it a foolish notion to think there was anything to be learnt from the white man about war. Aijang should go with the patrol if he must, but as soon as he could he should return to his own people. If yellow men came from outside and picked a fight with the whites he should just leave them to it.

When the patrol was finally out of sight Ellen sent Aino to check that everything was well with Onyx. As he raced away she said to Ivor that the boy was indeed Carl's son. Ivor showed little reaction to this admission, so Ellen asked if he already knew about Aino.

In answer Ivor said that circumstances dictated that there were quite a few half-castes in New Guinea; if he were honest he might be responsible for some himself. Every man should be allowed a few moments of weakness. It was usually just a matter of luck whether these moments had serious consequences or not.

Ivor took a moment then admitted, 'I have two daughters by native women. I don't interfere, just keep an eye out from a distance.'

'Do your daughters know you?' Ellen asked.

'They have their fathers in the villages. It's better that way.'

Ellen went to Ivor and put her arms around him. His response was awkward but eventually his arms came to rest in a suitable place. The embrace lingered for several moments.

'You'll have me blubbering like a child if you keep this up,'

Ivor began when they stepped back from each other. 'That wouldn't do.'

'You're a good man, Ivor. But why do you deny yourself so much? After everything you've been through.'

'I see it more as freedom. I like to be outside, looking in.'

The conversation returned to Carl. Ellen said that she still couldn't believe that he had slept with a native woman, but she was grateful that his son had become her child. 'I would like to take Aino back to Australia, but I worry he might face prejudice, even from my own family. I don't think I could bear that.'

Ivor said that in his experience the highlanders were much more open-minded about race than Australians, which was a good reason for Ellen to extend her stay in the highlands. And perhaps it would be no bad thing for the boy to grow up in the place of his birth. The people would accept him; in time he might even become a leader. The highlanders would surely be in need of strong leaders.

Ellen insisted that, since Carl was white and she was white, Aino should also be considered white. He should therefore grow up in the white world.

Six

After numerous conversations on the radio Luke had agreed to visit the Wahgi again. With no local help and few trade goods left Ellen struggled with the preparations, but she told Aino that Pastor Luke would be satisfied with whatever they were able to give him.

'He's looking well, Ellen,' Luke said as soon as he saw Aino. 'How old is he now?'

Ellen said that she estimated Aino's age at around four, whereupon Luke suggested an impromptu birthday party. With some tinned food that he had brought, a quickly baked cake, a game of hide and seek and a selection of simple songs, a celebration was improvised that lasted well into the evening. At Aino's behest Luke performed several tricks, making a playing card appear in and disappear from his hand at will, then unerringly finding a card that Aino had selected and returned facedown to a pack that was then shuffled. Finally, Aino was presented with a magnet and a collection of small metal objects that he took happily to his bed. When he was asleep Ellen said that she could not remember the last time she had enjoyed herself so much.

Before leaving for the west the next morning Luke said that according to enquiries he had made Alfred Fiebiger and the other German missionaries were faring well enough in Australia. It appeared that their greatest tribulation was boredom. Luke hoped that they would receive a report he had sent on developments in the missions since their departure. They would surely take comfort from the fact that their converts were eagerly awaiting the day of their return.

*

Luke was back from his journey to the west sooner than expected. An evangelist he had intended to visit had disappeared, having taken a local woman without paying a bride price, and as a result the people had proved hostile. They had demanded payment if they were to listen to what Luke had to tell them, and without Aijang to interpret he had lacked sufficient means of communication to convince them of his good intentions. The parting had been on poor terms.

There was still another day until the plane was scheduled to return for Luke and Ellen suggested a picnic at the swimming spot. She said it was a beautiful place where they could forget the troubles of the world. As they walked, each holding one of Aino's hands, Ellen provided Luke with a truncated version of her first experience of the place.

'The native girls were fascinated by my swimming costume and by the especially pale parts of my skin. I'd forgotten how white I am.'

Luke began a light conversation with Aino that continued until the river became audible and Aino ran to meet it. Ellen and Luke hung back and watched as Aino picked up some loose stones and threw them into the water. Then Luke spoke.

'You're doing very well with him, if I may say so.'

'But deep down you disapprove. You think he should be with his real mother.'

An urgent call from Aino to hurry up cut the discussion short. Luke was quickly at the river, where he demonstrated with sharp movements of the palm of his hand how the water could be turned into a projectile. Aino practised the manoeuvre several times then called for a competition. Ellen spread out a blanket and unpacked the picnic as she watched the game.

Aino's excitement carried over into the picnic lunch. He asked where Luke had learnt all his tricks, to which he replied that they went back to the practicalities of growing up on a farm. This led Ellen to ask for his best memories of childhood, and he talked about winter in Nebraska—of the snow that blanketed the land and of the exhilaration he felt as he and his brothers and sisters, wrapped up against the freezing cold, sped down the slopes near their house on toboggans. Ellen sensed that Aino's imagination was struggling and sought to help, but she quickly left off with the admission that snow and toboggans were also quite foreign to her. Luke said he hoped that one day she and Aino would be able to experience these things.

When Aino had finished eating and gone back to the water Ellen told Luke about a letter she planned to write to her parents. She recapitulated the reasons she had previously given her family for her delayed return, primarily a claim that she was needed because of a new outbreak of disease among the highlanders, then said that it was now time to tell the truth. She would write about Aino, but while he was the initial reason there was now something else keeping her in New Guinea.

Luke was quiet and Ellen waited. Finally, Luke said that he was glad she had spoken; he had also wanted to speak but feared being rebuffed. He would write to Hilda to ask her to release him from their engagement, but with the war interrupting everything they would need to be patient.

Aino was demanding permission to swim, and Ellen and Luke joined him. The water was cold but with energetic activity their bodies acclimatised and they spent a delightful time splashing and swimming. At one point Luke dived and stood on his hands with his legs protruding from the water. Aino laughed and shouted as if such a sight was beyond his imagining, then Ellen had to restrain him from trying to emulate the feat. There were tears and the beginnings of a tantrum before Luke lifted Aino onto his shoulders and calmed him.

On the walk back to the house Ellen reached for Luke's hand but he said they should wait. She would think him very straitlaced, but he would not feel comfortable until he had Hilda's permission. After this they were studiously solicitous of each other, staying close but avoiding even the slightest touch.

In the middle of the night Ellen got out of bed to confirm that Aino was asleep then tiptoed to the back bedroom. She whispered Luke's name and he responded. She quietly closed the door behind her then sat at the end of the bed.

'I think Carl would approve,' she said.

Luke said that when the war was over he and Ellen would go

to America. He would introduce her to his family, who would be sure to love her, at first for his sake and then for her own. He would meet with Hilda to explain what had happened. Then he and Ellen would decide on their future, which might involve a return to New Guinea.

'And Aino?' Ellen asked.

'He will come with us to America. But it might be easier if he had a new name. I was thinking of Adam.'

The discussion moved to Ellen's immediate future. Luke said that if she came to Madang the authorities there might pressure her to return to Australia. It might therefore be best if for the time being she remained in the highlands. He would arrange for trade goods and medical supplies to be sent to her, and he would visit again as soon as possible.

After a period of quiet sitting Ellen said that after her first meeting with Luke at the Fiebigers' house she had sometimes found herself comparing him and Carl, often to the latter's disadvantage. She had known that these comparisons were not fair to Carl, because his competitor was largely a creation of her imagination. But as she had come to know Luke better, through their radio conversations and then in person, she had found that what she had imagined had been very close to the truth.

Seven

When Ellen was next in the village she was asked whether the man with the strangely coloured hair who had twice come and gone in the aeroplane would return to replace Pastor Carl. She explained that there would be no replacement until the big fight far away across the ocean was finished, which led some of the women to suggest that she take Pastor Carl's place herself. She replied that she lacked the necessary knowledge and experience, saying that she had been baptised only after she had met Pastor Carl. After taking some time to digest this information the women said that it didn't matter; she was sure to know more about Jesus than they did.

When Ellen returned to the house she searched through Carl's papers and found translations into the local language of a number of stories from the New Testament. She spent the rest of the afternoon admiring Carl's work and remembering the comfort she had taken from these stories when she had first heard them.

The following Sunday the parable of the good Samaritan and the miracle of Lazarus's resurrection were generally well received, but after the inevitable questions some of the women said that they had already heard these stories several times from Pastor Carl. Ellen promised something new for the following

Sunday, having in mind a translation of the story of Christ's birth that Carl had begun but not finished. She spent several afternoons completing the translation, taking great trouble over words such as 'sheep' and 'angel' for which there were no local equivalents.

The idea that a baby born to an ordinary woman was the son of the one and only God aroused scepticism among the villagers, and the justifications Ellen offered, including the idea of a virgin birth, made little headway. She was relieved when one of the women asked if she would play the harmonium so they could sing hymns, which they had enjoyed doing with Pastor Carl.

Ellen had deliberately chosen the open air for the bible readings, fearing the state of disrepair and the memories she might find inside the church. But when she entered she saw that the interior was in good order; there were even fresh flowers on the sheet of protective bark that covered the harmonium. The memory of Carl that came was of his legs pumping furiously at the harmonium's pedals.

After taking a few minutes to familiarise herself with the foibles of the instrument, which included several keys that produced little to no sound, Ellen played some simple hymns to which she sang the English words. The crowded church clapped in time and applauded loudly at the end. She promised that she would practise her playing and find the hymns that Pastor Carl had translated before the following Sunday.

Over the subsequent weeks hymn singing replaced bible stories as the centre point of the village's Sunday mornings. The enthusiasm of the singers was often not matched by an ability to hold a tune, and Ellen found herself adopting the instructive attitude of the conductor of the university chorus, correcting mistakes and coaxing those who were struggling through the more difficult passages. Increasingly she concentrated on a small group of women and girls who demonstrated true singing voices, encouraging them to stay behind to practise more intensely when the others had gone. In addition to hymns she taught some English carols and folk songs, and she was impressed by the capacity of her pupils to pronounce the foreign words and to learn by heart the initially incomprehensible texts. The idea formed in her mind of transforming these voices into an accomplished choir; she even imagined conducting a performance that was received with thunderous applause in the Adelaide Town Hall. This dream gave way to the thought that a nativity play would be a suitable goal for herself and the choir. Christmas was still some months away, time enough to write a script, select and train a cast and ensure that the music was rehearsed to the point of perfection.

Eight

When Ellen saw the woman approaching the house her heart began to race. Ivor was there and she asked him to tell the woman to go. She found Aino and together they went to the dining room and waited.

'She says she knows Carl has gone for good,' Ivor said when he was back inside. 'Her husband has withdrawn his objection to her keeping the boy, so she's come for him.'

Ellen asked Ivor again to tell the woman to go, but he said he doubted she would take any notice. In response Ellen took Aino by the hand and went out the back door of the house and up the hill. They were past the garden when the sound of the woman's voice prompted Ellen to look back. Aino wanted to know where they were going and Ellen asked if he knew who the woman was. He said she was his first mother who had brought him here from their village in search of his father.

For several minutes there was a stand-off, Aino's mother and Ellen staring in each other's direction, before Ellen yielded and led Aino back to the house. She approached the woman, and Ivor came to translate.

'He's mine now,' Ellen began.

The woman held out her arms to Aino, but he clung tightly to Ellen. The woman spoke to him in a native language, but he did not respond. Ellen used the empty moment to justify her claim to Aino. His father was white, which entitled him to a life in the white world where he would have access to all of human knowledge and culture. If he were to stay in New Guinea his life would be narrow and stunted.

When Ivor had finished translating he said that Ellen needed to speak of more familiar, less abstract things. She sought out and held the woman's eyes. 'I lost my first child in the womb. After I came to New Guinea my husband was often away and there was no child. Aino came to me as a gift from God.'

The woman was unmoved. She said that in her world the loss of a child was a common thing, while white women had medicines and a hospital down on the coast. And Ellen was young; she would find a new husband and have children of her own. She should give back the child who was not hers.

The woman snatched at Aino, but Ivor restrained her. She spoke again and Aino muttered a few words in reply that the woman seized on. 'She says Aino remembers her and acknowledges her as his mother,' Ivor translated.

Ellen took the slender bracelet she was wearing and held it out to the woman. There was no reaction and Ellen hurried Aino back inside the house, keeping him close as she grabbed pieces of jewellery from a box in her bedroom. She was soon outside again, approaching the woman, holding out the additional pieces of jewellery.

'She insists Carl is not the boy's father,' Ivor intervened. 'She concocted the story because she thought he would be better off with Carl. She says the father is another white man, a *kiap*.'

Ivor suggested that they go and sit on the verandah and talk about what to do. Ellen gestured to Aino. She felt a moment of hope when he took her hand, but this feeling was short-lived.

'You believe her, don't you,' Ellen said to Ivor when they were sitting.

He shrugged his shoulders. 'Sometimes I think they have a different view of truth from us. I've never been able to get to the bottom of it.'

'But you think I should give him up?'

'There might be a fight if you don't. She says her husband and a troop of warriors are waiting nearby. A word from her and they will come and take him by force.'

For a moment Ellen imagined herself seeking out Mbagl in the village. He would immediately gather together a group of village men to protect her and Aino with spears and axes. The mission house would become an impregnable fortress.

When she returned from this interlude Ellen let her fingers touch Aino's face. 'My darling boy,' she said.

War

(1941–1943)

One

Luke met Ellen at the landing strip and they drove in and out of the sight and smell of the sea. As she sat in the rattling car she described the Adelaide beaches she was reminded of, the warm sand and the soft ocean stretched out like a lightly ruffled sheet on a large bed. Then she fell silent again, looking vaguely from side to side, picturing Aino's reactions if he had been there.

When they reached the compound Luke stopped the car in front of the place where Ellen was to stay, a building of native materials on stilts standing over pieces of lawn and beds of bright flowers edged with white stones. He said they would eat together in another building close by where meals had been taken by the students when the school had been in operation. Now Ellen had come they could think about restarting the school, which would give her something to do.

The pair continued to sit, occasionally acknowledging the native children who competed for their attention by rapping on the car windows. Luke eventually spoke, saying his letter to Hilda was long gone on a ship to Sydney. In normal times it would now be well on its way across the Pacific, but in current circumstances who could say where it was.

Near the compound were gardens belonging to the mission.

Ellen was introduced to the women working there but was left at a loss when they spoke to her in pidgin. Luke explained that pidgin was entrenched on the coast and too useful to ignore. He would teach her the rudiments and she would see what he meant. She might even come to enjoy the bluntness of the language, its refusal to beat around the bush. As if to demonstrate Luke spoke to the native women and a lively discussion began. Ellen's immediate impression was of an adult talking to small children, but as the conversation proceeded she found herself concentrating so hard on the words that this impression dissolved.

While she quickly acclimatised to the conveniences of her new home Ellen found the heat and humidity difficult to cope with. The presence of the ocean on her doorstep was only partial compensation. And when darkness came the mosquitoes descended, leaving her struggling to sleep huddled under a mosquito net. Despite the precautions she soon fell sick. Luke fetched a stout white woman who sat beside her and asked if she was experiencing any nausea, whether she had headaches, ringing in the ears or loss of hearing. The woman examined her thoroughly and concluded that it was a standard case of malaria from which she would almost certainly recover. She adjusted the dosage of quinine and said there was nothing more she could do.

When her strength returned Ellen went for regular walks along the beach. She swam in the tepid water and gave herself up to the buoyancy of the ocean. She stood with her eyes shaded to watch the imperceptible progress of an occasional ship against the horizon and imagined herself and Luke on their way to America. Sometimes Aino was there with them, and she cried until all her tears were gone.

On subsequent walks more and more ships were to be seen, heading in one direction then the other. Luke explained that preparations were being made all along the coast for war with Japan. If war did come the remaining white women would be evacuated. Ellen should return to Australia until the fighting was over. He would continue at the mission as long as he could.

*

There was an outpost of the mission in the hinterland, along a tributary of the Ramu river. One of Luke's evangelists was in charge and urgently in need of help. It was difficult country and no place for a white woman, but Ellen said that she would take medical supplies and provide what help she could. Luke agreed that she could accompany him.

The journey to the river was through oppressive heat, humidity and heavily vegetated country, and by the first afternoon Ellen was close to exhaustion. An improvised stretcher was made from a piece of canvas and two poles cut from the bush. As she lay she listened fitfully to the pidgin conversation between the carriers and Luke, which centred around how impossibly light her body was, almost as if it was made from air.

Ellen's exhaustion and a mosquito net soaked in peppermint oil enabled her to sleep through the night, and the next morning she had sufficient strength to walk unaided. Her long pants and high socks were not enough to protect her from the leeches that surreptitiously attached themselves to her, but one of the carriers was quick to use lighted matches to force the greedy creatures to loosen their grip. She shared a pleasant moment of accomplishment with the man.

Ellen's relief at reaching the river was dampened by the sight of the cut-out log that was to transport them to the mission station. Half-jocular warnings about crocodiles heightened her anxiety. Luke handed her into the vessel and warned her against making any abrupt movements, and when she sat she reduced her body to its smallest possible size.

Two young men, one at each end of the log canoe, stood as they paddled, expertly adjusting their weight to maintain their balance. As the vessel increased its speed a breeze began to flow, bringing coolness to the skin and a freedom from pestering insects. The paddlers started a low chant and Ellen felt her body lighten and expand as she joined in. It was all she could do to stop herself plunging an arm into the flowing water to feel its texture and pressure and to watch the ripples that it would create.

After half an hour of exquisite freedom the canoe was manoeuvred into a small indentation in the shore below a sharp rise. Ellen was lifted onto a piece of brown sand where she was instantly submerged in a dark, buzzing cloud. Waiting men used large banana leaves to slap away the mosquitoes, beating the backs and heads of the new arrivals in the process. Multiple hands assisted Ellen and Luke up the steep incline.

At the top of the cliff the insect clouds partially dispersed and the beating with the leaves was scaled back to a gentle brushing. The party was led through a bevy of children and animals to a hut that consisted of a high roof and half-height walls on two sides. A crude cross was tied to one of the walls. There was nothing but bare ground to sit on. The only movement of air came from the continued light brushing of backs with the banana leaves.

Ellen understood none of the excited words that were spoken, and to begin with Luke also seemed lost. A stocky man sitting next to them with teeth and gums reddened by betel nut provided a precis that was unintelligible to Ellen, but after several short exchanges with the man Luke nodded his understanding.

The assembly waited. Luke found his voice in the local language and before long he was engaged in a lengthy monologue. An elderly man gave a brief reply, full of gesticulations that seemed to Ellen to indicate confusion or dissatisfaction. Others joined in and the discussion threatened to become a free-for-all, the speakers interrupting or talking over each other.

When order was restored several questions seemed to be addressed to Ellen. Luke responded on her behalf and there were follow-up questions and answers before the men were satisfied.

Things to eat and drink were brought on plates made from leaves and in cups fashioned from bamboo stalks. As she toyed with the food Ellen asked Luke about his speech. He said he had told the villagers that yellow men from far away who did not believe in Jesus might sometime soon appear in their land.

If these men came near they should run away and hide in the bush. If white men came they should help them. Before long the white men would drive the yellow men away and the village would be richly rewarded.

The stocky man hovered nearby and Luke introduced him to Ellen. His name was Hune; he was an evangelist who came from a village near Madang. He said he had done his best, but the inhabitants of this place were too backward. They had asked for proof of the power of his god and he had demonstrated the cutting ability of a steel axe and the fire-making capacity of matches. For a time this had satisfied them, but now they were demanding more and he had nothing to give.

'I don't think I can convince Hune to stay any longer,' Luke said to Ellen when he had finished translating. 'He says he's been preaching the Gospel of peace and now the whites are preparing for war. The people will laugh at him.'

Luke went on, 'I doubt anyone from here has been as far as the coast. The labour recruiters rarely come this far. There's an occasional *kiap* and a few crocodile hunters but hardly anything more. You're probably the first white woman they've ever seen.'

Ellen reached for Luke's hand. She said she could never have imagined a place as primitive as this. It was truly the end of the earth. Then she reminded Luke that she wanted to examine the children.

Protracted negotiations with several elderly men followed, after which a line of children escorted by their mothers began to file past Ellen. She ascertained with mixed feelings that there were no signs of yaws. Some of the children showed indications of undernourishment and all were in need of a good wash, but by and large they seemed healthy enough, although bewildered by the process they were being subjected to.

After the inspection an old man came up and pointed at the untouched food and drink. As Ellen ate and drank the man sat down and watched then started a conversation with Luke. At various points he laughed and Luke joined in half-heartedly. The man smiled at Ellen and reached to touch her, but she shrank away.

'It was men's talk, wasn't it,' Ellen said when the man had wandered off.

Luke adopted a lightly ironic tone. 'He says I should leave you here and they'll put flesh on your bones. When I return you'll be ready for my bed and we can make a white child. We should bring the child to show them.'

When the eating and drinking were finished an offer came through Luke's evangelist to spend the night in the village. After a fitful conversation with some of the village men Luke returned to say that they were insistent and it would be disrespectful not to comply. They were shown a place where they could sleep then taken to a stinking pit toilet submerged beneath swarms of insects. Ellen asked Luke to stand guard while she went further into the bush.

Two

By the time Ellen and Luke got back to the coast the Pacific War had begun. The Europeans from the government post and the missions were busy seeking out each other to discuss the implications. Ellen told everyone she met about her nursing training, hoping that this would exempt her from the repatriation of European women that was certain to take place.

Days passed and no word came from the administration, and attention turned to preparations for Christmas. Ellen did her best with the local help, putting up decorations in the place where she and Luke ate and supervising the cooking of cakes and biscuits, but she admitted to Luke that she was no great shakes as a cook. She suspected that as an American he would be used to something more elaborate than she was capable of. Luke said that there was never much money in his family, but his parents had always succeeded in making Christmas a memorable time, largely due to their inventiveness. Thankfully there had always been enough to keep the cold at bay; this in itself had been sufficient to create a mood of celebration.

An invitation came to Christmas lunch at the government post and Luke suggested they attend. There would be plenty to eat and there might be news about evacuation plans. Ellen hesitated, saying she did not have anything suitable to wear and wondering whether there would be awkward questions about her and Luke. But eventually she agreed.

The lunch was held in an airy building set back from a beach with a wide view of the ocean. There were large tables loaded with European food in tins and local vegetables and fruit, along with copious supplies of alcoholic drinks cooled in a pair of refrigerators. There were streamers draped from the ceiling and party hats for each person. Ellen counted only a handful of women among the nearly forty guests who congregated around, although at the far end of the room a group of nuns all in white sat at a separate table and entertained themselves with quiet conversation. The nurse who had treated Ellen's malaria came and asked after her health then introduced a man of middle age with whom she said Ellen would have a lot in common.

'Father Denze has also recently come down from the highlands,' the woman told Ellen as she left them alone.

Ellen accepted the man's hand and he said she should address him as 'Tom'.

'You're German?' she asked tentatively. 'I thought all the Germans had been sent to Australia.'

'Some of us have managed to hang on here, by the skin of our teeth.' There was acknowledgement on both sides of the clumsy image.

Tom Denze explained that the new government man in Mount Hagen had introduced severe restrictions on the movement of German missionaries and as a result they were unable to minister to their people. He had come to Madang to argue the case for greater freedom with the district administrator, whom he knew from his years on the coast before he had gone to the highlands. But with Japan's entry into the war he now feared further restrictions, even internment. He had nothing against spending more time in Australia, which he had passed through on his way to New Guinea, but not as a prisoner.

'Sometimes I almost forget that Australia exists,' Ellen said. She glanced around the room. 'Except on days like today.'

'Unfortunately, I do not have the luxury of forgetting that Germany exists.'

A man with an authoritative voice called for everyone to find a place to sit. Ellen saw that Luke was immersed in another group and she allowed the priest to lead her to a table.

Food was brought and Tom Denze gave his attention to a large steak. When he drew breath he said, 'We brought cattle into the Hagen area last year. You can imagine the impression they made on the locals.'

'There are no cattle yet in the Wahgi Valley. Just my husband's horse, which is famous throughout the district.'

When the exchange of small talk had ended Ellen asked the priest about the Catholic presence in the highlands.

'A handful of us, Germans and Americans, went south from Madang in 1933, across the Ramu then up through the mountains to the Wahgi. From there we spread out to the west, eventually as far as Hagen. Your people were in the highlands well before us, but they came from the east, first to the Upper Ramu, then the Goroka Valley and the Wahgi. Later they also used the northern route into the highlands, and like us they spread out to the west.'

Ellen mentioned Pastor Sven Jonsson and Tom Denze said that he knew this man mainly by reputation, which was that of a loner. On the only occasion they had met Jonsson had been distant and awkward, and what he had said had made it clear that he wanted as little as possible to do with Roman Catholics.

'But I knew your husband well,' the priest went on. 'He was cut from a very different cloth.'

Ellen waited for an upwelling of tears to subside. Then she asked about the priest's relationship with Carl.

'We met as competitors for souls, but over time we were able to put our rivalry aside. We talked about what had led us to New Guinea, about our expectations for our missions, about Germany and what has gone so badly wrong. He told me about his father, and he told me about you.'

Father Denze waited before replying to Ellen's unspoken question. 'He worried that his own struggles would weigh you down. But he said you had a great capacity for happiness.'

The priest pointed to a bottle of wine and Ellen accepted a small glass. He poured himself a similar amount. The volume of the surrounding conversation indicated that the consumption of alcohol was elsewhere in full swing.

'A small island of whites,' Father Denze remarked, 'huddled together for comfort and courage.'

Ellen brought the conversation back to Carl, asking if the priest had any idea what might have happened to him.

'I can only think it was a terrible accident. Such things are always possible in New Guinea, even to someone as capable as Carl.'

A voice called out that Tom Denze should not monopolise the female company, him being a priest and she not even a Catholic. Ellen waited for the ruction to die away before continuing.

'Some of Carl's colleagues thought he was more interested in understanding the people than in bringing them to Christ. Was that your impression?'

'We talked a lot about the great variety of languages in New Guinea. Carl thought this variety was the result of a long process of divergence from a few original forms, perhaps a single form, caused by the isolating effect of the country's mountainous terrain. I could follow him in this. But he was in the process of extending his thinking beyond languages and beyond New Guinea to the development of different life forms, including human life. There he left me behind.'

Ellen remembered writings of Carl's that she had found among his papers, bold headings followed by long paragraphs of tight script that started tentatively, built up momentum then fell away. A recurring theme was regret at the lack of what Carl called 'useful knowledge'. 'I've wasted much of the time I've spent on this earth,' he had written.

Tom Denze continued. 'He also wondered about the different levels of civilisation of the New Guineans and the Australian Aborigines with whom his father had worked. He had come to believe that these differences were mainly due to the reliable rainfall of New Guinea, which made it a much more hospitable place for human life than the arid lands of Australia.'

A Santa Claus dressed in an improvised costume with a sack over his back bounded into the room to loud cheers. He made immediately for the far table where he ceremoniously presented each of the nuns with a piece of military attire—a slouch hat, a belt, a shirt, a lanyard—to stand them in good stead if the Japs came. Ellen was next, receiving a string bag with tins of food including marmalade and a plum pudding. When it came to the men, one of the *kiaps* received a voluptuous pin-up draped in an Australian flag, another a cartoon of a superior with his tongue uncomfortably close to the rear end of the top man in Lae. For the American clergy there were cigarettes made from bits of newspaper and local tobacco and small denomination coins hidden in shoe boxes full of sawdust. For the few Germans there was a map of Europe with Germany shrunk to the size of Luxembourg and the mangled text of a well-known German poem. Father Denze by contrast received an official-looking certificate conferring on him honorary Australian citizenship.

When the hubbub died down the priest told Ellen that the certificate meant a lot to him. He thought that by and large the Australians were doing their best to bring New Guinea into the modern world with as little violence as possible. Most of the *kiaps* he had come across seemed to have the interests of the locals at heart, even if many were too young and inexperienced to understand the complexity of the task confronting them. Of course, there were some who let their power over the people go to their heads, who were too quick to grab for their rifles at the first sign of trouble, and others who seemed to go out of their way to make things difficult for the missions.

Boisterous Christmas carols made further conversation difficult. When the singing ended Ellen was pressed by several *kiaps* in turn into dancing to music from a gramophone. She whirled in the men's arms until she was exhausted, all the time hoping that Luke would rescue her.

As the party began to dissolve the district administrator read out a message directing all women and other non-essential personnel to prepare for immediate evacuation. A plane would shuttle them to Kainantu in the eastern highlands, from where they would be flown south to safety. The only luggage allowed would be one small suitcase.

Ellen told Luke that once in the highlands she would find a way to avoid being sent further south. She would return to the Wahgi Valley and wait for him there.

Three

Mbagl said that he had kept a careful watch over the house and Misis would find everything just as she had left it. The garden had also been well maintained and the berries on the coffee trees had started to change colour. If Misis could explain what should be done with them he would follow her instructions. She said she would look in Pastor Carl's books for an answer, but first she needed to rest.

The return to the mission house had been beset with difficulties. The man in charge at Kainantu had initially insisted that Ellen travel on to Port Moresby with the others, and it had taken several interventions from Leo Fiocchini to bring about a grudging change of mind. In the absence of available Europeans Leo had assigned a pair of native policemen to accompany her on the long walk to the Wahgi Valley, but despite his assurance of their reliability they had failed to win her trust. She had been constantly on the alert for any signs or sounds of danger and had slept little, and she had dreaded the calls of nature that had emphasised her vulnerability. She did not understand the men's language and had imagined their conversations to be full of demeaning assessments of her capacities in the bush and the value of their assignment. Her attempts at pidgin had been met with offhand answers that deterred further conversation.

It had been agreed with the Kainantu authorities that she would gather essential things from the mission house then travel on to Mount Hagen, where a plane would take her to Port Moresby. From Moresby she would travel by ship to Australia. Leo had assured her that, with the Japs coming closer, the remaining white civilians on the north coast would soon be evacuated to Australia. She had deflected the implied question about Luke by asking why the Japanese would bother with New Guinea. Leo's answer had been that it was a stepping stone to Australia, or part of a strategy of isolation. Whichever way, they would not succeed.

*

After a deep sleep Ellen woke to a strong sense of homecoming. She savoured the clarity of the air, the beauty of the mountains, the perfection of the house and her own sense of safety. She was less sure about the memories of Carl and Aino that surrounded her, alternatively indulging and resisting them.

Over the next few days several women came up the hill with food to exchange. In the rush of her departure from Madang she had forgotten to stock up on trade goods, so she had to limit her purchases, but she was prevailed upon to accept eggs and other delicacies on credit. Her admission that she was not sure when she would be able to repay the loan was waved away, as was her attempted explanation about the Japanese and the war. She gave assurances that she would soon resume her health clinics, although she knew that the supply of medicines would not last long. She also promised that the Sunday hymn singing would start again.

The next morning Kubun knocked on the front door and asked for his job back. He explained that his wife had been unfaithful, he had sent her away and he was not looking for another wife because wives were too much trouble. He said that when the bride price was returned by his wife's family he would be wealthy. All he asked was to be allowed to live in the hut at the back and work in the house alongside Misis. The no-good man who was constantly watching her had been living in the hut; Misis would have to tell him to leave.

Later in the day Ellen spoke to Luke. He told her that the authorities were setting up a network of coast watchers and were about to commandeer the mission's radio. If she needed to reach him she could send a note with a native runner; he would keep in touch by the same method. Ellen pleaded with him to join her in the safety of the highlands, but he replied that if the Japanese came the people would hide him. In the meantime, he must continue the work of the mission.

*

Ellen was in the front room when she heard muted noises from outside. A small group of whites was climbing the hill, making hard work of it. Ellen went out to the verandah to greet them.

'They told us down below that you were still here,' a voice panted.

Marjorie Stebbins, the bulky nurse from the coast, was with two of the other women who had left at the same time as Ellen. She had imagined them weeks ago in Port Moresby or Australia and asked what had happened. When Marjorie had regained her breath, she explained, 'The aeroplane that was to take us south crashed on landing. The pilot escaped serious injury, but the plane was extensively damaged. Before a replacement could be found the Japs came over and bombed the airstrip. Initially the strip could be repaired, but finally it all got too much. After lots of dithering it was decided that we should go overland to Mount Hagen and fly out from there. A party of natives is guiding us.'

Ellen explained her own continued presence in the Wahgi Valley by saying that she was perfectly safe and there was always something to be done for the people. The visitors replied that the Japanese now had airfields on the coast and their bombers could easily reach this far. Marjorie elaborated, 'At first, they took Rabaul; now they're at Lae and Salamaua. Apparently, they've even bombed Madang.' She was quick to add that she was sure the whites there would have retreated inland, so Pastor Sommer would be safe.

Ellen could sense that Marjorie still felt the need to justify her decision to join the exodus from Madang, despite the shortage of nurses there. She repeated what she had told Ellen during the flight to Kainantu. She had already overstayed her time in New Guinea; her health demanded a return to Australia.

The visitors were encouraged to stay and rest but they stressed the need to get to Hagen as soon as possible, given uncertainties about the availability of planes and the state of the landing strip. Marjorie did her best to convince Ellen to come with them. She said a young *kiap* named Leo had told her that if she found Ellen still at the mission house she should use every means possible to convince her to join the trek to Hagen.

'He's obviously carrying a torch for you. I told him you were spoken for, but he said he hasn't given up hope.'

Ellen gave Marjorie a brief note for Luke, on the off chance that he would find his way to Mount Hagen. She helped Kubun prepare bundles of food that could be easily carried then watched as the women made their way down the hill and disappeared. In the distance she heard the drone of an aeroplane, but it soon faded and she thought nothing more of it.

Four

In the months that followed Ellen felt herself in a state of limbo, cut off completely from the white world and the affirmation of identity it provided. She gradually returned to the village and its language, allowing herself to be drawn into the currents of its life, for long periods forgetting the collapsing world outside. Even when she forced herself to imagine battles being fought and won, lives being maimed or lost, the images lacked purchase on her feelings and quickly faded. Her memories of people and places beyond the highlands seemed diaphanous and weightless—although sometimes with effort she was able to conjure an image of Luke that would comfort her before fading away. But throughout this time she was not unhappy. The diminished reality of her own self was compensated by a heightened sensitivity to the natural world and to the humanity of the villagers, with whom she interacted increasingly as an equal.

When not in the village Ellen often joined Yere, who had continued to work in the garden all through Ellen's absence. Together the pair picked the ripened coffee cherries and spread them out to dry on a large piece of canvas, regularly turning them with a makeshift rake and covering them when rain threatened. Ellen stored the dried cherries in the house, promising to include Yere in the next step of the process. The passionfruit vine was pruned regularly and the ripe fruit found favour with all who tried it. Small pieces of bark were carefully peeled off the cinchona bush and collected in a bowl, Ellen undertaking to prepare a special drink following a recipe of Carl's. The result was pronounced undrinkable by both Yere and Kubun and Ellen explained that some of the essential ingredients were not available to her. She would search for alternatives and repeat the process.

At intervals Yere asked questions that strayed from the immediate issues of the garden. She asked where Ellen had gone after she had left the mission house and why she had returned, what her relationship was with the white man with the yellow hair, and who the Japanese were and what they wanted. She also asked whether Aino was really Pastor Carl's child. Ellen answered that Aino had returned to his first mother where he belonged; the Japanese were invaders from far away who would soon be repelled; she had gone to the coast to visit the blond white man and eventually she would live with him across the ocean in America, which she had shown Kubun on a map. But, for now, she was content to wait patiently in the Wahgi Valley for the future.

The spell of this time was broken when a sustained period of tension between Kubun and the watching man erupted in a serious fight. Ellen called for order then listened as Kubun accused the man of having brought women to the hut behind the house when Ellen was away. The watching man countered that Kubun had taken things from the house and exchanged them for favours in the village. Ellen told the man that he would have to leave the hut in favour of Kubun; he should finally give up watching her and return to village life. She told Kubun that if she ever found that he had stolen from her she would send him away in disgrace.

When she was back in the house Ellen realised that this was the first time she had heard the watching man speak more than a single word. As she replayed his voice she revised her estimate of his age. He was probably closer to thirty than twenty, much older than she had thought.

Five

When Ivor Moore finally came Ellen asked immediately about Aino. Ivor said that he had followed the woman and her clansmen to a village in the Upper Ramu. He had regular contact with natives from the area and would be kept abreast of the boy's progress. He would provide Ellen with regular reports.

The conversation turned to the war but neither had any concrete news. Ivor said he doubted the Japanese would bother with the highlands, which was the important thing.

'You're not tempted to join up?'

'What is it I'd be joining?'

'They're called the New Guinea Volunteer Rifles.'

Ivor suggested that the rifles in question probably came from the Great War and had not been fired since. In any event he was too old for that sort of thing. If the Japanese left him in peace he would not stand in their way.

'Men are wanted to watch the coast and report on enemy ship and aeroplane movements,' Ellen said encouragingly. 'You could use my radio.'

'Sounds like a fool's errand. Anyway, it's a long time since I've been on the coast. Wouldn't know my way around down there.'

Ellen took the opportunity to talk about her time in Madang.

She said it had been like visiting a metropolis, with shops run by Chinese and goods paid for with money. There were cars in the streets, ships in the harbour and electricity in the houses. And other whites to talk to, face to face. She had even been able to get her hair cut properly. When she had finished Ivor said that he did not miss any of that.

'Why do you come to see me if it isn't to talk to someone of your own kind in your own language?'

Ivor acknowledged there might be something to that. Then he said, 'There are reports of a white man in the mountains to the north, repairing bridges. From the description it could be Carl. Since no body has been found I thought you should know.'

Ellen withdrew behind an impassive face.

'I could try to find this man,' Ivor offered.

'I've asked the administration for a death certificate for Carl. I'm going to marry Pastor Luke Sommer and start a new life in America.'

'I'd heard there'd been a white man hanging around,' Ivor admitted. 'Things seem to have progressed pretty quickly.'

To explain herself Ellen provided details of Luke's background and his time in New Guinea. She said that he had a secure faith in God and his fellow men that encouraged her and gave her confidence in the future. He was a quiet man, but strong.

'I always thought Carl was strong,' Ivor said. 'But there might have been cracks somewhere, deep down. I suppose we all have cracks, deep down.'

'You think Carl took his own life?'

'I'd say he had a lot to live for. You shouldn't be reproaching yourself.'

'I tell myself it was the impossible goals he set or something inherited from his father. But it is very hard not knowing.'

There was an interlude of tea and small talk, then the conversation returned to the war. Ivor said that if the Yanks were serious they would win, just like in France the last time. It might take a while—he'd heard the Japanese were tenacious fighters—but America with all its might would eventually come out on top. And there could be no better place for Ellen to wait for peace to return than the Wahgi Valley, which would be well above the fray. Ivor would never be far away if she needed anything. All she had to do was to let one of the head men in the village know and a message would find its way to him in no time.

*

When Ivor had gone Ellen sat down to write a letter to Luke. She first described in detail the things she was doing to keep busy, occasionally embellishing the prosaic text in the interests of the story. Then she confessed that with the passage of time and without being able to see his face or hear his voice he was starting to drift away from her. She was beginning to wonder whether the time they had spent together and the commitment they had given each other belonged to the real world or were just figments of her imagination, a nervous reaction to Carl's disappearance. 'But then I remind myself of your many acts and words of kindness to me, and of your acceptance of Aino and your love for him. You are very real to me in these memories, and I regain my confidence in our future together.'

When she had finished Ellen put the letter in an envelope and called out to Kubun, but by the time he appeared she had changed her mind. She realised that a villager sent to the coast to find Luke might instead fall into the hands of the Japanese, and she did not want to take that risk.

Six

The aeroplanes flew in low and the noise was deafening. Ellen ran from the house and threw herself under a stand of trees. The noise screamed to a crescendo and threatened to shake her body apart before gradually retreating. The dull thud of explosions from the direction of the airstrip followed shortly after.

The first time the planes had come it had been early morning and they had been a tiny formation too high up to determine their markings. They had returned from the west an hour later, flying much lower. Ellen had been in the village and had tried to warn the people, but they had failed to appreciate the purpose of the planes and taken only half-hearted cover. When a barrage of bombs exploded nearby they had panicked and fled into the bush. Later on, a delegation had come to ask Ellen for an explanation. Some were convinced it was her presence that had drawn the attack and they demanded she leave. She countered that the airstrip had been the target; now that it was damaged the bombers would not come again.

After the second raid Ellen went straight to the village and convinced a number of the men to accompany her to the airstrip. Bomb craters in and around the strip confirmed Ellen's claim that it had again been the target of the Japanese. But a consensus formed among the men that since the landing strip belonged to the whites and Ellen was white she should leave or there would be more bombings. Ellen argued that America was strong and soon its planes would shoot the Japanese planes down, but she received nothing in reply but shrugged shoulders. She thought for a moment of getting out a map to show the relative size of America and Japan but realised it would be of no use.

A few of the women remained true to her, occasionally bringing food to the house and asking her opinion about problems they had. When she visited the village some children were still brought out to her, but her supply of medicines was exhausted and all she could do was re-emphasise the importance of cleanliness and keeping rubbish and excrement well away from the sources of drinking water. The reconvened reading and writing groups dwindled in numbers, swarms of boys raced around emulating attacking planes and Ellen wore herself out trying to restore order. More and more she found herself listening to the gossip of the women, occasionally intervening, asking questions and offering suggestions before withdrawing and leaving the women to themselves, only a little later to be drawn back into the conversation.

Sometimes before returning to the house Ellen would watch Waiya as she played with her friends. Waiya's mother was usually in the vicinity and Ellen had to stop herself seeking forgiveness for the suffering she could see in the girl's future. On one occasion the mother came and sat next to Ellen, asking amid their small talk why the medicine had failed in the case of her daughter. All Ellen could do was to promise that when the big fight against Japan was finished she would search everywhere to find help for Waiya, if not a remedy at least some amelioration. But whatever happened Waiya should be encouraged to continue her reading and writing. These things would become increasingly valuable as the outside world pushed deeper and deeper into the highlands, as it inevitably would.

Occasionally to pass the time Ellen would take long walks up the hill behind the house into the mountains, to the point where the lower reaches of the valley and their veneer of humanity became a pleasant blur. She would listen for bird calls and animal noises and remember how expert Aino had become at identifying each sound. At other times she would go to the swimming hole and immerse herself in the water, remembering Aino's attempts to emulate Luke by standing on his hands with his legs protruding above the surface. When she returned to the house she would help Kubun to prepare food and when night came she would read, often Carl's *National Geographic* magazines. When the topic was America she would remember telling Aino after Luke's last visit that this man would be his new father after all, and that one day soon they would all travel together to America. There they would live among white people, not the dark-skinned people pictured in the magazines they read together, and it would be important for Aino to remember that he was white and that his name was Adam.

Seven

Ellen had almost lost track of the days when a message came from Luke, brought by an exhausted lowlander who asked only for food and a place to sleep as payment. The note said that Japanese soldiers were in Madang and Luke had retreated to the hinterland. Together with a handful of others he intended to strike out over the mountains for Mount Hagen. Ellen should make her way to Hagen as soon as possible. From there they would be flown to safety.

Ellen asked Kubun to go to the village and find recruits to accompany her; there was little to carry so two strong men would do. Kubun stood to his full height and said that he would go with her, and he knew another suitable man who was sure to agree. He had heard that Mount Hagen was somewhere to the west; they could ask directions along the way, as long as the people were not hostile and their language comprehensible. He finished his plea by offering to put some of his returned bride price at Ellen's disposal to purchase food on the journey, provided she promised that he would receive what he had lent her and more when they reached their destination.

Ellen was still weighing up whether to put her fate in Kubun's hands when she saw a patrol winding its way up the hill to the house. Leo Fiocchini was the sole white man, leading a contingent of twenty New Guineans, half of whom were policemen with rifles, the other half carriers with food and equipment. As Ellen stood on the verandah Leo called up to her that he was on his way to rescue a group of nuns from the north coast who were in trouble. The nuns were no longer young and might need to be carried for some of the journey out, hence the size of the patrol.

Ellen invited Leo inside, but he said there was no time. She should pack a few necessities and come with him; he would escort her to Mount Hagen, from where she would be flown to Port Moresby. To Leo's obvious surprise Ellen agreed without hesitation, asking only for the opportunity to say her goodbyes in the village.

Most of the women were in their gardens when Ellen arrived, but word travelled quickly and soon a large group had assembled. Ellen explained that she had to go away again because of the big fight with the Japanese invaders. When asked when she would return she just shook her head. The women began to sing, to clap their hands and to sway from side to side, and Ellen succeeded briefly in emptying her mind of everything except the immediate sights and sounds. When thought returned she looked for Waiya, giving her a wide smile when she caught her eyes. She repeated this smile with the girl's mother. Then she started to leave, touching the many hands stretched out to her.

'Take her, Misis.' Waiya's mother was pushing her forward. 'Take her.'

When Ellen realised what was meant she said that she

couldn't; everything was too uncertain. She did not know if she would ever return, or if white doctors could help Waiya.

The woman waited and Ellen squatted and asked Waiya if she wanted to come with her to a place where she might be healed. The girl replied that she would go if Misis wanted her to, although she was frightened of flying in an aeroplane.

Ellen said that to begin with they would walk. Then they would go in an aeroplane, and Waiya would discover that it was a wondrous experience. She asked if there was anything Waiya would like to take with her for the journey, favourite things to remind her of home. Her mother said on her daughter's behalf that she would make do with whatever she was given.

When she returned to the mission house Ellen put aside her misgivings about Waiya and convinced Leo to do likewise. She gave the girl something to eat then found a pen and paper and sat down to write to Ivor Moore. She told him that she had greatly enjoyed his visits and would not forget him. She was sure he had been a true friend to Carl and for this she was grateful. She asked him to keep watch over the house, perhaps even to make it his home for the time being, since it would be a pity if such a fine structure were left to go to wrack and ruin. He might even find time to oversee the garden, and he might also know what should be done with Onyx. She ended by saying that when she reached her destination she would find a way of contacting him; then he could send her whatever information he had about Aino. She added as a postscript that Ivor should consider making himself known to his daughters, who might give him love that would sustain him as he grew older.

*

When they were underway Ellen told Leo she was glad that the policemen who had escorted her back from Kainantu were not part of the patrol. Leo said that these men had gravitated to Keith Dawes, with whom they saw better prospects of adventure and promotion. They were now with Keith and a small band of other Australians observing Japanese movements around Lae from the mountains north of the town. Leo had volunteered for the operation but had been given this guide job instead. Ellen said she was glad he was out of harm's way.

There was news of other mutual acquaintances. Gordon Davenport and Reg Thompson were in senior positions with the administration in Port Moresby, while Chas Noble had long since left New Guinea to join the air force. Murray Saunders and Dick Lacey were with the New Guinea Volunteer Rifles, last heard of recuperating in the hills around Wau, not far from the famous goldfield of Edie Creek.

Leo then talked more generally about the war. The Japanese had been stopped in the mountains north of Moresby several months before, but they still controlled large areas of the coast. They might try to take the highlands to prevent possible attacks from high ground on their coastal positions. The patrol would need to keep an eye out for Japanese planes.

Over the next several days the party adopted a regular rhythm for their journey through the grasslands, starting out each day at dawn, pausing after a few hours for food and drink then walking on until early afternoon, with some of the company scouting ahead for a camp site and for settlements where they could purchase food. The local villagers were wary, fearing that the patrol might bring Japanese planes down upon them or might abuse their women, but after some cajoling they brought food from their gardens and were reasonable in what they demanded in return. A large evening meal would be prepared around a campfire and the patrol would be asleep by ten o'clock. Ellen would sleep soundly and then wake, listening for Waiya beside her. She would fall back to sleep to the rhythm of the girl's breathing.

On the third morning Leo remarked that a native man appeared to be stalking them. He had sensed the man in the shadows of the night and during the day his shape had come and gone behind occasional trees and bushes. Some members of the patrol had been sent to find out what the man wanted, but he had eluded them. Ellen said it was bound to be nothing. Sometimes local people took it into their heads to follow her, but before long they realised that there was nothing extraordinary to be found in her behaviour. They inevitably grew bored and returned to their previous lives.

As the journey continued Waiya gravitated towards some of the younger native policemen who amused themselves by teaching her pidgin, in which she made quick progress. Leo spent most of his time walking next to Ellen, talking about his life before New Guinea and asking about hers. Then as they approached Mount Hagen Leo said that if it were up to him they would keep going past the government post into the mountains further west. It was rough country, but he knew of populated areas where sufficient food could be found. He then expanded on the prospect, saying that each day there would be a new goal—to reach a particular mountain or river, to sight a new animal, to communicate with a band of local people without ulterior motive and win their friendship. At night he and Ellen would sit together and write down what they had done and felt during the day. Then they would plan the next day.

Ellen asked if this was what had happened on the Davenport expedition. 'You and Gordon Davenport sitting together at the end of each day, reflecting and anticipating around the fire?'

Leo said that the expedition had contained exhilarating moments where he had stood at the edge of all he had previously known, excited by the challenges and possibilities. But there had also been difficulties. Thieving raids by local natives had threatened to get out of hand and Gordon had told Chas Noble to put a stop to them. Noble had resorted to excessive punishments and he and Gordon had fallen out. Then some of the policemen had been found to be running their own show, pillaging gardens and abusing women. Discipline among the line had started to fray. The need to keep the expedition from unravelling had become a constant preoccupation.

'The public reports made no mention of this,' Ellen said.

'Gordon had to be careful what he put down on paper. The administration wanted nothing negative getting back to Canberra, which was already unhappy about the expense. A lot was left between the lines.'

Leo concluded by casting back to an earlier topic. He said

that Gordon Davenport knew what had happened with Keith Dawes and the rogue German, but he had kept it quiet to protect Keith. 'He thought Keith's career was more important than a dead German.'

*

An extensive effort was being undertaken to upgrade the Hagen aerodrome, but the Japanese had sent in bombers to disrupt the work. When Ellen and Leo arrived a large contingent of natives was at work on repairs, but the harried officer in charge said it was a thankless task. As soon as the strip was patched up the Japanese would doubtless bomb it once more. He wasn't sure when it would be serviceable again.

Ellen's enquiry about Luke was met with a firm shake of the head. She was given directions to a nearby mission, but when she arrived there she found that the missionaries had gone, the house now surrounded by jeeps—the first motor vehicles Ellen had seen in the highlands—and occupied by a contingent of resting American airmen. The men were not aware of any white civilians in the vicinity, Australians or Americans, but they suggested that Ellen wait around to see if the lucky man she was asking about turned up. In the meantime, they would be more than happy to show her the sights around Hagen, which was a real beautiful place. Ellen demurred politely, and the men replied that this was too bad.

Ellen and Waiya slept in a tiny room in the government post. The night grew cold and Ellen got up to put an extra cover over the girl. Before going back to bed she went outside, where she found Leo sitting on the verandah with a blanket around his shoulders. He told her that news had come on the radio that Keith Dawes had been killed by the Japanese. He had been betrayed by some of the locals who had gone over to the other side. 'Fuckin' *kanakas*,' Leo cursed in a voice that was new to Ellen. 'Fuckin' Japs.'

Ellen put her arms around Leo. He reciprocated then pressed harder and harder until Ellen was forced to extricate herself and hold him at arm's length. He apologised in a flurry of tears, saying that he did not know what had come over him.

The pair continued to sit together through their embarrassment. In the midst of further apologies Leo said that ever since he had first met Ellen at the missionaries' meeting he had envied Carl. He still envied him, which he knew was not logical. And now there was another man standing in his way, someone seen only from a distance. He did not wish this man ill, but he could not but wish he had stayed in America, or at least on the coast well away from the highlands.

Ellen ignored the comment about Luke, instead asking whether Leo had seen or heard anything while Carl was with the Davenport expedition that would help to explain his disappearance. Leo overcame obvious reluctance to say that there had been an altercation between Carl and Chas Noble that had threatened to get out of hand. Carl had questioned the behaviour of some of the native policemen and Noble had derided him as a do-gooder. Carl had lashed out and would have beaten Noble half to death if he had not been forcibly restrained. Carl had broken down and wept, and soon afterwards he had turned his back on the expedition.

The next morning Ellen was confronted with the choice of heading directly back east with a few Hagen men as escort or continuing on with Leo and his patrol. She chose the latter course, encouraged by Leo's confidence that if Luke Sommer were still on his way to Hagen they would cross paths with him or hear of his whereabouts from local villagers. Leo said that he had quinine tablets and if all went to plan they would spend only a few days in malaria country before returning to the safety of the mountains.

As the patrol prepared to set off the throb of aircraft engines sent everyone racing to a deep trench hidden in the bush away from the compound. There were just a handful of planes and a handful of explosions before one of the soldiers announced the end of the morning's entertainment. Ellen calmed Waiya and told her that before long their side would shoot the enemy planes from the sky. Waiya asked who their side was and Ellen said it was Australia and America, big places full of good people who would do their best to help her. Soon they would visit Australia in an aeroplane. Waiya said she could still remember when Misis first came in an aeroplane and was carried up the hill to the mission house. At that time many of the people had not been sure she was real.

Eight

Ellen slipped and slid on the clay track, occasionally holding onto Leo to prevent herself from falling. There were steep ascents followed by sharp descents, the only positive the heavy covering of trees that shielded them from any danger from the sky.

For the first few days they came across no villages and they began to run short of food. Scouting parties were sent further and further forward to locate a settlement where food could be purchased and a guide procured to smooth their passage. A tiny hamlet was finally found but the inhabitants were only willing to part with a small amount of their meagre surplus, despite the abundant trade goods on offer. Rations were reduced for all but Ellen and Waiya.

At first the guide they had procured in the village exuded quiet confidence and competence, taking them on paths through the heavy undergrowth that were visible only to his trained eye. For an afternoon and a morning they made good progress, but then it became apparent that the guide had reached the limits of his knowledge. The paths he chose suddenly ended in a wall of impenetrable bush or at the edge of a precipitous cliff and they were forced to backtrack, losing valuable time and placing increased strain on their supply of food. The line members accused the man of deliberately leading them astray and eventually he admitted that he was afraid of the tribe whose territory they were about to enter. He was sent back to his village and the party returned to reliance on Leo's compass and the sketchy map he had been given in Mount Hagen.

There was heavy rain for a day and a night and the ground underfoot became treacherous. Leo called a temporary halt and the line huddled around a fire under a hastily constructed shelter, some of the men smoking foul-smelling tobacco and joking without humour about the cold and the dim prospects of decent food. Ellen took some spare clothes and wrapped them around Waiya, at the same time warming the girl as much as she could with her own body. There was coughing among the men and Ellen turned her face away and covered Waiya's mouth and nose.

The night brought an alarm when armed natives appeared silently at the edge of the camp. The sentries scared them off with a volley of rifle shots. Leo warned that an all-out attack might come with the dawn and they needed to be on their guard. The remainder of the night brought little sleep.

The next morning the patrol made its escape under a blanket of heavy mist that had descended in the night. There was no rest until mid-morning when a meagre breakfast was prepared. When they moved on any hope of easy progress was thwarted by a series of fast-running creeks without bridges. Waiya was carried across by the patrol members and Ellen stepped from rock to rock, holding onto Leo and banning from her mind any thought of what would happen if she slipped.

Then after a steep climb they were confronted by a rudimentary bridge swaying high above a fast-running stream. Leo directed two of the policemen to strengthen the bridge with rope, a task they performed slowly and methodically. When the bridge was declared ready Ellen inched her way across, part of the way on all fours, collapsing with exhaustion when she reached the other side.

Leo gave Ellen water to drink and sugar cane to chew. He offered to have a stretcher made so she could be carried, but she assured him that she would soon recover. She explained that seeing the policemen at work had reminded her of Carl repairing a bridge on the journey to the missionaries' meeting, but unlike these men Carl had taken unnecessary risks that had aroused a deep anxiety in her. She still felt this anxiety whenever she thought of Carl.

Leo said that some of the *kiaps* he knew went out of their way to expose themselves to danger, as if compelled to match their behaviour to the wild landscape and primeval humanity of New Guinea. He added that risking unnecessary danger was not the only eccentric behaviour that New Guinea encouraged in white men, but stopped himself from saying more.

*

'They're watching us, *masta*,' one of the policemen called out. 'I'll shoot over their heads.'

Native men were standing free from the cover of the bush, slight silent figures with hair piled up on top of their heads.

There were a few women as well and Leo said that this was a good sign. He gestured to the natives that the patrol needed food, displaying shells to indicate a willingness to pay. The onlookers seemed to need time to process this information.

As the line walked on the number of bush natives steadily grew to more than a hundred. Some began to speak and others made gestures that indicated the possibility of friendship. The volume of human noise increased until it was deafening. Leo demonstratively covered his ears several times and the noise began to abate.

The village they arrived at in the early afternoon was large and seemingly prosperous and it took little encouragement for food to be brought and traded in abundance, pig meat as well as vegetables. An earth oven was quickly dug for the pork with green leaves added, sweet potatoes were prepared for roasting and vegetables made ready for boiling.

During the wait for the meat to cook Ellen asked the villagers if they knew of a party of whites heading into the highlands from the coast, but none of them spoke pidgin and their vernacular was indecipherable. Gestures and signs were tried, but Ellen was left unsure whether the vigorous shaking of heads meant lack of comprehension or no knowledge of other whites in their territory.

The cooking time stretched on and the line struggled with its hunger, but when the feast was finally ready the mood became euphoric. With food in his belly Leo proved himself a gifted mimic, providing versions of various *kiaps* including Reg Thompson, Chas Noble and Gordon Davenport. The line natives laughed uproariously and urged Leo on, some even joining in the mimicry, while the wiry local men added to the entertainment with vigorous dances in a clearing beyond the campfire. Ellen joined in the merriment despite herself, laughing even when Leo parodied people unfamiliar to her. Then she busied herself with Waiya, who was falling asleep beside her.

Later in the night Ellen found Leo at the edge of the camp. He said that he needed time to regain his equilibrium after such a performance. He pointed out several specks of light on the surrounding hills and said they were campfires. Ellen remarked that it was a comfort to be surrounded by these signs of humanity, but Leo was sceptical. 'For all we know the natives sitting around these fires are planning to attack us and take our heads as souvenirs.' Ellen replied that this macabre thought did not suit him. His light-hearted mimicry had revealed a truer side of his nature, and in the future when she thought of him it would be this that she remembered.

*

They were several more days in the mountains, at the mercy of guides of varying degrees of communicativeness and competence. At various points Ellen was sure they had reached the summit, but a descent would be followed by another steep climb, on one occasion into a dusting of snow that she pressed into a tiny ball for Waiya to throw. The fatigue was unlike anything she had ever experienced but she pushed herself through, reassuring Leo each time he asked that she was capable of more. At least she felt no anxiety about Waiya, who was being well looked after by the patrol, carried when need be and constantly encouraged in pidgin.

There were no further villages until they were well into the final descent, and when after another full day they reached a settlement they were greeted with suspicion that contained a new element of threat. After an extended period of hand gestures, stamping of feet and incomprehensible shouting a pidgin speaker was finally found. The man arranged for food to be brought and oversaw the exchange process then sat with the line as the food was prepared and eaten. He said he knew about the war and speculated that the Japan men might win. He scratched at the ground and at his body as he asked whether the Japan men planned to stay and whether they would be worse or better than the whites who were already there. Leo said that the Japan men were not whites and warned that any cooperation with them would be severely punished when they were driven away, as they certainly would be.

In response to Ellen's question the man said that from time to time word came of groups of foreigners heading into the mountains, usually further to the east. A group had been reported not long ago. At other times there were lone whites who went in circles, either lost or forever revising their destination, sometimes shooting randomly into the bush. And recently a white man had come down from the mountains and begun to repair every native bridge he came across, gathering in the process a crowd of local followers, some respectful, others contemptuous. The villager said that he knew by now that not all whites were the same, but with new arrivals it was not always easy to tell the friendly from the hostile or the sane from the mad, so he was cautious.

Ellen asked what the man repairing the bridges looked like, but the villager replied that he didn't know. He didn't even know if the story was true; stories about whites were often exaggerated for effect. Ellen then asked if among the recent whites was a strongly built man with yellow hair. 'Maybe, maybe not,' the man replied, extricating himself from the conversation by slowly backing away.

Leo tried to calm Ellen's exasperation by saying that they would rendezvous with the nuns then take a shorter route back to the highlands. They would come out in the centre of the Wahgi Valley where Ellen could confidently expect to find Luke, who had doubtless got word that it was not possible to fly out of Hagen and would hope to find Ellen still at the mission house.

As they walked on the heat began to build, the air became heavier and the insects swarmed in greater numbers and with greater ferocity. Ellen thought she could smell a river, a sickly smell that insinuated itself into her senses and her mood. Despite the heat she covered as much of her skin as possible with clothing and wrapped Waiya up until only her eyes were visible. She listened as the chatter around her dried up and watched as the members of the line moved their rifles to various stages of readiness. Leo offered assurances that the Japanese would not come this far inland, but the tension in his face belied his words.

*

The rendezvous point was a collection of dilapidated huts not far from the river, hardly sufficient to constitute a village. There was no sign of life, but Leo ordered the patrol to stay concealed in the bush and to maintain silence. He observed through a pair of binoculars then whispered that the place was deserted. The patrol struggled to maintain its discipline. Leo indicated to two of the men that they should approach the huts and when they gave the all-clear the others followed.

The place showed signs of recent occupation, the earth at various points black with the remains of cooking fires and dark red with the expectorated juice of betel nut. Rotting food scraps, predominantly pieces of chewed sugar cane, lay around. Leo searched thoroughly inside and out for a message. He ordered the company to scour the surrounding bush for a bottle or other container where a note might be hidden, but there was nothing.

The line reformed and moved on parallel to the river. After an hour another village was found. It too looked deserted but gradually a few women appeared, moving about uneasily. The line walked slowly, stopping at regular points to allow Leo to use his binoculars. After each observation he motioned the group to proceed. As soon as the women saw the line they disappeared, but Leo said there were a few old men sitting and waiting. The patrol fanned out and Leo and Ellen moved forward.

Language was again a stumbling block. Leo asked Ellen to adopt a praying pose, but the charade was greeted with silence from the old men. One of the women reappeared with agitated arm movements and a gust of words, pointing into the distance, but what she was trying to communicate was unclear. Leo shook his head and the woman raised her voice to the point of a scream, again throwing her arms about.

'Do you think the Japanese have been here?' Ellen asked Leo when the woman quietened down.

Leo said the villagers were frightened and not because of them. He thought they should put as much distance as they could between themselves and the river as quickly as possible. If the nuns had set off by themselves they would have gone south. From what he had been told about their age and condition they could not have gone far.

One of the line members called out to Leo to come. He was standing with a scrawny local man and conversing in pidgin. The man seemed constantly on the point of running away and had to be restrained.

'*Masta*, he says the Japan men took the white women, some time back. They came up the river in a boat and took them. The Japan men said they'd be keeping a close watch, and if they found out that the people had helped the Americans or Australians they'd shoot them dead and burn down their village.'

'Does he know where they took the nuns?'

'He doesn't know, *masta*.' The man was pushed away. 'He's too scared to know much. He's shitting his pants.'

Another member of the patrol said to peals of laughter that the man didn't have any pants to shit, and if they gave him a pair he would probably wear them on his head.

Leo gathered the patrol together for a council of war and Ellen took Waiya a few steps closer to the river, which sat motionless like a slick of brown sludge. The air shimmered in the heavy heat, Ellen's clothes grabbed at her skin and the murmured sounds of voices seemed to pulse in time with her heart. She looked up and was startled by the sight of the watching man standing impassively next to a stretch of bush. She raised an arm in muted greeting and took a step towards the man, but from one moment to the next he was gone. Waiya recognised the man as the one who spent all his time watching Misis and who everyone said was not right in the head. Ellen replied that he was a brave man who would stay out of sight but always be there to help them if trouble came.

An urgent voice brought Ellen back to the present. '*Masta*, listen.'

The chugging sound of a motor was soon unmistakable. Leo motioned everyone to the ground then issued an order to crawl away from the village into the surrounding tall grass. Rifles were made ready to fire and aim taken at nothing that could be seen. Ellen put a finger to Waiya's lips and mouthed silence. The sweet-sour smell of the earth invaded her nose and mouth, causing her briefly to gag.

The motor was cut and its vibrations replaced by the staccato sounds of a language that was entirely new to Ellen. Then accomplished pidgin separated itself from the general noise and was answered by rudimentary pidgin, saying no Americans or Australians had been seen and the consequences of assisting any who did come were well understood. After a series of variations on this theme the pidgin conversation stopped, the motor started up again and the boat chugged away downstream.

Leo gestured to the patrol to stay down so they waited, lying silently on their stomachs or their sides. The sound of the motor faded and a pidgin voice from nearby called that it was safe to come out. Leo motioned that no one was to move. Ellen pressed Waiya closer to her.

The next sound was a shouting voice warning that soldiers were coming through the grass from the rear. Almost simultaneously there was a barrage of gunfire and the voice abruptly stopped. The next few moments were a cacophony of bullets and shouts. Then the noise subsided, leaving nothing but a groaning hush.

Home

(1943)

One

The nuns welcomed Ellen and Waiya with a small portion of rice and a soggy green vegetable. There was weak black tea without sugar. The eldest of the nuns, a tall woman well into middle age, began the conversation while Ellen and Waiya ate. Her accent was Australian.

'We saw you at the Christmas party.'

Ellen seemed not to remember, so the nun continued. 'We sat at the back and watched. But we enjoyed ourselves.'

'Yes of course,' Ellen said eventually.

The nuns asked Ellen about the circumstances of her capture and she described the ambush on the river. The leader of the patrol, the only white man, a fine young man, had died of his wounds as she knelt beside him. Some of the New Guineans in the patrol had fought bravely; some were wounded and taken prisoner, others had run away. A Japanese soldier had also died and a comrade had severed the man's little finger, burnt away the flesh in a small fire and preserved the charred bones in a knotted piece of cloth.

'One of the Japanese soldiers spoke perfect English. He explained the ceremony to me. Then he intervened on behalf of Waiya and me with the officer, who wanted to leave Waiya behind in the village. The soldier told me that he had grown up in New Guinea and knew many Australians.'

The nuns exchanged looks then knelt, saying they would pray for the dead. Ellen indicated to Waiya that she should leave her food until the prayer was finished.

When everyone was sitting again, on boxes of varying sizes, the tall nun said that their capture had been their own fault. After the order to evacuate had been given they had been allowed to return to their mission inland from the town to make arrangements for their absence. At first it had been quiet so they had unobtrusively continued with their work, but they had miscalculated the speed with which the Japanese would finally come. At the last minute they had set off to walk to the highlands but had found the going difficult. Word had been carried to a coast watcher, a radio message had been sent and they had been waiting to be rescued when they were taken by the Japanese. The fate of the rescue patrol would forever be on their conscience.

When this thought had settled the nun sought to change the tone, saying that there were still things to be thankful for. So far, the Japanese hadn't treated them too badly.

'They haven't beaten us, Sister Anthony, that's true. But if we keep going as we are we'll starve to death, in this land of plenty.'

'I've heard about what the Japs have to eat, Sister Teresa. It's also very little.'

A third nun, Sister Claire, explained that the food shortage was due to the bombing. The Americans were coming with increasing frequency and causing extensive damage. They seemed to be deliberately targeting the gardens, and of course any ships in the harbour. The Japanese had taken to bringing in supplies by submarine, but it was not enough.

Waiya had fallen asleep and several of the nuns fussed around her. A nun who introduced herself as Sister Marie Louise said that the girl's disfigurement was a sign that God had singled her out for a special task. There would be further signs as to what this task was. She kissed Waiya on the forehead and the other nuns followed suit. A mosquito net was spread over the girl.

When darkness came there were shouted voices from outside, at first sporadic but quickly building to a persistent chant. After several rifle shots the voices died away, but they soon returned. One of the nuns explained to Ellen. 'Our people are shouting words of encouragement in their language. They are saying we should not worry, the Japs will soon be gone. We will be free to return to our mission, where we will be joyously welcomed.'

*

The next morning Sister Anthony was again the first to speak. 'You must forgive us, but we were curious after the Christmas party so we asked about you. We're very sorry for the loss of your husband.'

The nuns had finished their prayers and were sitting with Ellen and Waiya, eating their rice in the half light. When Ellen trusted her voice sufficiently she said that, while she had largely come to terms with her husband's death, when she talked about it with new people the grief rose again to the surface. But since she was soon to remarry she was not sure she still had the right to grieve. Some of the nuns nodded their understanding, but one of their number who had hardly spoken before said emphatically that the one thing did not preclude the other.

'Sister Hedwig knows Pastor Sommer,' Sister Anthony explained to Ellen.

Sister Hedwig said that Pastor Sommer came from the same American plains country as she did, and although he was a protestant he was a God-fearing man of good character. But it was her understanding that he was betrothed to an American woman who was to join him as soon as circumstances allowed.

Sister Anthony spoke before Ellen could find the words to justify herself and Luke. 'We have heard from our natives that Pastor Sommer is in the men's camp. Alongside our priests and brothers and the planters who, like us, left it too late to leave.'

Sister Hedwig said that the imprisoned men were being worked like slaves with little food and inadequate shelter. There was a lot of sickness, but the Japanese would not use any of their medical supplies to treat the men, nor ease their burden of work. Sister Anthony laid a hand on Sister Hedwig's arm and said quietly that you could never tell with the Japs. One minute they were brutal and pitiless, the next minute almost reasonable.

The order to work came. The party was escorted past abandoned gardens to a patch of sunken land further from the coast where they were given rough implements and required to dig, under the supervision of a pair of guards who alternated between long periods of indifference and brief moments of high agitation. Local women who were at work nearby occasionally smuggled items of food to the nuns under cover of snatches of pidgin conversation. Ellen worked alongside the nuns but after an initial burst of energy a profound exhaustion overtook her, at which point the nuns did their best to shield her and Waiya from the sun and from the gaze of the guards. After a meagre lunch of tasteless rice there was a brief rest period. Ellen fell into a deep sleep and when she woke she felt refreshed. She was able to continue working until the nuns put aside their implements and camouflaged their work with branches from trees and cuttings from shrubs. It was late afternoon when they arrived back at the hut.

The cursory search the nuns had been subjected to before leaving the gardens had found nothing, and inside the hut they bubbled with excitement as pieces of fruit and sweet potato were removed from deep within their habits. Sister Hedwig gathered enough flammable material to build a small fire and found water to boil their rice, to which she added the sweet potato. When supplemented by the smuggled fruit the meal was as satisfying as any Ellen could remember, even if she was forced to eat with her fingers.

After the meal when Waiya was asleep Ellen was questioned about the highlands. The nuns said that they had heard about the wildness of the highland people but had met very few themselves and were curious about her impressions. Ellen surprised herself by defending the highlanders, saying that their invention of settled agriculture showed what they were capable of. If the oppressive control exercised by the men over the women were loosened and the power of sorcery exposed as an illusion she could imagine a flourishing society needing only minimal guidance from whites. She concluded by saying that the most backward people she had encountered were not highlanders but the inhabitants of a village on a tributary of the Ramu, not so far away from their current location.

'We've grown very attached to the people we consider to be ours,' Sister Anthony responded with a tight smile. 'You must forgive us if we refuse to think of them as especially backward.'

As if on call the chanting began outside. The nuns exchanged smiles and Ellen smiled as well. She said that it must be a wonderful thing to inspire such loyalty. Sister Anthony replied that the early years had been hard, but now God's spirit was at work in the people. This was a blessing that far outweighed the benefits of civilisation.

Sister Claire said that she had been in New Guinea so long she doubted she would fit back into civilisation, although she would welcome the opportunity to use a flushing toilet and to wash free from the gaze of prying eyes. The other nuns added things they missed from the white world—window shopping at a department store, borrowing a book from a library, visiting a picture theatre—but when they finished there was general agreement that these things did not amount to much.

Ellen continued to sit with Sister Anthony. She asked about the American bombers, what time they came and whether there was much warning.

'They come whenever it suits them, not always from the same direction or with the same strength of purpose. The

Japanese have threatened to force us to keep working out in the open during the raids, but so far they haven't followed through. They're probably too worried about their own skins. So they herd us into the bush.'

Sister Claire joined the conversation, telling Ellen that the Japs were forcing the white men they had taken prisoner to dig a network of tunnels behind the town. But you could bet that the whites would not be allowed to shelter there; they would be left to take their chances out in the open. Ellen said she would prefer to stay above ground. The thought of being buried alive terrified her.

*

The door of the hut was eased open and a Japanese soldier came inside. A moment of consternation was replaced by half smiles when the man was recognised. He was invited to sit down.

'Ken Noda, is it really you inside that uniform?'

'It's me, Sister Anthony.'

'Have you come to gloat over us?'

'I just wanted to see you're all right, Sister.'

The nun said they were being worked too hard and given insufficient food; if it wasn't for the help from their natives they would be hard pressed to survive. She asked Noda to intercede with his superiors on their behalf. He replied that the Japanese themselves were short of food.

Ellen recognised Ken Noda from the river and thanked him for his intercession. Sister Anthony explained to her who he was. 'Ken was a pupil at one of our schools when he was younger, a good student although a poor Catholic. When Japan entered the war we heard he'd disappeared before he could be imprisoned and sent to Australia for internment, as happened to his parents. We suspected he had hidden himself somewhere, waiting for the Japanese soldiers to come.'

Sister Anthony then asked Noda if he had played any role in the nuns' capture. His answer was that he was doing his best to protect them. He had come to tell them that his superiors were growing tired of the nightly chanting of the natives. The nuns must put a stop to it or the natives would be punished. His superiors also suspected that the nuns were receiving smuggled food. If they were caught their rations would be reduced and their working hours extended. The blacks involved would have their hands cut off, or they would be shot.

When Ken Noda had gone Sister Marie Louise began to shake uncontrollably. The nuns responded with assurances that what Noda had said was an exaggeration designed to frighten them. It was left to Ellen to hold Sister Marie Louise in her arms until the shaking subsided.

*

As soon as the planes were heard the nuns and their guards hurriedly camouflaged the gardens then fled into the bush and pressed themselves to the ground. The camouflage seemed to have the desired effect because the bombs fell well away from them. When the attack was over Ellen could not keep from her mind an image of Luke buried alive in a collapsed tunnel. She remonstrated with a guard, the man prodded her vigorously with his rifle and she fell back into line.

Later in the day a message came that the Catholic cathedral in Madang had been bombed. The Japanese guards insisted that this demonstrated the barbarism of the Americans, but Sister Anthony was dismissive. She told them that everyone knew the Japanese were storing military supplies in the cathedral, so they shared responsibility for its destruction.

When darkness came a native man appeared at the hut to announce that the tabernacle and monstrance had been salvaged from the ruins of the cathedral and taken to safety. When the Japan men were gone the cathedral would be rebuilt and the holy things returned to their proper place.

*

Over the subsequent weeks the bombing raids intensified and the behaviour of the guards deteriorated. They became more niggardly with the distribution of rations, they demanded longer and more intense labour in the gardens and they searched more invasively for smuggled food. Sister Anthony's request to speak to Ken Noda was ignored.

During the next raid the gardens were hit. The damage was extensive and the Japanese were hysterical with anger, accusing the nuns of guiding the bombers and refusing to accept the impossibility of this. They threatened again to leave the nuns unprotected to face the bombs. Ellen was impressed with the eloquence of Sister Anthony's pidgin response, which questioned the manhood and courage of the Japanese. A furious guard made to strike the nun with his rifle, but at the last moment he thought better of it.

As the days passed and the bombing continued hunger began to dominate. One by one the nuns fell sick. Several attempts by local people to smuggle in additional food were thwarted, with those involved beaten in full view of everyone. The nightly chants were increasingly interrupted by rifle shots. The nuns pleaded with the people to pay more attention to their own interests and needs. They asked only for their prayers.

Despite the quinine that she had begun to take in Mount Hagen the malaria returned to Ellen and she burned with fever. She had episodes of convulsive vomiting and her head threatened to burst with pain. She covered her ears with her hands and curled up in search of relief. The nuns knelt beside her and prayed while Sister Anthony demanded that the guards fetch clean water, towels and a doctor.

Eventually a doctor did come, a stooping European from the men's camp. He questioned Ellen about the number of bouts of malaria she had suffered and the colour of her urine and seemed relieved to hear that her urine was of no particular colour and this was only her second bout of malaria. He said he knew Luke, who was bearing up as well as could be expected. He promised to tell him that she would be there when the boat to America was ready to leave.

Local people were increasingly being herded into labour gangs to rebuild the gardens and the nuns and Ellen were allowed to spend more time in the hut. They were given saltless rice and an occasional vegetable, and from this inadequate diet each provided a portion for Waiya. Despite this generosity Waiya began rapidly to lose weight, she slept fitfully and was listless when awake. Her bowel movements produced nothing but a thin dribble of yellowish slime. Ellen did her best to keep her amused with stories that she remembered or invented, while Sister Teresa sang songs in a native language in a thin but true voice.

At regular intervals during the day and night Sister Anthony led the nuns in periods of devotion. In Ellen's ears the words of the prayers would often separate themselves from their meanings and assume the character of pure sound, papery like the rustling of dry leaves, but the simple conviction in the drawn faces of the praying women encouraged her not to give way to despair. Her own prayers, when she could find the energy and words for them, were interspersed with fury at her captors and at her inability to fight back.

One evening at Ellen's request Sister Anthony talked about her time in New Guinea. 'I've been here for nearly twenty years, for much of that time away from the thin veneer of civilisation on the coast. I've come to realise that the life of even the most backward New Guineans is not so different from our own. I won't say they are closer to the essence of things—they have their terrible superstitions that hold them back—but their lives contain fewer distractions than ours and I've come to value that.'

'Will you ever return home?'

'If my superiors call me back I will have no choice but to go.'

Ellen expressed her admiration for such dedication and obedience, qualities absent from her own life. She was ruled by desires that in hindsight seemed trivial, her will was weak and easily overruled and she was not sure there was anything but emptiness behind the things she felt and the words she spoke. Sister Anthony took her hand and counselled her to conserve her strength.

From across the hut Sister Marie Louise whispered that a little rice had been put aside for Waiya if she woke during the night.

Sister Anthony and Ellen continued to sit quietly. Eventually the nun spoke. 'I doubt our doctors would be able to do anything for Waiya. I think her own village is the best place for her. When all this is over we will see to it that she is returned there.'

Ellen said that she supposed Sister Anthony was right; Waiya should go back to her own people as soon as possible. Then from some inner compulsion she started to talk about Aino. She said she had loved him as a son and it had been a terrible wrench to give him up, although she knew it was the right thing to do. Sister Anthony said they had heard about Aino, and she agreed that Ellen had done the right thing. She offered calm assurance that in God's good time Ellen would be generously compensated for everything she had lost.

Two

A native man had been caught again trying to smuggle food to the nuns and was facing execution. Sister Anthony tried to reason with the Japanese officer, but he was unmoved. She ended by offering herself as an alternative, and the officer eventually accepted the offer with a curt nod. He pointed to the front of the hut and the nuns filed out. Ellen remembered the officer from the ambush at the river and pleaded with him to show mercy, but his only reaction was to signal that Ellen and Waiya should stay inside.

Ellen wrapped her arms around Waiya, covering as much of her eyes and ears as she could. She then moved her own attention to the front of the hut, where a contingent of Japanese soldiers stood at attention with rifles at their sides and chins jutting out. A young native who had been released by the soldiers was kneeling on all fours and sobbing. In response to a shouted order Ken Noda stepped forward and drew a tentative circle on the ground with his boot to indicate where Sister Anthony should stand. He offered her something to cover her eyes, but she shook her head. The nuns began to pray out loud, ignoring the officer's demands to stop until Sister Anthony intervened with a raised hand.

Ken Noda took up his position some distance away from Sister Anthony. He raised his rifle to his shoulder and took aim.

A period of silence was broken not by the anticipated crack of the rifle but by the harsh sounds of the Japanese officer admonishing Noda. Ellen watched transfixed as Noda continued to hesitate. Then in time with a series of shouted commands the remaining soldiers raised their rifles and took aim, at Noda and at Sister Anthony. Noda suddenly lifted his rifle again and fired almost in one movement. Sister Anthony slumped to the ground.

As the detail of Japanese soldiers marched away a crescendo of wailing welled up from the surrounding bush. Men and women appeared from all directions, beating their heads with their hands and tearing at the bits of clothing they were wearing. They said Ken Noda had lost his mind or had been taken over by an evil spirit the Japan men had brought from across the sea. As punishment Noda would soon die the most painful death possible and his spirit would hang around like a piece of stinking pig meat until all his family members were dead or the Japan men had been driven away.

The grave that was dug for Sister Anthony's body with sharp sticks was deep and the earth tipped on top of her was stamped down vigorously, the grave diggers saying they did not want the soldiers to dig her up and eat her flesh to still their hunger. By the side of the grave Sister Teresa recited a simple prayer and a hymn was sung, the voices of the nuns drowned out by those of the surrounding congregation. The nuns then returned to the hut, where they ate their tasteless rice in silence.

With the onset of darkness the nuns knelt to pray, their repetitive monotone blending into an external chorus of lamentation that ebbed and flowed in a regular rhythm. Ellen lay down next to Waiya and whispered that the terrible things she had seen and heard since leaving the highlands did not belong to the normal life of white people. The Japanese had come to New Guinea and picked a fight that the whites did not want. When the Japanese were gone she would see that whites were people of peace.

*

'What are you doing, Sister?'

Ellen had woken with a start and seen a figure bending over Waiya. She propped herself up and repeated the question. Sister Teresa was also awake; she was slowly approaching Sister Marie Louise and encouraging her to return to sleep, but the bending nun seemed impervious to her surroundings. Her attention was solely on the crude cup she was carrying, from which she was pouring a thin stream of water on Waiya's head as she recited the words of baptism.

'It's not necessary, Sister.'

Sister Teresa took the cup from Sister Marie Louise and led her back to her sleeping mat. Ellen lay down beside Waiya and calmed her agitation then fell back into sleep.

In the morning Sister Marie Louise explained her actions to Ellen. She had become convinced that they were all about to die and she wanted to ensure that Waiya would be taken straight to heaven. The thought of the child suffering any longer was too much for her to bear. Ellen assured her that their own soldiers would soon drive out the Japanese; they just needed to hold on a little longer.

Sister Claire sought to lighten the mood. 'When our soldiers come I'll kiss the first one on the lips and ask him for a cigarette and a bottle of beer.'

The other nuns exchanged weak smiles. Sister Teresa told Ellen that to the best of her knowledge Sister Claire had never smoked or drunk alcohol in her life. As for kissing a man, she doubted Sister Claire would know where to start.

'I could always learn, Sister,' the nun responded.

Sister Marie Louise said that as soon as they were free they would ensure that Sister Anthony was given a proper burial. Then they would return to their mission house where they would call their people together and ask them to renew their pledge to Christ. Any who had helped the Japanese would be forgiven, as long as they repented. Even Ken Noda would be forgiven, if he were truly sorry and gave himself up to God's mercy.

Three

When the Japanese had attacked on the river Ellen had assumed that the warning voice had come from the watching man, and although she had not seen his body she had assumed he had been killed. So she was taken aback when late the next night he appeared at the hut, a warning finger to his lips. He wasted no time in explaining why he had come. She thanked him but said that if she escaped the Japanese would punish the nuns and she could not have that on her conscience. And if he were caught he would be cruelly tortured and killed. The man produced a steel knife to show the seriousness of his intent. Then he said that the nuns could come as well, provided they were prepared to follow his instructions without question.

Ellen explained the proposal to the nuns, adding in support that the man had followed her all the way from the highlands, a prodigious feat for a lone villager. He had somehow escaped the Japanese ambush near the river and had continued to follow her. She was sure that he was prepared to give his life for her. Sister Claire argued in favour of going with the man, saying that he might be able to lead them to food, and Sister Hedwig agreed. Sister Marie Louise said she doubted she had the strength to walk even twenty yards, but she would not stand in the way of the others. The last word was left to Sister Teresa, who concluded that she could not in good conscience consent to a plan that might implicate her and her fellow nuns in the taking of human life. They would wait until the Japanese set them free or they were liberated by their own side. But if Ellen decided to go with the highland man, she would have her blessing.

Ellen took the watching man aside and asked if he knew where the Japanese had their camp for white men. He confirmed that the camp was not far away and that among the prisoners was the man who had twice visited the mission house after Pastor Carl had gone. It would not be easy to rescue this man, but if she wanted he would try. Ellen explained that she only wanted to see the camp. Then she would return to the nuns and he would go back to the highlands.

After Ellen had informed the nuns of her intention the watching man easily manoeuvred her past the single guard who was dozing outside the hut. He indicated that she should scoop up some mud and smear it over her face then with a finger to his lips he led her forward, skirting a pool of light and sound that indicated an encampment of Japanese soldiers. As they penetrated more deeply into the bush, Ellen's dilapidated shoes sucking at the wet earth, the man engaged in a barely audible monologue in which he exhorted himself not to fail in this task, the most important of his life.

After a period of indefinite length the man indicated that they should slow down and keep absolutely quiet. A few moments later he moved his hand back and forth to his mouth to indicate the smoking of a cigarette. Somewhere ahead human voices made themselves heard, then a burst of laughter splayed out and quickly died away. The watching man looked at Ellen and smiled, his teeth an incongruous smear of light in the darkness.

They carefully skirted the compound and found a mound of damp earth that offered some protection. Through the screen of a haphazard fence Ellen made out a dozen huts, each one only large enough to hold a handful of prisoners, and there were several ghostly armed figures that she assumed were guards. She thought she could hear undercurrents of conversation coming from the nearest hut, but her sharpened attention only brought into relief the beating of her heart. She focussed her gaze on a stray Japanese soldier who seemed to be sleepwalking along the camp's periphery then turned away as the man laid down his rifle and went to relieve himself in the bush.

The watching man touched Ellen on the shoulder and displayed his knife. She instinctively shook her head and the man put the knife away. She resumed her watching and listening, unsure of what she hoped to see or hear.

A man appeared at the doorway of one of the huts and stood there in a halo of weak light. He was tall and thin and almost naked. He called out something in pidgin and Ellen recognised the voice of the doctor who had come to treat her malaria. The figure spoke again, one of the guards approached the hut and a conversation began. Ellen could hear enough to know that there was a sick prisoner who was unlikely to last the night without proper treatment, but that despite the relative proximity of the town's hospital he would not be taken there.

The conversation seemed matter-of-fact, both parties stating their positions in flat and lifeless pidgin. Before long the figure and the light disappeared inside the hut and the guard went back to his comfortable dozing position against a tree.

The watching man again displayed his knife, but Ellen indicated that she had seen enough. The man got silently to his feet and Ellen replicated his movements then carefully followed in his footsteps until they were well away from the camp. In a sunken place of thick bush she asked for a moment to rest. She sat on the ground and the watching man squatted beside her, his features gradually reassuming definition in the darkness. She asked whether he had understood the conversation at the camp. He answered that he could now understand some pidgin.

'I'm afraid that the prisoner who is close to death is the man I am to marry.'

The watching man said that the prisoners were weak from digging, from lack of food, from sickness and beatings. From what he had seen they were all close to death. After a short pause he asked where the Japan men came from, why they had picked a fight with the other whites and when the big death that was happening all around would end.

Ellen said that the Japanese were not whites. They came from a different place, far away to the north. They needed more land for their people so they wanted to take over New Guinea, but the whites would never let them.

The watching man said he had heard of New Guinea, but he was not sure where it was. He thought it must be on the coast because down here there was lots of talk about it. Ellen explained that the coast and the highlands were all part of New Guinea and that one day all these places and other places days and weeks away in all directions, islands and valleys and mountains with different clans and languages, would become one country, perhaps a great country.

The watching man accepted this information blankly, then said that they should move on because the Japan men got up well before the sun. When Ellen was on her feet she asked the man why he kept watching her. He replied that he watched her because it made him feel light in the heart. He had been with many women and at the beginning the feeling was light but before long it became heavy, but when he was watching her he always felt light, even when she was sad. He would watch her for as long as he could.

'I don't even know your name,' Ellen said as they began to walk.

'My name is Wamdi,' the man replied.

Four

Ken Noda came for Ellen. The nuns tried to resist but they were easily brushed aside. Ellen hugged Waiya, assuring her that she would not be away for long. She farewelled the nuns with brittle lightness, whispering to Sister Teresa that if she did not return they should do everything they could to reunite Waiya with her mother in the Wahgi Valley.

A pair of soldiers was waiting outside the hut and the party set off in the sweaty night in the direction Ellen had taken with Wamdi. She walked with small steps, her senses on high alert. She wanted to ask where she was being taken but could not bring herself to speak to Ken Noda. She did not respond when he held her back and whispered that he was sorry for what he had done, but he had been given no choice.

They came to a hut built up from the ground on stilts, one of a number of similar huts scattered around a clearing. Noda climbed a short ladder to a porch then reached out a hand and helped Ellen to climb. He indicated that she should go inside and out of habit she brushed down her clothes and tidied her hair as best she could before following his direction.

The officer from the river and from the day of Sister Anthony's death, his forehead surprisingly high without the peaked cap, stood up as Ellen entered. He gestured at a low table where two places had been set. He called out and a woman appeared with food that she put down on bamboo mats—sweet potato, corn, green vegetables, rice, a pair of medium-sized fish nestled around their backbones and pieces of cut fruit. The officer poured a clear liquid from a bottle into a tin cup and offered it to Ellen. He said something in Japanese and Noda gave a short bow and left.

The man began to eat, gesturing to Ellen to do likewise. He said in pidgin that he was sorry if there was not enough to eat in the camp, but it was entirely the fault of the Americans, who seemingly did not care that their bombing was destroying the livelihoods of the people.

Ellen picked up the knife and fork, wondering where they came from as she allowed her hands to reacquaint themselves with their feel. She asked the man what he wanted from her, but he just gestured again at the food. A heavy smell of incense settled on her, infiltrating her throat and chest. She coughed to clear her lungs and the man said that the smoke was effective in keeping away the mosquitoes.

Ellen began to eat, slowly and deliberately, wanting neither to fall too quickly or deeply into the man's debt nor to overburden her shrunken stomach. She watched the man over her knife and fork as he put his chopsticks aside and lit a cigarette. He took several deep inhalations of smoke then placed the cigarette carefully in an improvised ashtray and returned to his food, speaking between mouthfuls.

'I am an educated man, a lawyer. I had no desire to be taken from my family and sent to the Philippine islands and then to New Guinea. But Japan was left with no choice but to fight.'

Ellen felt that she was expected to acknowledge the justice of the Japanese cause, but she said that she knew nothing about Japan or its reasons for entering the war. All she could see was the destruction the Japanese were bringing to New Guinea.

'We will expel the Americans and the Australians, who have no right to be here. The people understand this. That is why they are supporting us.'

Ellen remembered Sister Anthony telling her that very few of the local people had fallen for the Japanese claim that they had come to liberate New Guinea from the white man. The people had quickly become expert at fooling the Japanese, spying on them and reporting back to the nuns. Ellen did not repeat any of this, instead asking the officer why he had made prisoners of the nuns, who had nothing to do with the war.

'They were watching our soldiers and sending word by radio to the Americans, who then came over with their bombers. We could not allow this to continue.'

Without any prompting the man went on to explain about Ken Noda. 'Private Noda has lived most of his life with white people, who lack the discipline of the Japanese. It was necessary for him to demonstrate that he has turned his back on the white world.'

Ellen said that Sister Anthony was now a martyr who would be remembered by the people long after the Japanese were forgotten. And Ken Noda would forever have the death of an innocent woman on his conscience.

The officer's chopsticks darted several times from bamboo mat to mouth. He poured more drink and tipped it into his throat, urging Ellen to follow his example. He sat back and said, as both a statement and a question, 'You have no husband.'

Ellen looked away.

'The Australian soldier at the river; was he your husband?'

Ellen shook her head.

'The blond man in the camp who continually asks about you?'

'My husband is dead.' Ellen's words sounded to her distant and disembodied. 'He was lost somewhere in the highlands and has never been found.'

The officer said that the highlands must be better than this place of heat, disease and war. When the fighting was over he would go there. He would sit on the side of a mountain, breathe the clear air and remember his fallen comrades. Then he would return to Japan and resume his life.

Ellen thought of Ivor Moore. She was only half listening to the officer. 'My men get satisfaction from local women, but I refuse.'

She could hear the man's breathing, heavy through his nose.

'No need to be hungry again,' he went on.

Ellen picked up the tin cup in front of her and drained it. She waited for the burning sensation in her chest to abate. 'If I do as you want will the nuns also get enough to eat?'

The man broadened his shoulders and gave his solemn word that she, the disfigured girl and the unmarried white women would be transported further along the coast to safety. The gardens there were out of range of the American bombers; there would be enough to eat.

The man stood up and said Ellen should wash, adding that she had no need to worry, he was entirely free from any transmissible disease. He produced a small pouch that he said contained all the protection that was needed. He excused himself and went to the back of the hut, returning with a neatly folded cotton nightdress, a pair of sandals and a small canvas bag, all of which he handed to Ellen. He then escorted her out of the hut and down the ladder to an improvised washroom where there was water in buckets, strips of cloth for towels and discoloured slivers of soap. As she scrubbed the grime and sweat from her skin Ellen could hear the man pacing up and down outside, his hypnotic tread contributing to her sense of unreality. She finished washing, mechanically dried herself then put on the nightdress. She slipped her feet into the sandals and bundled her sweaty clothes and worn out shoes into the canvas bag.

There was a brief look of approval from the officer as he replaced Ellen in the washroom, leaving her to stand outside and wait. She thought she heard a shout of encouragement from the direction of the nuns' hut, but more focused listening yielded nothing but the menacing whine of mosquitoes. Ken Noda appeared out of the darkness with a mango leaf that he folded and handed to her, indicating that she should use it to clean her teeth. He then sought to assure her that his superior would treat her well. The food prepared for her at enormous cost was a clear sign of the man's esteem. She should put out of her mind the ambush on the river and the death of Sister Anthony. These things belonged to an entirely different world.

When the officer reappeared Ellen asked him if the

prisoners in the men's camp would also be moved to safety. He replied that when the men had completed their job of building a network of tunnels he would do his best to have them sent to a better place.

Five

After hours of standing without shade while Japanese soldiers engaged in a frenzy of seemingly pointless activity the party finally set off in the direction of the ocean. The air was as dense as melted butter and the nuns soon begged for a slower pace and for food and drink, but the soldiers said there would be nothing until they arrived at their destination. When a short rest was finally allowed an exhausted Waiya lay on the ground and immediately fell asleep. A heavy bank of clouds cast a shadow over the ground and a few large drops of rain promised refreshment, but the clouds quickly dissolved in a funnel of fierce sunlight. Ellen closed her eyes and briefly imagined herself clean and fresh at the swimming hole.

When the order came to resume the march one of the soldiers nudged Waiya with his foot then quickly repeated the action with more force. Ellen remonstrated and a sharp blow to the chest with a rifle butt sent her reeling. Through the pain and shock she watched as a crouched figure rushed in slow motion from the bush and made a flailing attempt to stab the offending soldier, then she recoiled in horror as a series of bullets tore into Wamdi's body.

'Crazy *kanakas*! Crazy place.' A visibly shaken soldier

fired another shot into the dead body, then pointed his rifle at the nuns.

The women knelt in prayer and refused to move until the man was buried. The soldiers complied, using bayonets and knives to scratch out a shallow grave before covering the body with a mixture of soil and leaves, anxiously scanning the surrounding bush as they did so.

As Ellen lingered at the graveside several aeroplanes screeched in low and the soldiers pulled her and the nuns into the surrounding bush. As the noise abated one of the soldier's declared in broken pidgin that they would soon be in range of Japanese planes and there would be nothing more to fear.

The sea could be smelt before it could be seen. Waiya showed a flicker of excitement and Ellen let herself relax, but the Japanese soldiers seemed increasingly anxious. They kept to the tall grass and spread out in a snaking line. Their sporadic verbal exchanges dried up and their feet became completely silent. Ellen moved more quietly too, feeling herself part of a line of ghosts ascending from the underworld, unsure if they were visible to the earth's inhabitants, ready to descend again at the first sign of hostility.

In the fading daylight a dull slender shape sat close to the shore with voices and small boats ebbing and flowing around it. Sister Marie Louise's voice insisted that she would not be put into such a claustrophobic thing, leading Sister Teresa to call for calm. A soldier said that soon there would be food and rest.

They were marched past the submarine to a second vessel, a steamer that squatted in the water alongside a jetty. A stream of dark figures was moving up and down a swaying gangplank, unloading cargo under the supervision of impatient soldiers. When the party arrived the gangplank was cleared and the women were channelled on board and directed to the foredeck, where a solitary anti-aircraft gun pointed defiantly into the distance. Ellen comforted Waiya by telling her that they would soon be in a place of fine gardens and plentiful food.

Sudden engine noise caused Ellen to look back at the submarine. For a time the engine seemed to vibrate to no effect, then the vessel began to manoeuvre away from the shore. As she stood watching the matt shadow slipped past and quickly disappeared, in the failing light or beneath the water.

The women were allowed to sit and they spread out on the deck, searching in the unfamiliar surroundings for something secure to prop themselves against. Small portions of rice wrapped in banana leaves were passed around, along with water in metallic flasks. Pockets of conversation arose but quickly faded. One by one the nuns dropped into an exhausted sleep. Ellen held Waiya in her arms until she settled. She tried to sleep herself, but the memory of Wamdi's bullet-ridden body gave her no peace.

The boat's engine started, a thrumming somewhere deep below. Soldiers and sailors moved quickly from one place to another making last-minute preparations. A hushed group of figures was hustled along the quay and bundled on board, then the gangplank was hastily drawn up. The boat edged away from the jetty before turning and chugging out towards the open sea. The land sank from view, leaving the vessel alone in its own sounds and vibrations.

'Luke, are you there?'

Ellen was on all fours, peering into the semi-darkness. She edged her way towards the stern of the boat, but a soldier aggressively blocked her progress. She could hear subdued male voices speaking in familiar tones, but she could not make out the words. She called out Luke's name again and received a sharp blow to the back of her head. Her hands were fastened behind her back and a piece of stinking cloth was roughly tied around her mouth, leaving her struggling for air through a congested nose. There was a scuffle and someone untied the gag, freed her hands then helped her to her feet. She recognised Ken Noda and thanked him grudgingly. She asked if Luke Sommer was on the boat, but Noda did not answer. She allowed herself to be guided back to the foredeck where Waiya was still asleep, nestled between two of the nuns.

During the long night Ellen floated in and out of consciousness, occasionally aware of a vague nausea in her stomach. At one point she thought she heard Carl's voice telling her that he was on his way back to her, but she woke before she could ask where he had been all this time. She drank from a flask that was held against her lips, then took the flask and urged a few sips on a restless Waiya. A remote voice offered assurances that they were now safe, out of the reach of bullets and bombs.

*

At first the aeroplanes were two silent specks on the dawning horizon, but they soon assumed sound and shape. The boat surged into activity, the soldiers and sailors frantically urging Ellen and the nuns to their feet, exhorting them to wave their arms to make themselves conspicuous. Ellen positioned herself next to the gun, which was manned but silent, shielding Waiya with one arm and waving the other arm as instructed. To distract herself from the danger she speculated about the pilots, hoping they had children of their own, or younger brothers and sisters.

The planes roared overhead, deafening everything in their path. Ellen thought she caught the eyes of one of the pilots, who seemed to acknowledge her before screaming away. There were no bombs and no bullets, just retreating sound. The Japanese soldiers and sailors waited in seeming disbelief before bursting into laughter, clapping vociferously and jostling each other.

The heightened mood had not completely dissipated when the planes reappeared, tracing a path across the horizon before turning and heading in towards the boat. Without urging Ellen stood up and began to wave, her arm seeming to move of its own accord.

As the approaching sound reached a crescendo the water around the boat erupted, filling the air with spray. The boat's gun fired several bursts but quickly fell silent. The vessel was covered in a sheet of machine gun fire then buffeted by a series of explosions. Ellen crashed down under a heavy weight. As she lay there the boat began to list, causing the body covering her to slide to one side.

When she came to herself Ellen saw Ken Noda clearly dead beside her, a neat line of bullet wounds along his torso. She called out desperately for Waiya, then saw her wedged beneath a prone Japanese sailor. She dragged her free, quickly examined her for wounds then wrapped her intact body in her arms.

Sister Claire lay slumped and motionless against a coil of rope, but the remaining nuns seemed unscathed. Sister Teresa knelt praying beside Sister Claire while Sister Hedwig and Sister Marie Louise offered comfort to the wounded. Ellen joined their efforts, using pieces of torn clothing to stem the flow of blood. She closed the eyes of a soldier with a pinched face who was beyond help, then reassured a young sailor with a flesh wound that he was not going to die. She pressed a water bottle to the lips of an older man who gripped her arm and muttered in a mixture of Japanese and pidgin that the American pilots must be blind or insane. She loosened herself from the man's grip and made her way back to Waiya, telling her to stay close to the nuns until she returned.

*

The scene at the stern of the boat was one of ghostly figures and an eerie near silence. A rough circle had formed around a priest with a white stole who was praying over a prostrate body. Ellen joined the circle and recognised Father Denze, then saw without surprise that it was Luke Sommer he was ministering to, a shrunken Luke with a face reduced to little more than skin and bone. She waited for the ceremony to end before she spoke.

'He's gone, Father?'

The priest looked up and said that Luke had been struck by a piece of shrapnel, but he had been close to death before the attack. He had contracted malaria in the camp and it had gone to his brain. The shrapnel was probably a blessing.

Ellen knelt next to Luke and Father Denze comforted her by saying that her love for Luke and his love for her could never be taken away. Nor could Carl's love, which she should never doubt.

Several clanking noises deep below deck were followed by the boat's engine spluttering briefly into life. There were several more failed attempts before the engine found a halting rhythm. To shouts of encouragement from several of the crew the stricken boat began to eke out a path through the lapping water.

When Ellen returned to the foredeck she found the nuns shielding Waiya from the surrounding sights and sounds of suffering and death. A place was made and Ellen sat down next to Waiya's bony frame, her ears alert for any sign of returning planes. But the sky remained peaceful and she closed her eyes, finding comfort in the boat's listing progress.

A call from Sister Teresa that they were in sight of land startled Ellen out of a half sleep. She roused Waiya and took her to the railing, where through a mist of salt spray they watched the heavily wooded coastline with its sliver of sandy beach come fully into view. For a brief moment Ellen thought she could hear muffled voices calling to her over the water. 'Misis, Misis.'

Sister Teresa declared that soon they would be safe from attack and there would be plenty to eat. The Japanese would be defeated and the nuns would resume their missionary work. Waiya would return to the highlands and Ellen would go with Pastor Sommer to a new life in America.

Ellen waited for a few moments then explained about Luke. There were tears and awkward embraces under the gaze of a pair of bemused Japanese sailors, then a solemn promise from the nuns that they would pray for the repose of Luke's soul, alongside their prayers for Ellen's deceased husband.

When she regained her composure Ellen drew Waiya to her side and said to the nuns that now Luke was gone she would remain in New Guinea and make her life there, close to the men who had been close to her. She would honour these men by dedicating her life to the women and girls of New Guinea, who were the country's best chance.

Sister Teresa suggested that she take more time to consider her future, which might look very different in peacetime, but Ellen insisted that her mind was made up. As soon as the Japanese were gone she would return with Waiya to the highlands, where a fine house and garden awaited her. A visit from the nuns would be most welcome at any time.

Chronology:
New Guinea 1884–1944[1]

1884   Germany annexes north-eastern New Guinea and several islands off the New Guinea coast. The colony is named Kaiser-Wilhelmsland.

1886   The first Lutheran missionary arrives in Kaiser-Wilhelmsland.[2] In October the first mission is established at Simbang near Finschhafen on the Huon Peninsula.

1887   The first Protestant missionary from the Rhine Mission arrives at Astrolabe Bay on New Guinea's north-east coast. In November the first mission station is established at the village of Bogadjim, south of present-day Madang.

1897   The Catholic Divine Word Mission opens its first school in Kaiser Wilhelmsland, near Madang.

1914   At the beginning of World War One an Australian expeditionary force takes control of German New Guinea.

---

1   Lutherans and Roman Catholics were not the only Christian churches to have missions in the Mandated Territory of New Guinea, but given the focus of the story these are the only denominations included in this chronology. Only a couple of events from the Japanese occupation of New Guinea in World War Two are included. The references to Madang reflect the fact that this town figures prominently in the latter part of the story.

2   This was Johann Flierl, a representative of the Neuendettelsau Mission in Bavaria. Flierl had spent most of the previous seven years at the Bethesda Mission in South Australia, working among the Dieri people.

1919   First contact takes place between Lutheran missionaries and the people of the eastern New Guinea highlands.

1921   German New Guinea becomes a Mandated Territory of Australia under the League of Nations.[3]

1925   An Uncontrolled Areas Ordinance is passed, restricting the areas of the Mandated Territory that private persons can enter without a government permit.

1926   Gold is found at Edie Creek in a mountainous region inland from the coastal town of Salamaua. The subsequent gold rush significantly increases the number of Europeans in the Territory and leads to the development of a thriving aviation industry.

1931   Lutherans open the first European mission station in the eastern highlands.

1932   The first government post is opened in the eastern highlands.

1933   An expedition led by government official Jim Taylor and gold miner Mick Leahy undertakes the first European exploration of the Wahgi Valley in the central highlands.

A small party of Catholic missionaries cross the Bismarck Range, becoming the first Europeans to reach the highlands from the north. The following year Catholic mission stations are established at Mingende and Mount Hagen in the Wahgi Valley.

---

3   The Mandated Territory was administered separately from the Territory of Papua in south-east New Guinea, which had become an external territory of Australia in 1906, having been under British control since 1884. The two territories were united as the Territory of Papua and New Guinea in 1949. In 1975 the Territory became the independent nation of Papua New Guinea.

1934   Several new Lutheran mission stations are opened in the highlands, setting the scene for an ongoing rivalry between Lutherans and Roman Catholics.

1935   Following the deaths of two Catholic missionaries at the hands of New Guineans the Uncontrolled Areas Ordinance is amended, restricting European entry into and movement within the highlands. The unsupervised activity of local evangelists is also restricted.

1937   Restrictions on movement in the highlands begin to ease.

1938-9 A patrol led by District Officer Jim Taylor explores the territory west from Mount Hagen to the border with Dutch New Guinea.

1939   The outbreak of war in Europe ushers in the beginning of the internment in Australia of German missionaries.

1941   In response to Japan's entry into the war Australian authorities order the evacuation of European and Australian women and children from New Guinea, although there are some exemptions, such as civilian nurses.

1942   In February Japanese troops occupy Rabaul and quickly gain a foothold on mainland New Guinea. Coastal towns including Madang are subsequently captured. Later in the year Japanese forces attack south towards Port Moresby over the Owen Stanley Range but are repelled by Australian forces with New Guinean assistance.

1944   Madang falls to Allied troops.

Background

Wagner & Reiner contains a comprehensive overview of the first hundred years of the Lutheran Church in New Guinea. Radford provides detailed information about the Lutherans in the eastern highlands in the inter-war period. Frerichs is the story of an American Lutheran missionary and his family in New Guinea, beginning before World War Two. Winter discusses the impact of World War One and the rise of National Socialism on the Lutheran missions in the field and on support organisations in Germany, America and Australia. Winter also discusses the New Guinea mission's language policy, as does Handman.

Farnbacher & Fugmann and Fugmann & Hauenstein contain first-hand descriptions of the early years of the Neuendettelsau Mission in New Guinea by two of its pioneers.

Mennis describes the early Catholic missions in the Madang area and in the western and central highlands.

Gammage, Leahy & Crain, Mennis, Radford and Winter discuss various aspects of the Australian New Guinea administration in the highlands in the inter-war years. Gammage provides a detailed account of the 1938–1939 Hagen-Sepik patrol led by James Taylor. This patrol is the inspiration for the story's Davenport expedition. Leahy & Crain and Waterhouse contain extensive discussions of gold mining in New Guinea.

Sinclair provides a comprehensive account of European penetration of the highlands, from the initial forays from Papua in the early twentieth century through the expeditions and settlements of the 1930s to PNG's independence in 1975.

Read and Reay analyse highland life from an anthropological perspective.

Daniels is the source of the idea of a missionary whose beliefs about human origins are challenged by reflections on the evolution of languages.

Ryan is the story of a young Australian soldier who spent much of 1942 and 1943 behind enemy lines in New Guinea, maintaining contact with local people and observing Japanese troop movements.

Ochi provides a Japanese perspective on the Pacific War in eastern New Guinea. A summary translation was provided for my benefit by Mariko Nakamura.

The story's ending is loosely based on the fate of the Japanese ship *Dorish Maru*. An account of this episode is provided by Tschauder.

Jared Diamond's *Guns, Germs and Steel* was inspired by the author's chance meeting on a beach in New Guinea with a local man in 1972. 'Why is it that you white people developed so much cargo and brought it to New Guinea, but we black people had little cargo of our own?' the man asked (p. 14). Diamond's argument—that environmental rather than biological factors provide the fundamental answer to this question—forms part of the background (albeit at several removes) to Ellen's story.

Bibliography

Daniels, KW, *Why I Believed: Reflections of a Former Missionary*, The Secular Web, www.kwdaniels.com, 2009.

Diamond, J, *Guns, Germs and Steel. A Short History of Everybody for the Last 13,000 Years*, Vintage, London,1998.

Farnbacher, T & Fugmann, G (eds), *Johann Flierl (1858 bis 1947): Ein Leben für die Mission, Mission für das Leben*, Erlanger Verlag für Mission und Ökumene, Neuendettelsau, 2009.

Frerichs, CE, *Desires of the Heart: A Daughter Remembers her Missionary Parents*, Cold River Studio, Tennessee, 2010.

Fugmann, G & Hauenstein, P (eds), *Christian Keyßer: Mission im Leben der Menschen*, Erlanger Verlag für Mission und Ökumene, Neuendettelsau, 2011.

Gammage, B, *The Sky Travellers: Journeys in New Guinea 1938–1939*, Miegunyah Press, Melbourne, 1998.

Handman, C, 'Languages without subjects. On the interior(s) of colonial New Guinea', *HAU: Journal of Ethnographic Theory*, 7(1), Spring 2017, pp. 207–228, DOI:10.14318/hau7.1.017

Leahy, M & Crain, M, *The land that time forgot: Adventures and discoveries in New Guinea*, Hurst and Blackett, London, 1937.

Mennis, MR, *Hagen Saga: The Story of Father William Ross SVD*, University of Papua New Guinea Press, Port Moresby and Madang, 2015.

Ochi, H, *Nyū Ginia senki*, Tosho Shuppansha, Tokyo,1983.

Radford, R, *Highlanders and Foreigners in the Upper Ramu: The Kainantu Area 1919–1942*, Melbourne University Press, Melbourne, 1987.

Read, KE, *The High Valley*, George Allen and Unwin, London, 1966.

Reay, MO, *Wives and Wanderers in a New Guinea Highland Society*, ANU Press, Canberra, 2014.

Ryan, P, *Fear Drive My Feet*, Text Publishing, Melbourne, 2015 (first published by Angus & Robertson, 1959).

Sinclair, J, *The Middle Kingdom: A Colonial History of the Highlands of Papua New Guinea*, Crawford House Publishing, Goolwa, 2016.

Tschauder, J, *Death on the "Dorish Maru"*, Dorish Maru College, n.d., https://www.dorishmarucollege.org.au/about-us/death-on-the-dorish-maru

Wagner, H & Reiner, H (eds), *The Lutheran Church in Papua New Guinea: The First Hundred Years 1886–1986*, Lutheran Publishing House, Adelaide,1987 (revised printing).

Waterhouse, M, *Not a Poor Man's Field: The New Guinea Goldfields to 1942 – An Australian Colonial History*, Halstead Press, Canberra, 2010.

Winter, C, *Looking after one's own: the rise of nationalism and the politics of the Neuendettelsauer Mission in Germany, New Guinea and Australia (1928–1933)*, PhD Thesis, Australian National University, Canberra, 2004. https://openresearch-repository.anu.edu.au/handle/1885/148219